Twice Upon a Wedding

Other Books by Jean Stone

ONCE UPON A WEDDING

BEACH ROSES

TRUST FUND BABIES

OFF SEASON

THE SUMMER HOUSE

TIDES OF THE HEART

BIRTHDAY GIRLS

PLACES BY THE SEA

IVY SECRETS

FIRST LOVES

SINS OF INNOCENCE

Twice Upon a Wedding

Jean Stone

Bantam Books

TWICE UPON A WEDDING
A Bantam Book

Published by
Bantam Dell
A Division of Random House, Inc.
New York, New York

ISBN 0-7394-5202-9

Printed in the United States of America

TO EVERYONE WHO
BELIEVES IN
SECOND CHANCES . . .

AND ISN'T AFRAID
TO MAKE THEM HAPPEN.

Twice Upon a Wedding

1

It was one of those smiles.

It was secretive, mischievous, almost happily naughty.

It was not the sort of smile Andrew would have expected of Elaine. Especially on the day she should have been married. Especially as she wore the gown of a bridesmaid, not a bride, and stood on the top of a grassy slope, overlooking the magnificent grounds of a magnificent estate, watching a wedding reception that should have been hers.

He crossed the lawn and moved next to her. She stood apart from her friends—Lily, Sarah, and Jo—yet was dressed like them in Vera Wang gowns of oyster and pearl. On Lily the dress looked like sassy haute couture; on Sarah, mysteriously earthy and sensuous; on Jo, heart-thumpingly gorgeous. On Elaine, it simply looked like a nice dress, more palatable than the clash of colors she often wore, more fashionable than the stretch pants and big shirts of the carpooling, PTO-president mom.

Elaine turned to Andrew, her smile unflinching. He knew that the past weeks had been tough, that she'd risked her future security, her children's happiness, and the success of her best friends' new business when she'd broken her engagement to Martin because "I just have to," she'd said.

"Lainey," he asked, "how are you doing?"

She tipped her head toward the crowd, her lacquered brown hair rigid in its French twist, as she'd called it ("An *updo,*" Lily had corrected). "Fine," Elaine said, "or at least I will be."

"When this wedding is over?" It was the celebration of Jo's mother's marriage to Ted, the West Hope, Massachusetts, town butcher. It was also the debut event for Lily, Sarah, Jo, and Elaine, once college roommates, now partners in Second Chances, second-wedding planners for second-time brides.

Elaine looped her arm through Andrew's and stood a bit taller. "I'm tired of being ordinary, Andrew. I'm tired of having a predictable life."

He kept his eyes on her. She didn't waver. "There's nothing wrong with being predictable, Lainey," Andrew said, because so many times he'd longed for just that.

"But my kids are practically grown and I'm unattached. I'm forty-three years old and I want excitement. I want pizzazz."

"Pizzazz," was an old-fashioned, Elaine kind of term, like "French twist," Andrew supposed. "Well," he replied, because, despite months of working to untangle the puzzle, he remained quite clueless about how a woman's mind worked.

Elaine paid no attention to his hesitation. She merely nodded with seeming resolve. "What I want is a makeover. Inside and out."

"A makeover?" His laugh seemed too quick, even to him. "You're going on TV? A reality show?"

But Elaine didn't laugh in return. She took a deep breath, touched her hand to her heart and said, "The only reality is going to happen right here. Elaine McNulty Thomas is finally going to be like everyone else."

Andrew fell silent. Then his eyes followed hers toward Lily, Sarah, and Jo, who stood twenty feet, yet light-years, away. "You want to be like one of them?"

Elaine shook her head. "I want to be like them all."

Andrew slowly smiled. He felt new material building on the gossip horizon, juicy new fodder for the magazine column he secretly wrote. "That would be a tall order for anyone."

Elaine nodded. "But I'm going to do it," she said. "What's more, I'll do it in time for the Benson wedding on New Year's Eve."

Andrew's right eyebrow cocked. "In less than twelve weeks?"

Her gaze still didn't waver. "I can do it. I will."

He patted her hand. "I'll tell you what, Lainey. If you succeed in your quest, I'll give you the first dance at the Bensons' reception."

"And if I don't?"

He smiled and looked back toward Lily, Sarah, and Jo. "Something tells me you will." There was no need to add that he had a goal of his own set for New Year's Eve, if he could just hold out that long.

It was odd to stand there on the grassy slope, while Vivaldi danced through the golden leaves of the linden trees that shimmered in the autumn air, while chatter rose between long puffs of laughter from gaggles of wedding guests gathered on the lawn, a small plate of pâté in one hand, a crystal champagne flute in the other.

It was odd to stand there in a pearl satin gown and realize that this was her mother's wedding, that after years of being single, Marion Lyons was now Marion Cappelinni, that she was once again someone's wife.

It was, Jo suspected, all about trust.

Shifting from one foot to the other, Jo wondered if, like her mother, it would take her decades to trust a man that much again.

2

Women call it a makeover.

I call it an act of not-so-divine desperation, a misguided adventure destined for chaos.

Andrew stared at the screen of his laptop later that night after he'd returned to his cottage from the wedding, said good night to Cassie, and hung up the rented tuxedo that he'd worn all day.

When Elaine made her announcement, he hadn't been sure if he should say, "You go, girl," or notify the others that she had lost her mind.

Guys, after all, don't do makeovers, he typed. *When a guy wants to change his life, he buys a new car or a Harley, or changes from beer to vodka martinis, extra dry.*

He sat back in his chair, clasped his hands behind his head, and wondered if he should add, "Or he leaves a high-profile job as a television journalist and escapes to the Berkshires and switches to an ambiguous career as a college professor where, if anyone thinks they recognize him, they surely can't justify their suspicions by his faded denim, his modest home, or his eleven-year-old daughter, an unspoiled (well, sort of) kid."

He couldn't, of course, reveal that information, not to his growing throng of readers.

As far as anyone in West Hope knew, Andrew Kennedy was a college professor on sabbatical from Winston College, who wrote his doctoral dissertation before and after hours at Second Chances, where he worked as the receptionist—and was supposedly gay.

He was not the anonymous A.K. of *Buzz* magazine, the man who had committed to write six months' worth of the now-famous "Real Women" column, a delightful task for which he'd gone under cover, so to speak, in order to get four women to trust him with their secrets, to spill the gender beans about the ways real women thought and acted and actually were, to share the riddles of their lives in ways they never would if they knew he was straight.

He was not *Andrew David*, whose face and whose voice Americans might (or might not) remember from TV news programs. He was not the same man (was he?) who had used his middle name as his last because the network had deemed "Kennedy" too overexposed.

He was not those men now. He was merely sensitive, regular-guy Andrew Kennedy by day; savvy, suave columnist by night. Clark Kent versus Superman. Two roles he adored.

Adored?

"Oh, crap," Andrew said, standing up and diving one

large hand into his sandy-colored, often unkempt hair. "Adored" was such a girlie word, such a gay word. He laughed. "The trouble with being Superman," he said into the screen, "is that you sometimes forget which one of you is in the room."

He shut off the laptop that sat on the old oak table in the alcove off the living room—"A cozy study," the real-estate woman had hyped it five years ago. He liked it because it was nestled behind the natty but oh-so-comfortable overstuffed living-room furniture, and afforded two special views: one of his backyard garden, which now lingered admirably with a few bright pumpkins and burnished butternut squash; the other of the living-room stone fireplace that he'd soon crank up again for another New England winter. They were peaceful views, comfort views. He'd not had them in the Manhattan high-rise.

"Dad?" Cassie's voice beckoned from the doorway. "Are you talking to yourself again?"

His smile broadened as he turned to face his daughter, who had inherited her father's wit (well, most folks referred to it as "wit") and her mother's (God help him) international-cover-girl, breathtaking beauty. "I was just celebrating life," he said.

Cassie rolled her large turquoise, Patty-look-alike eyes. His daughter loved to do that. It was her teasing way of throwing up her hands at her father's errant ways. She'd been rolling them a lot since he'd joined the staff at Second Chances, since he'd trusted her with the knowledge of his undercover task. "Sometimes you are so lame," she said.

"I know." He walked to where she stood and gave her a bear hug. Her dark hair was damp, her scent was powdery and babylike; she must have showered after the wedding. "I thought you went to bed."

"Too much wedding cake. I couldn't decide if I should throw up."

A flash of panic sent his palm to her forehead. "Are you okay?" He hated this part of single parenthood. *Call me sexist*, Andrew thought, *but women know when a kid is sick or well with an instinct that God forgot to give men.*

Cassie laughed. "I'm okay, Dad. I just wanted attention."

He swatted her shoulder and crossed the hall to the kitchen. "It was fun today, wasn't it?"

"My first wedding," she said.

"So what did you think?"

"Mrs. Lyons was pretty for such an older woman."

The bride, Jo's mother, was seventy or so, Andrew had figured. "Ted is a nice guy. I guess there had been some kind of town scandal about them all these years, even though they didn't know it." He stopped himself. He often wasn't sure how much he should tell his daughter or what she was too young to be a part of. He went to the refrigerator and poured a glass of milk.

"Jo is pretty, too," Cassie said. "I wish you would tell her."

"That she's pretty?" Andrew said with a thin smile.

"Dad," she whined. "You need a girlfriend."

He swallowed the milk fast. Too fast. It lunged from his throat and shot out of his nostrils.

Cassie erupted. "Dad! Nasty!"

He laughed with her, then wiped his mouth, his nose. He secretly loved the way his daughter could catch him like that, her impetuous comments always a surprise. "You think I need a girlfriend?"

She shrugged. "You could do worse than Jo Lyons."

"You seem to forget that Jo thinks I am gay."

"Give it up, Dad. You need a life more than you need a stupid magazine column. Besides, if you wait too long, she might fall in love with someone else. She's already met a new guy, hasn't she?"

He digested Cassie's words, because, though she was a kid, she was wise. "It must be the wedding," he said. "I've never met a woman who didn't get all gushy over a wedding." He reminded himself to use that in his column. It was a good line, and it was probably true.

"It's more than that, Dad. I worry about you. What's going to happen to you when I'm out of school? When I'm out in the world on my own?" She swept her arms in a big arc around the kitchen, as if this were the universe and not a ten-by-twelve space with knotty-pine cabinets and an enamel sink and an awkward but bountiful collection of herbs in the kitchen greenhouse window. Cassie had started the herb "garden" as a school project their first year in the Berkshires, the first year on their own. Father and daughter had nurtured it to vibrancy—parsley, sage, rosemary, and thyme. "Like the song," Andrew had said, and Cassie had pretended to know what he had meant.

After another swig of cold milk, Andrew set down the glass. "You're only in sixth grade, Cassie. I think we have time to plan old Dad's destiny." It occurred to Andrew that maybe what she really wanted was a mother. It was something he thought about from time to time, then discarded the notion because he and Cassie were fine. Parsley, sage, rosemary, and thyme. "Besides," he added, "you know I plan to tell the truth about everything at John and Irene's bash on New Year's Eve. After that, who knows what will happen." He winked.

Cassie half grinned. "Right," she finally said, and his insides relaxed. "Still, it was a nice wedding. I liked the food and the band, even though they played OPM."

OPM was Cassie's acronym for Old People's Music: Andrew's kind of music; any kind of music that didn't involve artists preening the stage nearly naked, covered in sequins and small tattoos, and wearing one of those ridiculous microphones as if they were telephone operators instead of rock stars.

"You danced three dances with Burch," Andrew said, referring to Sarah's son, who was a year older than Cassie. "Shall I have the women start planning your wedding next?"

"They do *second* weddings, Dad," she said, planting her hands on her small hips and tossing back her long, damp hair in an exaggerated flirt. "Give me a little time, okay?"

Andrew laughed and hoped his daughter would never want a makeover, because she was perfect just as she was.

3

She was born in Saratoga Springs, New York, where the elite once went for mineral baths and the horses still ran in August. Elaine's father owned a restaurant—*the* restaurant—McNulty's, where reservations were required in season unless you were a Blakely or a Swanson, in which case your table was available any night at any time.

Elaine had been happy to wait on all of them, to remember their names and take their fussy orders and practically curtsy, because that was her job and her fat tips ultimately sent her to Winston College, where she'd been the first in her family to earn a degree.

It hadn't been a bad life.

When she'd been fifteen or sixteen she'd tried to emulate the ladies who wore subtle, chic dresses and stately, wide-brimmed hats, not plain, unimportant clothes like her mother's had been. But once racing season ended, Elaine's mother convinced her she looked out of place. It had been Elaine's last girlhood attempt to *spiff*, her father called it, to *buff*, her kids would have said.

"To look *ele-ghhhant*," would have been Lily's term.

Lily, of course, could have been any of the thoroughbred ladies. She'd always known what to wear and what to do to look perfect all the time.

But the truth was, Elaine had always felt more comfortable, more *Elaine*, in the bright colors and splash that her mother said were too gaudy but Elaine thought were simply cheerful. Once out of the house, once she was an "adult," Elaine had dressed as she had pleased.

So, maybe she'd been wrong.

She stared at her bedroom ceiling now, eyes wide open, despite the fact that it was two A.M. She thought about Lily: Elaine would ask her to serve as her fashion and beauty coordinator. Because no matter what Elaine wanted to believe, no matter what the magazine articles touted or what the PhD's said on *Oprah*, Elaine suspected that a makeover must begin on the outside, not on the in.

"How you look is who you'll be." It was a line Lily used often, but could have come from any of the ladies at the Saratoga restaurant thirty years ago.

She rolled onto her side and snapped on the bedside lamp, her adrenaline softly pumping with anticipation, just enough to prevent sleep, her thoughts awhirl with what changes she'd make and where on earth she would start.

She thought about the chic dresses and the wide-brimmed hats, Lily's kind of clothes. Then she thought about her walk-in closet packed with polyester in every color of the rainbow and some colors in between. She thought about the high-heeled ladies of Saratoga, and about her sensible sneakers and square-heeled pumps lined up according to shades of spring green and magenta and goldenrod for summer.

Tasteless, she sensed, but could not help herself.

She thought about the red patent leathers that matched the red-and-mandarin-striped dress she'd worn last Easter. Lily would have been horrified. It didn't matter that Martin had liked the outfit; she wouldn't think of Martin right now. Or Lloyd, either, damn him.

Out with the old, her adrenaline commanded. *You'll dance with Andrew on New Year's Eve, and you'll be the belle of the Benson ball.*

Bolstered by the voices of her imagination, Elaine flung back the comforter. There was only one place to begin this romp, and it was directly across the room.

One polyester, two polyesters. She yanked them from their hangers and dumped them onto the floor. With every yank and every clatter of every hanger, she felt absolved somehow, unburdened, free.

"*Out, out, damn spot!*" she shouted at a purple polka-dot shirt that she'd worn with purple pants.

"*Off with your head!*" That to a bright pink hoodie that her son said made her look like Peter Rabbit in drag.

She stopped when she reached the royal-blue suit that she'd worn for her justice-of-the-peace wedding to Lloyd over twenty years before. She stared at the tiny pinholes where her corsage had been: three tiny white roses, tied with a pink ribbon. She'd worn a hat, though they'd long since gone out of style. It was a small red pillbox with matching red netting that scooped across her forehead and was torn years later when her daughters were playing dress-up.

She wondered why the suit still hung there, as if the wedding had been yesterday, as if Lloyd had never left her.

The wedding hadn't been like Marion and Ted's. It hadn't been like the one Elaine and Martin would have had yesterday if she hadn't broken the engagement because she'd realized in time that Martin was merely a Band-Aid, that even kindly Martin could not ease the pain deep in her heart. She simply hadn't dared to let herself love him enough.

Her marriage to Lloyd had not been elaborate. It had been a simple town hall ceremony, with only Lloyd's brother, Russell, and his sister, Celia, as witnesses. Elaine's parents hadn't come down from Saratoga, because she hadn't told them. They thought she was in the middle of her final exams. They didn't know that she and Lloyd were getting married. They didn't know she was pregnant.

She reached inside the suit jacket and touched the waistband of the skirt. She remembered it had been too tight that day—her belly had swelled above average.

Throw it out, the new voice inside her urged.

Her eyes widened, her mouth dropped open. "*Out!*" she commanded, then pulled the suit off the hanger and hurled it past the closet door.

"Mother! What are you doing?" Karen, her youngest, had always been a light sleeper. Like her mother, she was the one always on alert, waiting to be sure no one in the house needed anything, because serving others was what she gladly did. Karen was just like Elaine in all those selfless, get-you-nothing-but-headaches and nowhere-but-miserable ways.

"Sorry, honey," Elaine said. "Did I wake you?"

"Of course you woke me. Who are you shouting at?" Her head rotated around the haphazard piles of polyester. "Good grief. What are you doing?"

"I'm starting my new life." Elaine stopped her purge for a moment. Karen was sixteen, the last child at home: Kandie and Kory were at college. Karen was also the most like Elaine, dressed now in a flannel nightgown and kneesocks, her face shiny with night cream from the supermarket health-and-beauty-aids section because it was more economical than the department store kind. Karen had watched Elaine shop economically long before Elaine's checkbook was reduced to a modest alimony: the girl now hoarded baby-sitting money the way Elaine hoarded coupons and reused plastic baggies.

Karen stooped down and retrieved the purple polka dots. "But Mom, you love this shirt." She clutched it to her breast as if it were her firstborn.

Elaine laughed. "You're right, honey, I did. And I loved your father once, too." As soon as she'd said those words, she wished she could take them back. She wished she could rewind the moment and erase the sting now visible on her daughter's face.

"I hate it when you're mean to Daddy," Karen said.

Elaine sighed. She returned to her hangers, some of the fun now gone from her energy burst. "I'm not mean to your father, honey. I'm sorry I said that. It's just that my clothes are out of style and so am I. It's time for a change."

Karen disregarded her mother's apology and continued to rummage another pile. "Your wedding suit," she said. "You're throwing out your wedding suit?" Elaine might have chosen to toss the family jewels, given the pain in her daughter's voice.

"Honey..." she began.

Karen's eyes narrowed. "Are you trying to be like her?" She did not have to elaborate on whom she meant by "her." *Her* was Beatrix—Trix—as Lloyd had called her, a county court judge who happened to be pretty and smart and rich, and who happened to have stolen Lloyd from Elaine.

And married him.

And left him after a year and eight months, right after Elaine and Martin got engaged.

"No," Elaine said. "I'm not trying to be her." Elaine didn't know if Karen would think that was a good or a bad thing; the issue was simply too sensitive to ask. The divorce, after all, had been hardest on Karen. Kandie, who was as much like Lloyd as Karen was like Elaine, had not hidden her approval of the new Mrs. Thomas. Then again, Kandie and Elaine hadn't gotten along well since the girl had turned twelve. Kory, Elaine's son, had tried to stay in the middle, not wanting estrangement from his mom or his dad. Karen, who'd been only thirteen the night Lloyd walked out, still believed her parents would get back together, still tried to encourage Elaine to wait for him.

Especially after Elaine broke up with Martin and the second Mrs. Thomas broke up with Lloyd.

Especially now that it looked like Elaine might have a chance with her ex-husband, as if she wanted one.

"Life changes," Elaine said quietly. "Sometimes we need to move on."

Karen threw the suit back on the floor and stomped from the room.

Of course, she slammed the door.

From the darkness of her bedroom, Jo heard the dings of the elevator ticking off the floors. She was on four, the top floor, in a two-bedroom unit identical to forty-seven others in the brick building whose residents might or might not hear the elevator or the trash chute or the footsteps in the hall as clearly as she did; whose residents might or might not hear the snores that resounded through abutting bedroom walls, or the quarrels between neighbors, or the theme song from back-to-back episodes of *The Golden Girls* that began every evening at six.

To Jo, the noise was an ongoing reminder that she no longer lived in the soundproof penthouse in Boston, where all that she'd heard was silence after Brian had left.

The dings stopped on four. She pulled the bedsheet closer around her neck and waited, as if the footsteps that followed might stop at her door.

When they did not, Jo opened her eyes.

Brian was finally out of her life. She was back in West

Hope where she belonged, at least for now. She was back with her friends, in an exciting new business; she was back with her mother, who'd become a joyful bride yesterday. She was living in a modest apartment, though it had been suggested she should move into her mother's house, the house where Jo had been raised, now that Ted had bought Marion a new condo, now that they were husband and wife.

Jo had said "No, thanks." The house was too big. It needed work. Her furniture wouldn't match. She did not tell her mother there were too many memories.

Marion hadn't applied any pressure. "We won't put it on the market just yet," she'd said. "It will take me forever to clean it out, and in the meantime, you might change your mind." Marion's procrastination, however, might be for other reasons. How could she walk away from the home where she'd lived all her life, the house her father had bought as a wedding gift for her mother?

Marion had known no other home. When she'd married Sam Lyons, he was in the army, shipping off for Korea. It only made sense for her to stay in West Hope. When he returned, he took a job on a heavy-construction crew that worked all around the northeast and had him away more than he was home. Then Marion became pregnant with Jo, so the little family stayed put in their rooms on the second floor of the colonial house.

Nine years later Sam ran off with Doris Haines, the junior-high-school science teacher. He never returned.

For a few years Jo received cards on her birthday and at Christmas, with gifts like stuffed animals and dolls made in Taiwan. Jo spent many hours watching out her small bedroom window, hoping her father might come by for a visit. But Sam never came, and after a while, the gifts and the cards dwindled, then stopped.

And now Marion wanted her to live there again.

Jo supposed it was that, not the emotions of the wedding or the noise of the building, that kept her awake that night.

The elevator dinged again. She closed her eyes. It took seventeen average footsteps to get from the elevator to her door, number 411. Eight steps to 409; twenty-five or -six steps to 413. She counted eight, then nine, ten...

The steps stopped at sixteen.

Jo held her breath. Was someone coming to see her? At two in the morning?

There was no knock, only a soft, swishing sound. A new sound. Then footsteps again, this time growing fainter. The fire door opened, then closed with a hollow, steel thud.

Her heart came to life. Slowly, Jo slid from beneath the covers and put her feet on the hardwood floor. She reached for her robe and quietly slipped it on. Inhaling a silent breath, she stood up. She tiptoed down the short hall to the front door in the three-by-three area that the sales-manager-on-duty had called a "foyer."

In the dull glare that leaked in from the outdoor security lights, Jo noticed a small piece of paper on the linoleum floor. She snapped on the overhead light; she picked up the paper.

"Six o'clock, Sunday night" was neatly written. "I hope you like Chinese food. Jack."

Jo smiled. After all, she had a date—a first date, an

as-yet-unopened treasure chest of possibilities—in a matter of hours. She reminded herself that no matter where she lived, or what she did, like her mother, Jo had a new life.

She turned off the light and tiptoed back to bed, thinking it had been nice that the footsteps in the hall had, that time, been for her.

4

Elaine called Lily in the morning.

"Get over here," she barked into the phone. "I need your help." Barking was new, like the rest of her plans.

"It's nine o'clock on Sunday morning," Lily whined. "Is this life or death?"

"Some people wouldn't think so," she replied. "You, however, will."

An hour and a half later, Lily was at the door. "Sorry it took so long, but you know I loathe mornings." She brushed past Elaine and went into the family room, the mauve and peach and blue family room that Elaine supposed she'd want to make over after she was done with herself.

Me first, she thought a bit giddily as she padded after Lily.

Lily sat down on the sectional sofa. "What's all this about?"

Elaine stood there a moment, looking down at lovely Lily who, despite loathing mornings, was perfectly put together, her makeup on, her light wool pants and vest unwrinkled, her blond, wispy hair wispily in place. Suddenly the task seemed impossible, unattainable, hopeless. Elaine was just *Elaine*, after all, just a waitress-turned-mom. She fidgeted with the drawstring on her son's maroon-and-white Springfield College sweats, the clothes she'd thrown on because most of hers were cloistered upstairs in heaps for Goodwill.

"Coffee?" she asked.

Lily shook her head. She patted the seat beside her. "Sit down," she said. "Tell me what's going on. I assume it's about a man."

Everything to Lily had to do with a man, or the lack of one. Of the four old college roommates, Lily had always been the romantic. Even between marriages she'd not been manless for long.

Elaine said no, it wasn't about a man. It was about something much more important. Then she sat beside Lily and related her intention for a makeover.

When she was finished, there was silence. Lily didn't jump up and say, "Yes! What a brilliant idea!" Instead she sat there on the sofa, staring at Elaine. "Well," she said after a moment, "why would you want to do that?"

If one of her kids had music blasting or if the washer and the dryer were grinding in the background, Elaine might have thought Lily had not heard her right. But Karen was still asleep and the only sound in the house was a slow *tick-tick* of the battery-operated clock that had been free with her *Reader's Digest* subscription and now sat upon the mantel.

"You're joking, right?" Elaine asked.

"Well," Lily replied. "No."

Elaine laughed. "Come on, Lily. Look at me! Look at my life!"

"What about it?"

"It's dull. It always has been. Look at my clothes!" She tugged at the sleeves of Kory's sweatshirt. "This is probably the most stylish thing I've ever worn. Don't say you never wanted to get me to change my wardrobe."

Lily, sweet Lily, reached across and gently touched her arm. "Listen, Lainey, I've always thought the most important thing any of us could do is just be ourselves."

" 'Ourselves'? *Ourselves?* What about 'How you look is who you'll be'?" Her fingers returned to the drawstring of the sweatpants. She couldn't believe Lily was disagreeing with her.

"Well, do you think you'd feel better if you looked like someone who wasn't you?"

"But wouldn't it be better for our business? If we're selling style and elegance, wouldn't it make sense for all of us to look the part?"

"Everyone has their own sense of what style is, Elaine. You've had your own style all your life. It's worked for you, hasn't it?"

It had seemed so simple. She'd never expected Lily to react the way her daughter had. Elaine stood up and tightened the drawstring. "Never mind," she said. "Andrew thought it was a good idea. Maybe he can help me out."

Lily stood up. "No, he can't," she said. "I can."

"But you said—"

"I only wanted to be sure this is something you really want."

Optimism sparked. "I do want it, Lily. I want to change the way I act and look and am. I want to be smart and clever and *attractive*, for godssake. I want to be a more positive asset to Second Chances. Please help me. Please?"

Lily put her arm around Elaine. "Of course I'll help, you silly goose. We'll start by going to Laurel Lake Spa for a few days."

Laurel Lake Spa was the latest exclusive resort in the Berkshires whose trademark was privacy. It catered only to "mature" ladies with "mature" issues, often celebrities in search of rejuvenation. It also had a price tag as big as its following. "Whoa!" Elaine said. "I can't afford—"

"My treat," Lily added, as she pulled her cell phone from her purse. "After all, you're right about one thing. I've been dying to do this for years."

Half an hour later, standing in her foyer with a tote bag on one wrist ("You won't need a thing, Lainey," Lily had said. "I'll buy your starter clothes and your cosmetics and the like."), Elaine patiently awaited Lily's next command. She didn't have to wait long.

"Shavonne will do your hair if we get over there right now," Lily announced as she clicked off her cell phone again.

After Shavonne's they would check in to the spa. Elaine had never been there; she'd only seen the winding driveway from the stone-pillared entrance and the long limousines and big black Mercedes coming or going. She'd never seen faces behind the heavily tinted car windows.

She'd never been to the spa, but she'd spent many nights on the grounds there before there had been a spa, back when the most noteworthy thing at Laurel Lake was Edith Wharton's estate and the old ice house down by the water. Elaine and Lloyd used to go often: She'd lost her virginity right there in the ice house; it hadn't been long before she was pregnant with Kandie and they'd gotten married. And now she was returning to the lake, almost to the scene of the crime, a place that would again spin her life into unknown directions. Like preparing to have sex the first time (she'd known it was inevitable from the first time Lloyd touched her *down there*), the thought of what lay before her was exhilarating, almost dizzying.

"Karen, we're going now," she called to her daughter, who'd finally crawled out of bed and made her way downstairs.

Karen meandered from the kitchen into the front hall. She wore the purple polka-dot shirt that Elaine had loved, and a decided frown.

Elaine ignored the attire and the facial expression. "You'll be all right while I'm away?"

Her daughter shrugged.

"Of course she will," Lily said. "She's almost seventeen."

"You'll call if you need anything? I'll only be a couple of miles down the road."

"She won't need anything," Lily said. "She'll be fine."

Before Karen could respond, the doorbell rang.

"I'll get it," Elaine said. She stepped in front of Lily and opened the front door. If she'd taken a minute, just one lousy minute, to think about it, maybe she would have pretended that no one was home.

The old man stood on the front steps; the same old, short, bald man who'd stood there every Sunday morning since Beatrix Thomas had dumped Lloyd the same way that Lloyd had once dumped Elaine.

Except that there were no kids.

Except that a year and eight months could hardly compare with twenty years.

Over the khaki pocket of the man's khaki shirt was embroidered the name "Leonard." Leonard was the deliveryman for West Hope Florist. In his hand he held the usual Sunday delivery: three tiny white roses, tied with a pink ribbon. She didn't need to read the card to know that it read "Thinking of you, Lloyd."

She took the flowers in the awkward moment that followed. She reached into her tote bag, took out two one-dollar bills, and paid the man named Leonard so he'd return to the panel truck sitting in her driveway and go away.

She closed the door.

"Well," Lily said. "That's a nice surprise."

Elaine could have said, "It's no surprise," but she just nodded. Instead of tossing the flowers into the trash, she tucked them in her tote. No sense pissing off her daughter more than she already had.

5

The next wedding to plan was for New Year's Eve, the John-and-Irene Show, Andrew liked to call it. After all, it would not be a wedding, exactly, but a fortieth-anniversary renewal of their vows. Forty years of wedded bliss—well, mostly bliss—was a concept Andrew had once longed for. Unfortunately, he'd married a woman who had not agreed.

With Cassie safely ensconced at the stables for her Sunday trail ride, Andrew sprawled across the living-room floor and poked through the Sunday styles section of the *New York Times.* Lily said it was required reading for the success of their business. Not that they'd need much inspiration for the Benson event. Irene Benson had been at the top of the social register for years and the woman always knew what she wanted. She hadn't, however, known that she'd be renewing her vows.

It had been Andrew's idea. The Bensons were his friends. John was the editor of *Buzz*, Andrew's boss in his "other" life. The women of Second Chances needed a high-profile wedding to get their business off the ground.

It had seemed easy, harmless.

However, the women didn't—couldn't—know that Andrew knew John and Irene, let alone that they were Cassie's godparents, or that Andrew had more than a disinterested hand in the gala. The women didn't—couldn't—know about Andrew's past or his present, his two lives spent in one body. Sometimes it even confused the hell out of him.

He scanned the photos of the brides and grooms and brides and brides and grooms and grooms. He didn't recognize the names, but committed a few to memory for Lily's Monday-morning quiz.

"Did you read the profile about the couple that was wed in New Paltz?" she was sure to ask, and to which Andrew could definitively respond, "Yes. The arrival of the bridal party on an old steam train was a wonderful idea." The bride's great-grandfather had been an engineer on the old Boston and Albany; indeed, the couple had met on a commuter train that they both rode each day in and out of Manhattan, to jobs at opposite ends of that island.

"If it weren't for a train, we never would have met," the groom said while toasting his bride.

It was that kind of detail Lily said would help set Second Chances apart from their competition. "It's not unique enough that we plan second weddings," she said.

"We must get to know each couple and make the wedding special for them, special for their story."

If nothing else, John Benson would laugh and say the exercise helped Andrew get in touch with his feminine side.

He'd made it through the first page and on to the second when his cell phone rang.

"Speak of the devil," Andrew said when he heard Lily's voice. "I was just thinking of you."

"Good thoughts, I hope."

"Indubitably."

"Wonderful. They'll have to hold you for about a week."

As usual, Andrew found it difficult to keep up with Lily's brain. "Explain, please."

"Elaine and I are off to Laurel Lake Spa for a few days. Don't count on us until Friday. Or maybe Monday."

He closed the paper; the quiz apparently would be skipped until next week. "Feel a need to get away?"

"You won't believe this, but I'm at Shavonne the Stylist's right now."

Sometimes it was best to keep quiet and let Lily ramble.

"Elaine is having highlights."

He recalled Elaine's pronouncement last night. "She mentioned wanting to make changes. I didn't realize it meant going blond."

"That's not all it means, dear Andrew. Oh, this will be so much fun. For years, absolute years, I've wanted to lend a helping hand to our poor Elaine. She is so much more attractive than she ever let herself appear..."

He grunted an agreement, because Lily would want him to. He picked up the Sunday sports section and skimmed the article about the Giants beating the Jets.

". . . so I'm treating her to Laurel Lake. She'll come out of this a whole new person. It will be so wonderful for our business. Isn't it just divine?"

Andrew wasn't sure what any of this had to do with wedding planning, but he muttered, "Yeah, it's great."

"So we won't be there this week. And Sarah is taking the time off because her troubadouring musician-lover is home right now. It looks as if you and Jo will have to hold down the fort. Or I should say 'the wedding chapel.' "

"Mmm," he said, turning to page two. Then he stopped. "What?" Had she really just said what he thought she'd said?

"I said you and Jo will have to work alone this week. Think you two can handle it?"

The ink on the sports section blurred just a little. Alone. With Jo. Just the two of them, every day, for a week.

"Andrew?" Lily asked. "Did you hear me?"

He cleared his throat. "Don't worry about a thing, Lily. Jo and I can handle everything."

He hung up quickly and wondered if it was time to leave mild-mannered Clark Kent at home and go to work posed as Jo's hero.

"My daughter will never speak to me again," Elaine said later that day as she unlocked the door to her room, stepped inside, and genuflected at the first mirror she saw—a tall one across from the bed.

"Stop looking at yourself," Lily said with a laugh. "It's not ladylike. Besides, you're not the first woman in the world to go blonde."

Elaine flicked her eyes from the mirror to the newly laminated Laurel Lake photo ID in her hand. "But Karen will think I've flipped my old-fashioned lid."

"You have," Lily said. "Thank God." She backed out of the door. "Dinner is at seven; your massage is at eight. I'll be at the pool." She swept out of the room.

"Well," Elaine said, looking again at the photo, then back to the reflection that was supposed to be her, "you asked for it."

With a small sigh she turned from the glass and surveyed the large room. It was decorated in shades of celery and cream with touches of aqua—solid, soothing colors in soft, touchable textures, perhaps blended to evoke an aura of peace. A telephone sat on the bureau; next to it was a tray with an ice bucket, a pitcher, and two tall glasses. Elaine plucked Lloyd's roses from her tote, inverted a glass, and quickly plunked them in. She carried it to the bath that was equally, quietly restful.

She wondered how many women had begun new lives—or reinvented their old ones—in this room, in this bath. She wondered if she'd waited on any of them at Saratoga, so many years ago.

After filling the glass with water, she returned to the room, set the flowers on the bureau, then dropped onto the bed. Suddenly, Elaine was tired. But when she shut her eyes, images danced within the darkness.

"I'll have the lemon sorbet with your raspberry crème," a wide-brim-hatted lady was saying.

The raspberry crème had been made from the wild berries Elaine had picked in the morning on the slopes of the back track, where the mist met the dew and the only sounds in the stillness were the soft *neigh*s of the thoroughbreds and the muted hoofbeats that circled the practice track at the top of the hill.

Each autumn, after the horses had left and the berries had, too, it was near those same slopes that Elaine gathered chestnuts for holiday stuffing and for preserving for her father's special quail sauce next season.

She had loved her life in Saratoga. But then she'd gone off to college, had met Lloyd, and her happy memories soon became buried under layers of shame and guilt.

She missed her father sometimes. She missed her mother, too.

Turning onto her side, Elaine thought about her once fun-loving father, how lonely he must be since her mother died a decade ago. He'd closed the restaurant the next year, claiming, "By George, I deserve an early retirement." But Elaine knew that without the presence of his daughter, then without his gentle, steady wife, Bob McNulty had no doubt lost his spirit. An old horse no longer part of the race.

Over the years they'd drifted apart—more guilt on her part, Elaine knew. He sometimes traveled the two hours to West Hope for holidays, but Elaine had always been too busy to go to Saratoga. Too busy with the kids, too busy with Lloyd, too busy with the library board and the PTO and the Fourth of July parade committee.

Too busy or maybe too guilty, the good daughter who'd had a good life, who'd repaid her parents by getting pregnant when, no matter who said they didn't, people still talked.

Too busy because she missed her mother so much, and it was too hard to think about all the times she'd meant to tell her she was sorry but hadn't and now couldn't. She could still tell her father, but it would not be the same. Besides, it was too long ago now, too over-and-done-with. It was easier just to forget.

She rotisseried to her other side, hating that she was thinking these things when it was the beginning of her brand-new life.

Then from the corner of one eye, Elaine spotted Lloyd's roses. She sighed. She closed her eyes again and wondered if, despite what we do and how hard we try, the hooves of our past are never far behind, trotting us toward a future already determined by those things we've already done.

Her last date had been in April in Boston, the night she and Brian had gone to McNally's and Jo had gone home alone.

Six months later here she was, sitting in a red-and-gold-glowing Chinese restaurant on the outskirts of town, with a man named Jack Allen who lived in the apartment building where she lived, and whom she'd almost run down in the parking garage.

She hadn't seen him since the "fortunate incident," as he called it. They had, however, swapped a few notes, tucked under wiper blades, slid under doors. It was playful and sexy and safe. She'd learned that, as a kid, he'd broken his leg in a soapbox derby. She'd learned he was a pilot and that he was from Brussels.

She'd thought he was relatively good-looking, and he was, with very black hair and very light skin and very dark, liquidy eyes. But she hadn't really expected that they'd be well-suited, though his notes made her laugh and that had felt good. Nor had she expected she'd feel such an attraction as they'd driven to the restaurant, that between-the-lines thoughts would now have her thinking about sex when she should have been reading the menu.

It was foolish, of course. She hardly knew him.

She was on the rebound, after all, vulnerable to a quick way to dust off the ashes of Brian.

It didn't mean anything that her palms had grown moist and her mouth had gone dry and her brain didn't seem to know what to say. She'd simply had too many months between dates.

He passed on the wine. "I'm flying tonight," he explained, his accent lightly French. "But please, get something."

She ordered Chardonnay because she was nervous. She'd overdressed in a short fawn suede dress and high coffee-colored boots. He was in faded black denim and sneakers. She'd spent hours getting ready; he hadn't shaved.

"So how did you get from soapbox derbies to jets?" Jo

asked, when her wine had arrived and she began to settle down.

"The derbies didn't pay much of a living," he said.

It took Jo a few seconds to realize he was joking.

"I'm sorry," she said. "I'm out of practice. I haven't been on a date in a long time."

He smiled but didn't say that he hadn't either.

"Really," she asked, "how long have you been flying?"

"Twenty years for Global Paper. Only eight months out of here."

"Well. You must love it."

"What about you?" he asked without giving an answer. "What's a girl like you doing in West Hope?"

She sipped her wine. She wondered what her friends would think if they saw her now, trembling like a teenager.

"It's home," she replied.

He picked up his water glass and raised it in a toast. "To home," he said. "Be it ever so humble."

She supposed he was referring to the building in which they lived, to the working-class tenants that came and then went, to the white plastic chairs on the balconies and the rows of philodendron that lined the windowsills, struggling to survive like everyone else there.

"Humble," she said. "Yes."

He smiled. It was a nice smile. "Perhaps you need some adventure in your life."

"Adventure?" she asked with a laugh. "Yes, maybe that's what I need."

He studied her face. "You're lovely," he said.

She reminded herself that she didn't know him.

"Thank you," she said as she lowered her eyes, embarrassed that his words were so easily welcome.

"So," he said, as he leaned toward her slightly and brushed the edge of her hand where it touched her glass. "How would you feel about a weekend in Brussels?"

6

The dining room was decorated in the same shades as the three sets of "sumptuous silk lounge pajamas" (Lily's words) that Lily had given Elaine before dinner—one of which (the cream-colored one) Elaine was wearing now. Celery, aqua, and cream were apparently spa trademarks.

Rich mahogany furniture and thriving green plants completed the backdrop for fifty or sixty other ladies who were dressed in attire similar to Elaine's, and sipped mineral water between smiles that revealed scarcely a wrinkle, thanks, no doubt, to Botox and a steady hand. Lily fit right in.

Dinner itself wasn't much to write home about.

A small broiled lamb chop. A fresh mint salad. A few baby carrots. It wasn't exactly a gourmet feast at Elaine's father's restaurant, but the flavors were good and she wasn't hungry, anyway. She'd never had a massage and wasn't sure it should be done on a full stomach.

"You're a hoot," Lily said.

Elaine was afraid to ask what she meant. She popped a baby carrot into her mouth.

"Don't get me wrong," Lily continued, "I'm all for makeovers. But, Lainey, you've got an ex-husband who simply still adores you. Why else would he send you flowers? And you had Martin. You never explained why you called off the wedding. Wasn't Martin nicer than Lloyd?"

She swallowed the carrot whole. Thank God it went down. "Lloyd wouldn't have sent roses if Beatrix hadn't left him. As for Martin . . ." She pierced another carrot. "I don't want to talk about either one of them," she said. "I want a new life."

Perhaps because the topic was men, Lily was not eager to let it go. She leaned across the small table. "But you seemed so happy with Martin. What happened, Lainey?"

Elaine reminded herself that romance was Lily's life, Lily's world. Lily had never had to concern herself with teenagers or unfaithful husbands or whether or not the alimony check would last from one month to the next. There would be no getting around it, through it, or past it. Not until Elaine told Lily what she hardly understood herself.

She dabbed the corners of her mouth with the linen napkin. "All right," she said. "But the truth is, nothing happened. In fact, when I said it was over, Martin was wonderful. He never tried to force me to change my mind." Once or twice, Elaine had wondered what she'd have done if he had. There was no point in telling Lily that, though.

"Well, something must have been wrong."

Elaine shook her head. "No. Maybe that was the problem. He's nice and he's loving and he was good to my kids. He has his own business—the Chevy dealership out on Route 7—and he acts in Shakespearian plays in the summer. He's solid and dependable. And he's not bad to look at, though he's almost sixty."

"Was he good in bed?"

"Lily! Life is about more than sex."

Lily smiled a smug grin but didn't reply.

Elaine set the napkin next to her plate. "I changed my mind when the four of us started planning my wedding," she said quietly. "It was such fun to be together again." Lily, Sarah, Jo, and Elaine. *The Four Musketeers*, her father had called them in their early college days, when the world had been nothing but fun.

"When you decided to open the business, well, I thought about my life and how boring it was compared to yours. All of yours."

Lily's eyes grew wide. Her upturned mouth turned down a bit.

"Think about it, Lily. You're still so pretty and vibrant. You've had three husbands and you have lots of money and you can go anywhere in the whole world and do absolutely anything you want."

Lily didn't comment, so Elaine continued. "And Sarah. She's so successful with her jewelry designing. She has a famous guy who isn't her husband, but they've made a wonderful life and have a wonderful boy. She has that great Native American heritage, and she grows herbs and eats health foods and has all that inner peace." Lily might not agree with Sarah's choice of a life, but she couldn't argue with the tranquility Sarah had found.

"And Jo! Good grief. She'll always be gorgeous. She could have any man she wants. And she's so smart. She's so sophisticated. No matter what she wants or what she does, she'll be successful. That's intoxicating to others."

Lily set down her fork but kept her eyes on Elaine. "Shame on you, Elaine McNulty Thomas," she said. "Shame on you for thinking for one single second that any of us have a life that's better than yours."

Elaine was surprised and embarrassed. "I didn't mean *better*, Lily. I meant more exciting. Less tedious." She wasn't sure if that was what she'd meant at all.

Lily picked up her fork again and played with the mint. "More exciting to you, maybe. But we're all so different, Lainey. That's why we've stayed friends. That's why our business will succeed. Because we each bring something different to it."

Elaine shrugged again. "I don't want to get philosophical, Lily. I just knew if I married Martin my life would keep on being conventional. Predictable. Sane. And I'd never have a chance to experience the other side."

Lily's expression turned a tiny bit sardonic. She moved her eyes around the room. "Well, honey, we're in the right place for that."

Elaine's gaze followed Lily's with a tingle of anticipation, a glimmer of fear. Then she shrugged a what-the-hell kind of shrug, kissed Lily's cheek, and left the dining room in search of her first massage.

"Gunter, without an 'H.' "

He was tall and broad-shouldered and built like a boulder, a very big boulder. He wore navy sweatpants and a form-fitted tank top that hugged every muscle like a long-lost best friend. And when he turned to lead Elaine into the massage room, she couldn't help but notice that Gunter (no "H") had an awesome ass.

She fanned her face with her hand.

The table was high and layered with thick towels.

"You may undress if you want." He had big white teeth that flashed when he smiled and looked almost fluorescent against his tanned skin.

" 'Undress'?" Elaine asked. Her voice sounded tiny, as if it had come from a wind chime in a small breeze, not from her.

He smiled again. "Leave on as much as makes you comfortable. Many of my clients remove all their clothes. You can cover your essentials with a towel, don't worry."

She smiled back because she didn't know what else to do.

"I'll leave you to undress," he said. "When you're ready, get up on the table, facedown, on your stomach." He handed her a towel she assumed was to cover her "essentials." Then he left the small room.

Elaine was glad the lights were low. She stood there a moment, a long way from Saratoga, a long way from Martin or Lloyd. She inhaled the air, which seemed inordinately clean. She eyed a waterfall in the corner that gently cascaded over copper and stones. Somewhere in the ceiling, soft music played, Yo-Yo Ma, maybe.

She shivered a little, then took off her new silk pajamas, lounge suit, whatever Lily had called it. She hesitated a moment, then unclasped her bra. She began to slide out of her panties, but stopped. She stared down at them, at the white cotton briefs she supposed she'd have to trade in at some point for silky, pastel French-cut panties, maybe even a thong.

A thong? Were salesclerks allowed to sell thongs to anyone over forty?

She ran her hands over the small lumps and bumps safely ensconced beneath the forgiving cotton. She laughed at herself, knowing it would be best if she stayed with the briefs. It wasn't as if anyone would know.

Except, of course, Gunter. Because there was no way Elaine could have a massage without underpants.

Folding her new outfit, she stacked it onto a chair. She tucked her bra between the bottoms and the top, where Gunter wouldn't see the white cotton cups. As she climbed onto the table she noticed her nipples were hard. She hesitated a moment, then touched them lightly. She circled one tip with her forefinger, then the other. Rock solid, they were. It must be cold in the room. Yes, that was it, it was definitely chilly. It could not possibly be that her nipples had risen to the thrill of undressing in public—well, almost in public—for a muscle-bound, darkly tanned stranger.

A shiver of anticipation traveled to her "essentials."

She groaned a little groan and resisted the urge to touch herself more, to rub her taut nipples, to bring her hand down to the warmth that now swelled inside her.

Instead, Elaine shook her head, flopped onto her

stomach, and tugged at the towel, hoping it covered her back and her butt. Hoping it covered that unwanted need that had only ever spelled trouble for Elaine McNulty Thomas, first with Lloyd, then with Martin, because she'd loved both of their touches so much.

Gunter returned and she regained her focus. "All set?" he asked.

She closed her eyes and said yes, she was ready.

And then Gunter's big hands sank into her shoulders. She almost cried out at his unexpected strength.

"Oh," he said, "you're very tight."

Tight. Oh. Yes.

He lifted his hands. "I'll get the oil."

She opened her eyes. Was the room darker? She heard him rub his big hands together. She tried to command her nipples to return to a state of limp disinterest.

Then his fingers returned to her shoulders.

Her eyes closed again.

Deeply, tenderly, Gunter kneaded her muscles. Slowly, he stretched the length of her arms, loosening every muscle, every piece of tissue, every inch of her skin. Then he moved down her back, caressing her shoulder blades, massaging that small spot that curved under the bone.

The room was not cold. In fact, it grew warmer and warmer with each stroke of his hands.

She wanted to cry out. She wanted to cry out for how long it had been since she'd been touched by a man, by Lloyd or by Martin.

Not that sex with Lloyd had been very plentiful those last several years. But they'd had plenty early on. He had a big, happy penis that seemed engorged most of the time. *The hormones of youth*, she'd thought much later. But time and familiarity had interrupted their frequency, and maybe they both had become a little bit bored.

Then came Martin. It had been years since Elaine had felt passion, real, roll-in-the-hay sex that unleashed all kinds of good stuff.

Yes, Lily, Martin had been good.

Sometimes he'd been too good. Once, he'd wanted to perform oral sex. On her. Of all people. She had resisted because that seemed such an intimate act, to be shared only between husband and wife.

What a fool she had been. Because if Gunter suggested doing that right now, she would not stop him, no way, no how. No "I Do" involved.

Oooh.

Aaah.

All the way down her back, Gunter kept kneading. So gently. So firmly.

She wondered where the towel had gone. Not that it mattered.

Oooh.

Aaah.

And then, he touched the arc of her butt.

He pushed down her panties, her white cotton comfort. He began on the right cheek, stroking the large muscle, tracing its path from her waist to her thigh. Again. And again.

Her legs parted slightly, involuntarily.

Had he noticed?

He moved to the left cheek. He repeated the process.

Then—oh, God!—he took both cheeks in his hands.

Without hesitation, Elaine arched her butt. Tenderly, tenderly, yet oh, so firmly, he . . .

Jesus Christ, she almost shouted as the first throes of an orgasm threatened to shudder all through her.

She sucked in a sharp breath. Then, without pausing for one more racing, out-of-control heartbeat, Elaine scooted from under his hands, clutched the towel against her, and leapt from the table. She grabbed her neat pile of clothes from the chair, stuttered "Thank you, I must go now," then hurriedly flew from the room.

7

They could have had sex right there in the elevator.

After two glasses of wine, sesame chicken that she barely touched, and fried ice cream that they shared with one spoon, Jo could have had sex between the third and fourth floors.

She'd never had sex on the first date, but that wouldn't stop her. Jack Allen was frustratingly tempting, with his small crooked smile and a way of holding his eyes on hers just a little too long, as if he were exploring her down to her toes.

She lost all perspective about being on the rebound, or about having been without a man for too long.

She forgot that she didn't know him.

She leaned against the wall. He held his fingers to her mouth. He traced her lips, her cheeks, her eyes.

"I have to go," he said. "I'll call you when I get back from Brussels. Maybe then we can plan that weekend together."

Then his mouth was on hers, and hers was on his, and the elevator doors opened and it was over that fast.

She meant to ask how long he'd be gone, but in the heat and the madness, she forgot.

8

Word had already leaked out about the Benson nuptials. Well, not *leaked*, exactly, more like had been spread with the speed of an e-mail, thanks to Andrew's carefully planted hints at Ted and Marion's wedding.

"New Year's Eve," Andrew had whispered to local business owners of the florist shop, the restaurants, a string of bed-and-breakfasts. "It's going to be small, but it will be spectacular."

Buzz, buzz.

"Best of all, it's going to attract national media attention to the Berkshires."

Buzz, buzz, speaking of which, too bad he couldn't mention it in his column, too. Someone, however, might add up the *buzz*es and figure out that Olivia, Eileen, Sadie, and Jacquelin of his "Real Women" column were really Lily, Elaine, Sarah, and Jo, and that A.K. was really him.

When he walked in to Second Chances Monday morning, Jo was already hard at work. She seemed happy, immersed. He decided not to ask how her date went last night; he didn't really want to know.

He set his leather briefcase, which held his laptop, on the desk that he'd come to call his own. It was placed across from Jo's, a position that often was distracting. "Good morning," he said. "Busy so early?"

Jo laughed. She brushed back a shock of taupe-colored hair and blinked her green eyes. She wore a soft pastel sweater the color of beach grass or seafoam or one of those earthy colors that made her eyes look more seductive, as if they weren't seductive enough. Yes, she was happy.

He yanked out his laptop, shoved his briefcase in a drawer.

"There must have been thirty messages on our voice mail this morning," Jo said. "All kinds of businesses offering their services."

Well, at least he'd done that right. That, and the fact that he had sort of blackmailed John Benson into the wedding-vow renewal in the first place. ("Let's put it this way, John," Andrew had said, "either agree to do it, or I'm finished with the column. These women need a break to get their business off the ground.") He hadn't had to add that it was his fault—correction, it had been *both* their greedy faults—that he and John had surreptitiously extinguished the one good promotional idea the women had come up with, because it was too risky: It could have blown Andrew's cover and cost tens of thousands of dollars in magazine-ad revenues.

He unzipped his jacket and dropped it onto the chair. "It's about time we got noticed."

"Noticed isn't the word. It's sort of like when the Beatles came to America."

He smiled. "You're too young to remember that."

"I'm aging quickly. And Lily called to say it's just the two of us this week." She looked so damned pretty, he was tempted to flirt. But then the phone rang. *Just as well*, he supposed.

While Jo took the call, he attacked last week's paperwork with more vigor than necessary. Jo hung up and said, "That's the fifth bed-and-breakfast that wants us to see their rooms."

"We might need them all. Two hundred guests. Probably five hundred journalists and their entourages. Every available bedroom from here to the New York State line will be scrambling for a piece of the media pie." He laughed. She laughed. Laughter made her eyes sparkle all the more. He cleared his throat. "Any ideas for the venue?"

"Actually, yes. We had a call from The Stone Castle. It's a beautiful place north of town. Do you know it?"

It was the location for a summer theater: Andrew had heard of it, but had never been there.

"Well," Jo continued, "it's an old Scottish castle, and John Benson is Scottish. I'm sure Lily will think it appropriate."

So Jo had been doing her homework, looking for something unique and special. Something Sunday *Times* style section appropriate. Then she added, "They offered us lunch, to check the place out."

Lunch. With Jo. "As it happens," he said with a grin, "I am free."

It was known simply as The Stone Castle, which boasted thirty guest rooms and a grand ballroom and had been built in the 1800s for Lord Aitken and his bride. Reconstructed with the original stone and wood beams sent by clipper ship from the Scottish Highlands, the castle's turrets and winding staircases sounded like a perfect setting for the winter celebration. The fact that Lady Aitken had caught pneumonia while crossing the Atlantic added to the glamour and mystique, because the poor thing had died not long after arriving in the Berkshires, and rumor had it she still haunted the halls.

When Jo was young it had still been a private home, which hadn't stopped her and her friends from sneaking onto the grounds more than once, trying to peek in the windows and catch a glimpse of life inside, maybe even of the lady herself.

When Jo was in the seventh grade, half of her class went there at Halloween, hoping to have "the bejesus scared out of them," her grandfather had warned. But the lights were off and no one answered the door.

Owned now by Dave and Martha Holland, the castle was advertised as a respite extraordinaire. It had been featured in travel magazines not only for its charm but also because many who spent the night confirmed seeing a mystical presence, a woman dressed for walking through the countryside in a long cloak and a bonnet.

Unlike Lady Aitken, Martha Holland greeted them in Yuppie tartan pants and a crewneck sweater that had no doubt come from Talbots.

The place was exquisite.

Jo held her breath as they softly walked through the long, cool stone corridor into the enormous ballroom that had been recently renovated. The room had a thirty-foot buttressed ceiling with freshly gilded cornices and a full wall of tall stained-glass windows. Across from that was another windowed wall, this one offering a sweeping view of the lawn that sloped down to the lake. From there Jo could see two rowboats tied to a rustic old dock. They sat on still water against a backdrop of leaves that were orange and yellow and red: It could have been a canvas, painted artfully in oil.

"Lovely," Jo whispered, as if it were a dream and could suddenly vanish.

"The fireplace can be lit and monitored by two tenders," Martha said.

Jo turned from the view to the giant granite fireplace that three people could stand up in. Next to it several sets of full-body armor stood at attention, ready for battle. She thought of her long-ago elementary school classmates: None of them could have imagined the exotic world within.

"Look," Andrew said. "Balconies."

Heads turned upward. Jo thought of Romeo and

Juliet. King Arthur and Guinevere. "How romantic," she said. "It's perfect for a wedding." Not for the first time since they'd opened the business, her thoughts lingered for a moment on the fact that she'd never had a wedding of her own. She wondered if that might change, now that a new man was on the brink of entering her life. A small wave of anticipation rushed through her.

"Castles were like cities," Martha was explaining to Andrew.

With reluctance, Jo pulled her attention back to her job.

"Whole communities evolved inside," Martha said. "They weren't just living quarters. They housed doctors, weavers, potters, and God-knows-who-or-what else. They needed spacious rooms because they were self-sufficient."

"Self-sufficient enough for a wedding," Jo said. "I think it has possibilities. Do you agree, Andrew, that the Bensons might love it?"

"I'd put it at the top of the list," he said. "When is Mrs. Benson coming to review the arrangements?"

"In a couple of weeks. In the meantime, we can e-mail her information and talk on the phone. She said she'll trust our judgment."

"Well," he said, "there you have it."

"If you'd like to see the rooms, we can do that now," Martha said. "Then we can have lunch and talk about our services."

Martha led them from the ballroom while Jo fell into step beside Andrew, as if they were there to plan their very own wedding, as if she were the blushing bride, as if he was Jack Allen, the handsome groom.

9

Crunch. Crunch.

The leaves under her feet crunched the way leaves were supposed to when it was New England and it was October.

Elaine forced her chin up and marched behind a woman in front of her on the afternoon nature walk around Laurel Lake. Every footprint was a familiar—too familiar—reminder that she'd been there before, back in her Lloyd-life. The path, however, was well-tended now, the scraggly bushes and sprawling undergrowth had been groomed and landscaped from the boat docks to the ice house, her once-coveted ice house.

With a sliver of a smile, she wondered if the woman in front of her could possibly know the things the woman behind her had done right there. She couldn't, of course, which made Elaine's secret seem somehow delicious. She might not be one of them—not yet—but she had a few talents of her own.

She breathed in the crisp air and tasted the aromas of acorns and oaks and *autumn*. Her father used to say, "a pinch of autumn in every pot," while making his chestnut stuffing or his acorn-squash bisque.

Last night, she'd thought about leaving.

After returning to her room, she'd flopped onto the bed and stared up at the ceiling and wondered what on earth she thought she was doing, trying to be a woman she clearly was not.

An orgasm?

With a stranger?

In private, she'd groaned many groans at her near-miss. Surely she'd have to leave Laurel Lake. But what would she tell Lily? If she stayed, she might run into Gunter. Which choice would be worse? Elaine barely let herself have orgasms in her own bed, in her own home. Not because she feared getting caught, just because it didn't seem right. Small-town upbringing, old-town beliefs, which didn't include masturbation on the list of what a housewife and mom from West Hope should do with her free time.

Not that anyone still thought those kinds of things. It was just one more example of how the world had changed and somehow had left her behind.

All of which Elaine reminded herself over and over, and why she'd ultimately decided not to leave Laurel Lake. If she ran into Gunter she was determined to smile. She would give no excuses about escaping his clutches; if it had happened to Lily, Lily wouldn't have apologized, not that Lily would have ever found herself in such a precarious situation.

So, Elaine had Pilates that morning, followed by meditation and a soy protein shake for her lunch. And now she was walking, like everyone else.

Crunch. Crunch.

"An eagle!" their leader exclaimed, as one hand shot upward to the top of a cluster of nearly naked birch trees.

The necks of the dozen morning walkers swiveled to take in the sight, just as the wings spread and flapped and the giant bird soared to another part of the lake.

The woman in front of Elaine turned around. She was a platinum blonde with a slight gullet of loose flesh and teeth that were too white for their age. "I've never seen one before. Have you?"

Elaine smiled again. "Oh yes. Right here. Many times."

The woman nodded. "This is my first time at Laurel Lake."

"Not mine," Elaine replied, and the woman smiled back and Elaine realized she must think Elaine was one of them.

Like the sumptuous silk of her new outfit, the sensation it generated felt pretty good.

For two days Andrew savored the time alone with Jo. He happily discovered that, on top of those lust-filled feelings, he liked her, really liked her. He liked her clearheadedness, her unwavering energy, her ability to say "No, thank you" to solicitors who called offering one service or another, yet never leaving an impression that she was rejecting them.

He'd also thought about what Cassie had said, that he needed a life more than a magazine column. In order to attempt a life with Jo, he'd have to tell the truth, that he really was Superman and he wanted her, Lois Lane.

He couldn't possibly wait until New Year's. She hadn't said a word about the guy in her building (and he still hadn't asked), but that didn't mean Andrew hadn't already lost his chance.

Late Wednesday afternoon, he said, "I want to surprise Lily and Elaine." It wasn't exactly true. But it seemed a plausible excuse to get Jo out the office to a place much more quixotic. Then maybe he'd tell her the truth.

"Surprise them how?" Jo asked.

"Let's go to Laurel Lake. Check up on Elaine's progress. We can tell them about the castle. It's across the lake from the spa." Like other matters of the heart, Cassie surely would say his romantic attempts were pretty lame.

"I'm sure they know about the castle," Jo said. "It's been there practically forever."

"But not as a bed-and-breakfast. And not as the perfect setting for the Benson wedding."

Jo scanned the screen of her computer, giving him only half her attention. It was not the behavior Superman would have liked.

"It would be fun," Andrew pressed on, "to surprise them. Do you think Elaine has changed much?"

"In three days? Highly doubtful."

He was losing this battle and he didn't like it. He paced to the window and looked out on to Main Street, to the antiques shops and the bookshop and the old brick town hall. He wondered how A.K., woman-know-it-all, would handle it.

"Besides," Jo added, "the spa is only for women. They won't let you in."

Andrew jammed his hands into the back pockets of his jeans. He watched a few local vehicles and the boxy mail truck lumber by, not the big Lincoln Navigators or the zippy Miatas that drove around in season. Once Columbus Day was done, so were the tourists, at least until ski season, still two months away.

By then Jo might be married with a half-dozen kids.

"Unless," Jo said, "we went by boat."

Andrew turned from the window. Jo shut down her computer and rested her elbows on the desk. "What?" he asked.

She smiled. "When we were out at the castle, did you see the rowboats? I used to love to row across the lake when I was a kid. I'll bet Martha Holland would let us use one. We could sneak onto the grounds of the spa and track down Lily and Elaine."

He looked at her. A rowboat ride across a lake. With Jo. Andrew would have said okay, except for one problem: He didn't know how to swim. When he'd been a kid he'd never done the Hamptons or camp. His parents—both physicians—had taken separate vacations (his father to Ireland, where "his people" were; his mother to Vancouver the entire month of August, where she looked after an aging aunt and her half-dozen cats). When one or the other was away, Andrew visited lots of museums with whichever parent was home. Museums and galleries, but never the "Y."

"Oh, come on." Jo was the one who prodded now. She got up from the desk and walked to where Andrew was, hands still in his pockets. "It will be fun. Not to mention the added excitement that we might get caught."

He smiled. "It's kind of cold for boating, isn't it?"

She laughed. "Are you kidding? This is the best time of year. Not as much junk in the water—you know, weeds and lily pads. And tomorrow is supposed to be a beautiful day—Indian summer. Come on," she repeated, lightly touching the sleeve of his beige denim shirt. "The new man in my life says I don't have enough adventure. This will be an adventure, won't it?"

There it was. *The new man in her life.*

"You're on," Andrew said, because he was a man, too, and his brains were not up in his head where they belonged.

He wondered if Cassie was too young to have her father committed.

10

"I have one word for you," Cassie said over dinner after he'd told his daughter of the absurd notion.

"No?" he implored, hoping that was the answer. It wouldn't be the first time he used his daughter as an excuse. "Sorry, but Cassie has a bad cold and I need to stay home with her." It had especially worked well when it came to faculty functions. Who could dispute that anyone—or their cocktail party or their luncheon or, now, a ride in a rowboat—was more important than the health of his daughter?

Cassie shook her head. "Life vest," she said.

"That's two words," he said with annoyance. He cleared the table of their now-empty hot-dog-and-beans plates. It had been his turn to cook and he hadn't been in the mood, having decided on the way home after work that he truly was nuts. A straight man in gay clothes, a master's degree in broadcast journalism, and a job answering phones for a bunch of wedding planners.

He didn't need a shrink to exact a diagnosis.

"Dad, you can't swim," Cassie said.

An image of Superman wearing a bright orange foam vest wasn't quite what he'd imagined in all his imaginings of Jo.

"I guess I should cancel."

"Cancel?" Cassie asked. "A boat ride with Jo Lyons?" She clasped her hands to her chest and rolled her eyes.

"Very funny," he said, then dunked the plates into the enamel pan of sudsy water, ruing the day he'd told Cassie that he had the hots for Jo. "You've forgotten something else. Not only can't I swim, but I can't row a boat, either. Mr. Macho, that's me."

"It doesn't matter, Dad. She thinks you're gay anyway. It's not as if you need to impress her."

He drowned the dishes with a hot-water rinse. "Right," he replied, and then the phone rang.

"I'll get it," Cassie announced. The cordless usually was in the living room, where Cassie bolted, as if Andrew could possibly beat her to it with his hands stuck in the water and his brains—well, he already knew where his brains were located now. He scrubbed the utensils as if the silverplate needed removal.

"Dad?" she asked as she returned. "It's for you." She smiled and held the phone out to him. "It's Jo."

He quickly wiped his hands on his jeans. He grabbed the receiver and shooed Cassie from the room. She stuck out her tongue and went into the hall, but peeked around the corner to let him know she was watching. He laughed in spite of himself, then tried to ignore her.

"Jo?"

"Yes, it's me, the adventure-lady. I called Martha Holland."

"And?"

"And she said we're welcome to borrow a boat. I'm so excited, Andrew! This will be such fun!"

"Oh," he said, "that's terrific." He ran his hand through his hair, turned back and stared at his daughter. This was the time to tell Jo that he couldn't swim. Instead, he said, "I can't remember when I've rowed a boat."

Cassie's jaw dropped; her little pink mouth formed a big O.

Jo laughed. "I'm told it's like riding a horse. You never forget how."

He did not mention that he didn't ride horses, either.

"I told her we'd be there around noon. That will give us all morning to take care of things at the shop. It should take about forty-five minutes to row across the lake. Hopefully we'll find the girls having lunch."

"Is there anything I should bring?" Andrew asked, because what else could he say?

"Maybe bottled water," Jo said, "in case we get thirsty." Then she laughed again. "That's funny, isn't it? To bring water when we'll be surrounded by it?"

Andrew agreed that, yes, that was funny. Then he clicked off the phone, turned his back on his daughter, shoved his hands back into the sink, and pretty much wished he was living on Mars.

Jack Allen had been gone three days. Not really that long, Jo supposed. After all, it was probably foolish to think he would fly to Brussels, turn around, then fly back.

Still, it would be nice if she knew when he planned to return.

She tossed a frozen dinner into the microwave and wished she were better at the man-woman thing. How did it happen that other women could casually flirt, casually date, casually slip in and out of relationships with the seamless ease of a model changing her clothes?

Lily was like that. Elaine and Sarah were not, but they both had the experience of long-term relationships with men that were present, not long-term fantasies like Jo had wasted on Brian.

She supposed it was because of her father.

"You're the prettiest girl in the whole wide world," he'd said when Jo would come in from playing outside and was covered in dirt and her hair was all tangled.

"You're the smartest girl in the whole wide world," he'd said when she brought home her report card and it had all A's.

"You're the nicest girl in the whole wide world," he'd said when she made Christmas cookies and took them to shut-ins like Mrs. Halsey on Park Street and Mr. Turrell on Dwight.

But it hadn't mattered that Jo was pretty or smart or nice. Her father had left anyway, and not said good-bye. In the few cards or gifts he sent those first years he was gone, he hadn't explained why, if she'd been so perfect, she hadn't been good enough to keep him at home.

So she'd spent a lifetime trying to maintain his

expectations, hoping it would matter to someone, at some time, aware that her demands on herself were too great, but not knowing how on earth she could stop, how she could be more like lighthearted Lily.

Lily . . . who would not have brooded one second over Jack Allen. She would have deftly moved on, would be out in search of another new man instead of standing in her kitchen, staring at the microwave.

The timer beeped; Jo retrieved the plastic tray and tried to focus on the next day. It would be fun to be with Andrew. He was so easy to be with, so happy, so unpretentious, with no hidden agendas or potential to betray her.

Manicures, pedicures, even a stone facial massage, where hot stones, then cool stones, alternately glided over Elaine's forehead, cheeks, and chin. By Wednesday night, she didn't know if she was in a trance or just exhausted.

Dinner was filet of sole with thin slivers of almonds, the tiniest green peas Elaine ever saw, and a delicate fan of bright orange mango slices.

"Tomorrow I'm going to take the cooking class," she said to Lily. "Maybe I'll learn how to create pretty dishes like this."

"But you were brought up in a restaurant," Lily remarked. "I'd think the last thing you'd want in your new life is food."

Lily, of course, had been raised like Eloise at The Plaza, where meals were served by white-gloved staff and snacks came only from room service. How could Elaine explain that being in the kitchen was therapeutic, comforting, like being home? "If I brush up on my cooking skills, maybe we can use them at Second Chances."

A tiny frown crossed Lily's forehead. "That's why we have caterers. Besides, if cooking is what you want, why not go see your father? He's the master chef, isn't he?"

Lily might be great at helping Elaine make over her looks, her clothes, and her confidence. But some things, like the ins and outs and ups and downs of family, Lily could never understand.

Stabbing another pea, Elaine didn't comment.

Lily sighed. "It's your life," she said, then added, "but while you're still in my hands, I have another surprise. When we leave here Friday morning, we're going to New York." Lily's eyes twinkled with her Lily-magic; her thoughts were off again on a Lily-escapade. "The limo will pick us up at eight-thirty in the morning. Then I'm taking you shopping for a new wardrobe. My treat. No argument."

Elaine laughed. "You are insane," she said.

"True enough. But in the meantime, you might reconsider switching that cooking class for another massage. I'm going to wear out your feet on the streets of Manhattan."

The cooking class, of course, was much safer than a massage. But Lily wouldn't understand Elaine's reasons for believing that, either.

Maybe it was Lily's mention of Elaine's father that got Elaine thinking about family again, about her kids, about her daughter Karen, who didn't like her now. She wondered if there were a way to salvage the relationship before it crossed the line into mother-daughter hell, before she and Karen drifted as far apart as Elaine and her father had done. *No one's fault, really*, an outsider like Lily might think. *It just happens in families.*

It happens, Elaine knew, because families let it.

After dinner she tried to ease her glum mood with a swim in the indoor pool. It didn't help. She thought about her father; she thought about her daughter. Clearly, the spa afforded too much time for too much thinking. Staying busy had always proved less painful. Like she'd heard on a talk show one afternoon, Elaine had become a *human doing* instead of a *human being.*

Except for the periods of depression following the dumping by Lloyd and the ouster of Martin, *to be* had not been an acceptable state.

When her mood didn't elevate, Elaine hauled herself from the water, wrapped the thickest towel she'd ever seen around her special-issue, Laurel Lake tank suit, stepped into the complimentary flip-flops, and went back to her room, feeling guilty that Karen might have eaten a Big Mac for dinner and probably sat alone now, listening to CDs.

After a quick shower, Elaine sat on the bed and knew she had a choice: strengthen the bond with her daughter, or let it grow weaker and weaker. She picked up the phone and asked for an outside line. In four rings, Karen answered.

"Did you have your music on, honey?" Elaine asked.

"No. I was watching TV."

"Anything good on?"

"No."

"You're not baby-sitting tonight?"

"No."

Of course Karen wouldn't ask how Elaine was doing. Elaine sighed. "Would you like to come clothes shopping in New York? With Lily and me?"

"Shopping?" At least it was a word she recognized.

"We're going Friday. Lily rented a limo." Lily's world attracted most every teenage girl. "You could take the day off from school."

"Okay. Sure."

It didn't matter whether it was the prospect of new clothes, a ride in a limo, or the day off from school. It was Elaine's first step toward rebuilding her family, and it felt better than a thousand facials or a million massages.

11

I'm beginning to think I should be writing this column about the trials of a man, not a woman, looking for love.

Andrew had barely slept through the night. He arose way too early, took extra time shaving, put on his most comfortable jeans and a new flannel shirt that was solid navy and Cassie had said brought out the blue in his eyes. He'd trundled downstairs and made pancakes for Cassie. ("On a weekday, Dad? Wow.") He watched from the window as she skipped to the big yellow school bus, then he sat down at his laptop. Baring his soul to his readers might help quiet the commotion going on in his gut. It also might help to kill time.

I felt this way once, he continued. *I was in over my head, out of my league, but I married her anyway and had a few years of heaven, then*—bang!—*it was done. Done for her, anyway.*

He thought about Patty, a luxury he rarely allowed himself lately. Besides, with Jo in his thoughts, Patty had moved to the proverbial back burner, the bottom of the list, no longer a priority.

If only Cassie didn't resemble her so much.

He'd been startled when he'd seen Patty's picture in the latest issue of *Buzz.* She was romping on a beach at her new home in Australia with her cowboy husband and their bouncing baby boy. They must have moved to the coast from the outback. Andrew had almost asked John why the hell he'd allowed the photo to be printed, why he'd given one inch of PR to the woman who had ripped up Andrew's life and Cassie's, as well.

Not long ago he would have; hell, he might even have told John what he could do with this job. But Andrew had merely grimaced, turned the page, and reminded himself he was lucky he had Cassie. The other guy had Patty and their baby named Gilbert, of all names, and good riddance to them all.

He'd also reasoned that John had known the photo would help sell magazines, because Patty could still create a sensation in her perky, ego-driven, own special way. Not to mention that, after all these years, John would probably have expected that Andrew had rid himself of her debris.

Well he had, and to prove it, he hadn't ditched the copy, but slid it under the old couch with the rest of the issues that held his "Real Women" articles, his private stash of the famous men's tutorials best left unseen by the eyes of an eleven-year-old girl. The issue and the photo were safe there: Cassie didn't vacuum, Andrew did, so she didn't know what was filed along with the dust.

Besides, he reassured himself, he was a professional. His job was to write about real women. It was not to create a forum for him to vent his frustrations with the opposite sex.

Glancing back at the laptop, he clicked on his mouse and highlighted his words. Without further reflection, he hit the DELETE button and shut down the power.

Yes, he said to himself, he was a professional. And he would start with the boat trip. It was, after all, an ideal chance for "Real Women" research: the city sophisticate, Jo, embarking in a rowboat because some guy had said she didn't have enough adventure in her life.

Andrew got up, threw on his denim jacket, and decided he'd show her some adventure, if he didn't drown first.

Martha Holland must have spent too much time hanging out with the ghost of Lady Aitken and her otherworld powers. How else could she have picked up on Andrew's interest in Jo?

"You two have a good time," she'd said as she untied the small boat and pushed it from the dock. "Don't do anything I wouldn't do." Then she winked at Andrew.

When they were out of earshot, Jo laughed. "She thinks we're lovers," she said. "Isn't that cute?"

Yeah, real cute. The truth was, Andrew was so focused on staying alive he could barely think about Jo, who now sat in the rowing position because she (thank God) had begged Andrew to let her row for a while. She wore jeans today, yellow rubber boots, and a thick fisherman sweater. They both wore the predictable god-awful orange life vests, courtesy of Martha Holland. Andrew wasn't convinced, however, that if the boat capsized, a hunk of canvas-covered foam would hold up his six feet, one hundred and eighty-five pounds.

He sat at the back of the boat (or was it the front?) facing Jo. He gripped the sides of rough, raw wood, and tried to act as if this was fun.

"We must have a barge here on the lake," Jo said as she stroked the water with the flat wood oars.

" 'A barge'?" He leaned first to the right, then to the left, trying to adapt to the gentle sway of the vessel.

"For fireworks. For the Bensons. It will look incredible from the castle."

"Oh," Andrew said. "Yes. Good idea, matey." He attempted to laugh, but that didn't work. He picked up a small stick that floated on the water. He dragged it over the surface, studying the small ripples, trying not to think about how deep Laurel Lake was.

A short time passed, then Jo quietly said, "I guess you haven't done much of this."

Had the fact that he'd seemed paralyzed been her first clue? "I'm a city kid," he admitted with a smile. No sense in adding that the only time he'd been on a boat was the Staten Island Ferry with his fifth-grade class, and then he'd stayed inside because of that swimming thing. No sense in adding that the closest he'd been to this much water was when Patty had the hot tub installed on the terrace of their high-rise apartment.

"I can't imagine what that was like," Jo said. "I grew up here, playing with snakes and frogs and eating fresh strawberries in June and blueberries in August."

He grinned and loosened his grip just a little. "We had fresh fruit in the city," he said. "It was called the Produce Department." He watched her now, with the sun on her face. She wore no makeup that day, none that was detectable. She didn't need any. Her skin was creamy and smooth and lightly bronzed from the leftover summer. He dropped his gaze back to the water.

"You know so much about our lives," Jo said, "but you've said so little about yours."

"Mine?" he asked. Was that a squeak in his voice? "Ha," he said, trying to mask his sudden discomfort, hustling his brain cells to come up with an answer. "There's little to tell." Little he *could* tell, was more like it.

He thought of the many times that, as a journalist, Andrew had reported that it wasn't the lies that ruined a career/appalled a nation/sent someone to jail; it wasn't the lies, it was the cover-up.

Nixon.

Clinton.

Martha Stewart.

Andrew David Kennedy?

He closed his eyes and tried to sync with the rocking motion. "Let's see," he said slowly. "I was born in Manhattan, an only child of two doctors who'd had me too late." Yes, that sounded good.

" 'Too late'?" Jo asked.

"Well, too late to be real parents. I often thought I was a hurry-up baby. You know, 'Hurry up and get pregnant before the clock runs out and we're old and wish we'd had at least one.' "

He thought he sounded rather amusing, but Jo stopped rowing and said, "Andrew, that's terrible."

He opened his eyes. "It wasn't so bad. They both worked long hours taking care of the poor. But we had a great doorman who looked after me. And there was a young couple on our floor who didn't have kids but claimed they liked being surrogate parents to me." He didn't mention that the young couple had been John and Irene Benson, or that John had become his mentor, often taking Andrew with him to whatever studio or newsroom or magazine he was working with, a media mogul even at a young age. It was then that Andrew found journalism, then that he'd been told he had the good looks to do network.

Of course, he couldn't tell her those parts.

"So that's it?" Jo asked. "What about college? When did you decide to become a journalism professor?"

He sucked in his lip because he—the man who led two lives—hated to lie. "I worked in the city at first," he said as evasively as he dared. "Then Cassie came into my life and I decided she might have a better upbringing out here in the country. Winston College had an opening... and here we are." It was sort of the truth.

"You have no family? Your parents are... gone?"

"They both lived past eighty. But it was pretty amazing. They'd been married sixty years, then they died less than six weeks apart."

"How sad," Jo said.

"Sad? I thought it was neat to have been that devoted."

She shook her head. "Sad that you have no one."

She meant, of course, that she thought it was sad that he had no partner, no *man* in his life. "I have Cassie," he said, "and now I have the four of you. What more could a guy want?"

She smiled a half smile. "Maybe he wants to row. My arms are getting tired."

Before Andrew knew what had happened, Jo had set down the oars, stood up and stretched, and tiptoed toward him with the grace of a gymnast.

Oh, shit.

He stood up on one leg, then on the other. He wobbled. He laughed. "I'm not sure about this sudden transfer of power," he tried to joke. The boat jiggled beneath him. Beneath *them.*

"Stay to my right," she said, taking him by the arms and looking into his eyes. "Steady now."

He tried to be steady, really he did. But before Andrew knew it, either he or the boat had wobbled too far, and Jo toppled to the bottom and he toppled, too, and he fully expected that next would come a mouthful of water and the scenes of his life flashing before him.

He heard a loud *crack,* followed by a series of splinters beneath him.

And then he landed on her, half on, half off her, really, their bodies separated only by their orange-covered foam vests, their faces separated only by a kiss.

12

She laughed.

Between that spark of a second when their faces touched and when Andrew had the chance to say a few words; between that flicker of an instant when his thoughts caught up with what had happened and when he knew this was the time, this was the moment, the one God-given opportunity for him to lay his lips on hers and taste her mouth and her tongue and her sweet breath and to disclose his true colors and his heterosexualness, Jo laughed.

"Well," he said, then awkwardly maneuvered from his post-sex-like position, rolling from her body so the poor woman could breathe.

"Well, indeed," Jo said, still laughing. She managed to rise to a seated position; she managed to not look disheveled, but beautiful still. "Let that be a lesson to those of us who've forgotten we're no longer kids and that it's been a while since we've rowed a boat."

Andrew just smiled. "Are you all right?" he asked. "God, I'm so sorry."

Jo nodded and half crawled back to the place where she'd been sitting. She pulled herself onto the plank, looked around, then back at Andrew. "Well, I'm all right except for one minor problem."

"Which is? . . ."

She reached down and presented him with one of the oars. Or at least with two halves of one oar. "We seem to be impaired," she said, then nodded toward the water. "And our other one went overboard."

His eyes moved from the broken oar—the obvious culprit that accounted for the splintering *crack* beneath his weight—out to the water, where the matching oar, though still intact, drifted in the opposite direction.

"Well," he said. He was stalling for time. She probably expected him to come up with a solution, because, gay or not, he was the man, wasn't he?

"Well, how are you at paddling with your hands?" she asked.

"All the way to the spa?"

Jo shielded her eyes against the Indian summer sun that didn't feel as nice as it had only moments ago. "It's closer than going back to the castle. Our only other choice is to sit here and wait for another ship to pass."

It took him a second to realize that was a joke, that Jo wasn't angry with him. "I'm sorry," he said again. "It was my fault."

"Just a little maritime accident," she said. She appeared to be studying the shoreline, where tall, looming pines crept up out of the water.

"We're close enough to shore," she said, "that one of us could swim for help."

Well, he supposed he should have expected that, what with the way this day, this life, seemed to be going for him. He sighed. "I guess the swimmer would have to be you," he said, his eyes closing, waiting for his humiliation to surface.

"No!" Jo said. "I'm not going to leave you alone in the boat. You're a city kid, remember?"

Oh, God, he thought. She actually thought it would be easier to be the swimmer than the one left behind. "Not to worry," he said. "I have plenty of water." He tapped the edge of the cooler that Cassie had reminded him to bring. "Besides," he added, nodding toward land, "I'll hardly be welcome at the spa. That man-thing, remember? Imagine if I wander into a Pilates class dripping wet and covered with seaweed."

Jo laughed. "It's a lake. There's no seaweed. A little algae, maybe. No seaweed."

But he shook his head. "It's settled," he said. "You swim. I'll go down with the ship."

She smiled and asked, "Are you sure?" as if she had the better end of the algae-covered stick.

"Quite," Andrew replied, folding his arms, staking the old wooden boat as his turf.

She unbuckled her life vest, then slipped her arms through it. She leaned down and tugged off her yellow boots. "Well, then, I won't want these weighing me down," she said with a laugh. Then Jo stood up, set her feet slightly apart, reached down and quickly pulled her sweater up over her head. She shook out her hair while Andrew tried to breathe.

The white cotton knit shell clung to her breasts the way he would have liked to. Then, with another small smile, she unbuttoned the top of her jeans, unzipped the fly, and slid the denim down to her ankles.

He flinched. He forced himself to look away, but not before he saw the long, lean, tanned legs and the clean whiteness of bikini panties looking back at him.

And then Jo turned sideways and plunged into the water.

The water was cool, cold, actually. Maybe the chill would help her come to her senses.

But as Jo sliced the surface and headed toward the shoreline, she couldn't push the questions from her mind: Had Andrew almost kissed her?

And what was worse, had she wanted him to?

She turned her head to one side, took another breath, and kept swimming.

They were learning to make Spinach-Mango *Insalata*—a fancy Italian name for "salad." Elaine was certain they'd served one like it at McNulty's in Saratoga: baby spinach leaves, crisp arugula, toasted pecans, and mandarin sections, all laced with a parsley vinaigrette.

Presentation is everything, her father often said. She wondered if Lily learned that from him.

She chuckled again, amused by the unexpected humor emerging from her. Which was why, when a familiar voice called out her name, interrupting her enjoyable task, Elaine was first annoyed, then quickly alarmed, when she saw the intruder was Jo. In a Laurel Lake bathrobe. With soaking wet hair that was glued to her scalp like Liza Minnelli's in *Cabaret*.

Elaine dropped the colander. "Jo! What are you doing here? What's wrong?" She maneuvered through the counters where half a dozen other women were busy with their *insalatas*. She wiped her hands on her Laurel Lake apron as she went.

Jo was shaking her head. "Nothing's wrong. Andrew and I came for a surprise visit. We got a little sidetracked." She laughed. She said she'd asked the first person she saw if she knew Lily or Elaine: She'd been given a robe then directed to the kitchen. She opened the robe, revealing wet underwear. "It turned out to be a surprise all right. Poor Andrew is stuck in the boat."

Elaine shook her head with a laugh, and knew that domestic diva-ness would just have to wait.

If his laptop were in the rowboat, Andrew could have worked on his column. If his cell phone were there, he could have called John, or at least Irene. If he had learned how to swim, he could have been on land.

He was glad he'd made sure that Cassie had swimming lessons back in the city, though it had meant giving up

Tuesdays and Thursdays from seven-thirty to nine. It was no sacrifice—at least, not for him. Patty had never once taken her, claiming a late booking or an early call, depending on which was more convenient. It took Andrew a while to figure out that while he sat on a damp, wooden bench in the chlorine-scented, tile room, munching Doritos for dinner and cheering for Cassie, his wife's off-hours appointments primarily happened when Lonnie Mack was in town.

Lonnie Mack, the playboy, cowboy son of one of Australia's largest sheep breeders ("The finest Merino," Patty had told him); Lonnie Mack, current husband of Patty, father of Gilbert.

Gilbert the Grape, as Cassie had called him.

"Andrew!"

His body twitched. He half expected to see Patty.

Holding his hand to shield the sun, he was glad it was Jo nestled in a shadowy cove, clutching a robe around her. On her left stood someone who looked like Elaine; on her right was Lily, no mistaking the tiny, excited sprite. All three women waved.

He waved back.

"Sit tight," Jo shouted. "Help's on the way."

He heard a *putt-putt* and saw an aluminum craft head toward him, then swing around, as the driver—a burly man—slowed the engine, dipped over the edge, and scooped the rowboat's lost oar out of the water.

The boat arced a U-turn, then came alongside Andrew. The man cut the motor and drifted close. He tossed Andrew a rope. "I work up at the spa," he said with a thick accent. "Name is Gunter, without the 'H'."

He looked like Arnold Schwarzenegger on the early side of forty. "Andrew," Andrew replied, picked up the rope, and wondered if he should tie it somewhere. He glanced toward the women. Was the new man in Jo's life as rugged—as muscled—as Gunter? And was that what women—*real women*—wanted?

"Tie it to the bow," Gunter said, pointing to the small end of the boat.

Andrew was grateful for the direction, but dismayed that the bow was at the opposite end of *him*, about ten feet away.

He got up slowly, gingerly. He stepped on one foot, hoping, praying that this time his balance would hold. He knew that the women were watching.

"Shit," he muttered under his breath, then took another step. The boat rocked slowly beneath his sneakers. He clutched the rope more tightly.

And then Andrew lost his balance. Both arms flew up; the rope dropped from his fingers. But the gods were on his side: He managed to stay upright. He dared another glance toward shore. Jo's hands covered her mouth.

Andrew laughed. He signaled for the women not to worry, that he had everything under control. Then he looked down and saw that the rope had fallen into the water.

Gunter pulled it out, then tossed it over again. "Maybe you should sit down," he said. "Just hang on to the rope. Don't bother to tie up."

Not to worry, Andrew thought. He knew when it wasn't his day.

Of all the people who could have rescued Andrew, Lily had dragged Gunter from the massage room where she'd been scheduled for a full-body rubdown.

Elaine didn't want to know more.

What she did know was that, as she stood on the shore watching the boats drawing closer, she couldn't be sure if the warmth in her cheeks was from the sun or from mortification.

She did not know what to say.

She did not know what to do.

So she did what she expected every woman in her Laurel Lake flip-flops would do: She kept her eyes totally fixed on Andrew, kept a smile on her face, and pretended Gunter did not exist.

In the morning, before they left, she'd leave a big tip in an envelope for him. No sense having him think she was ungrateful, in addition to being a fool.

13

Andrew didn't get home until suppertime. As he pulled into the driveway he noticed the kitchen light was on: Daylight savings time would soon be over and darkness would hurry the end of the day. The night somehow seemed sinister out in the country without high-rises glowing and headlights defining the streets.

He turned off the ignition and looked through the window. Cassie sat at the table. Her head was bent; she was no doubt doing homework.

She'd be eager to hear about his adventure with Jo. He wished he could tell her that it had been fine, but Cassie knew him too well. He'd have to tell her the humiliating parts: including when he trudged up the hill behind Jo and the muscle man, when he waited in the staff quarters until Jo had changed back into her clothes. He'd have to say he watched while Gunter hoisted the rowboat ("No tanks," he'd said, without the "H," to Andrew, when Andrew offered to help), then tied it into the back of the pickup truck, to return it to the Hollands'.

The closest Andrew had come to the experience of Laurel Lake Spa was drinking warm tea that Gunter said was loaded with good herbs, which he oddly pronounced "Herbs" as if they were named after men.

With a short sigh, Andrew got out of the car. Sometimes—not often, but sometimes—he had to admit that he missed the old days when the name Andrew David meant something in some places, when maître d's called him "Mister" as if he were someone important.

Cassie looked up at the window but she did not wave.

"Hey," he said, after unlocking the back door and stepping inside.

"Hey yourself," she said, closing a magazine—not a school textbook.

"What a crappy day," he said. He hung his jacket on a peg in the back hall. He noticed she hadn't made dinner. He sat down at the table and said, "How about Friendly's tonight? I'll tell you my woes over a huge root beer float."

Cassie pulled back her hair and lowered her eyes. And Andrew got that uncomfortable feeling in his gut that warned him he wouldn't like what was coming next.

She slid the magazine across the table to him. "Why didn't you show me?" she asked. The quick flash of her eyes was all it took for Andrew to know that she had been crying.

His eyes dropped. Crap. It was *Buzz.*

He covered the magazine with an open palm.

"Honey," he said, going for humor, because what else could he do? "I didn't know you were into such intellectual stimulation."

She didn't say anything.

He moved his hand over to hers. "I would have showed you," he said, "but I didn't think you'd love seeing a picture of your mother dancing around on some dumb beach, acting as if she's having the time of her life." There. When all else fails, Andrew thought, honesty was still the best goddamn policy.

"I know where you keep your magazines, Dad. I'm not stupid." Then Cassie's thick lashes glistened; tears dropped down her cheeks.

No, Cassie wasn't stupid. But she was curious. Of course she was curious. She was smart; she was eleven. Andrew needed to remember that more often. He went over to her side of the table. "Honey," he said, first patting her hair, then drawing her head to his chest.

"Is she trying to get back at us?" Cassie asked.

He had no idea why she'd think something like that. "Get back at us for what?" Had Cassie forgotten it was Patty who'd left, Patty who'd filed for divorce?

Oh, God, he thought, maybe she'd somehow learned the rest, the one thing Andrew would never tell her, that Patty hadn't fought him for custody because she said she didn't want Cassie to get in her way.

"She must hate that we have such a good life without her," Cassie said. "That must be why she got married again and had that kid Gilbert. I bet now she's trying to let us think her life is good, too. But it isn't, Dad, is it? I mean, it can't be as good as ours is."

Andrew hugged her again because he didn't know what to say. And suddenly the rowboat and Jo and Gunter the God and Jo's quest for adventure seemed a million miles away and not very important.

Jo slept. For the first time since she'd lived on Shannon Drive, she did not hear the sounds of other people's lives through the walls, she was not disturbed by thoughts of what would happen the next day or the day after that.

When she opened her eyes and realized it was morning, she knew something was different, but she didn't know what.

She showered and dressed and grabbed a quick breakfast bar, her thoughts fixed on the fun of the day before.

Jack Allen had been right: She'd needed some adventure; though perhaps he hadn't meant a rowboat on Laurel Lake. But to be away from the office, to laugh with her friends... even the collision she'd had with Andrew... maybe that most of all, for its unexpected, quicksilver, hormonal spark.

First Jack Allen, then Andrew.

Had Jo's interest in men returned in one week?

She applied lipstick over her smile, grabbed her Coach bag and went out the door, knowing that things usually changed without warning, grateful they seemed to have changed in her favor this time.

Though she would have doubted it was possible, Jo's mood escalated even more when she stepped into the parking garage and saw Jack leaning against her Honda. His arms were folded; his grin was smug.

"You're back," Jo said.

"I am," he replied.

She readjusted her bag on her shoulder. "Was it a good trip?"

"Uneventful. I thought of you often."

She didn't know what to say, so she just smiled.

"I thought we might do breakfast."

Jo laughed. "I'm on my way to work."

"I know. I've been waiting for you."

She winced at the thought that he might know her schedule. It felt a bit... what? Too close, too soon?

"Does that upset you?"

She pushed her fears away. Too many months between dates, she reminded herself. "No. It's okay. I was surprised, that's all."

He smiled. "So let's have breakfast. You can go in late, can't you?"

Yes, she could go in late. After all, Andrew would be the only one there.

14

This counted twice Elaine would be in a limo—well, three times if you counted their trip to New York for the television show as one time for each way.

At eight-twenty the phone in her room rang and the receptionist announced that her driver was there. *Her driver.* As if she were anyone special.

Lily had said any of the silk outfits would be fine, that they'd be in the city in plenty of time to shop for something appropriate to wear to lunch.

Lunch! Of course they would *do lunch*. Didn't everyone?

Elaine dropped her tip envelopes at the front desk (yes, one for Gunter—she hoped twenty dollars was the going rate for an orgasm), walked toward the front entrance and wondered about the bounce she felt in her steps, a little bit jaunty, a little carefree. She wondered if it was newfound confidence, and if so, how long it would last.

The driver—a young man in a stunning black suit with a waist-short jacket and high collar—held open the back door of the white stretch. Lily was already seated inside. Elaine glanced over her shoulder, disappointed that no one was around to witness her departure, like the woman from the nature walk, or even Gunter.

She climbed in and Lily said, "Oh, I should have suggested you pull your hair back in a knot."

Elaine's hands went to the sides of her head. She'd spent twenty minutes this morning getting it teased and lacquered in just the right way.

"Never mind," Lily said with a smile. "Karen can bring a brush and we can do it later." Elaine had told Lily about her plan to patch things up with her daughter; Lily had agreed that the small trip might help.

It was odd, riding through West Hope as if she were the Queen of Sheba. They moved through the center of town: the town green on one side, Second Chances on the other. Elaine waved and said, "Too bad no one's up this early to wave back."

The only shop open at that hour was the coffee shop and luncheonette. Elaine considered rolling down the window and having the driver blow the horn, but she supposed that was something the old Elaine might have done.

The limo moved through town then turned down Elaine's street. As it approached the house, Elaine noticed that Karen was halfway down the driveway. A good sign, Elaine supposed. Her daughter must be looking forward to the day.

"Wait just a minute," Lily instructed the driver. Then she flung open the back door and held out her arms to Karen. "You look divine," Lily said, and she was right. Karen wore jeans and a new white sweater and the tan suede jacket Lloyd had given her last Christmas. Elaine had been certain Beatrix picked it out. When Karen had opened the package, Elaine witnessed a look of glee on her daughter's face. It had been one of those tough-to-swallow moments that Elaine would rather forget.

Karen pirouetted for Lily. "I'm ready," Karen said, tossing her backpack onto the seat. "But is the Big Apple ready for me?"

Lily laughed and Elaine smiled, grateful that Karen was in a good mood.

"Do me a favor, dear?" Lily added. "Run back in the house and grab a hairbrush. Your mother changed her mind about the way she wants her hair today."

Karen climbed in after her backpack and patted the side. "I have a brush right here." She unzipped the main compartment, shoved her hand inside, rumbled around a few seconds, then came up with a hairbrush. Attached to the bristles were several one-hundred-dollar bills.

"That looks like shopping money! Hooray!" Lily laughed.

"Karen," Elaine said, as her daughter detached the bills and stuffed them back in the bag, "are you planning to spend your baby-sitting money in New York?"

The girl shrugged. She made no comment about Elaine's new hair, new makeup, new look.

"Karen?" Elaine asked again, because she was the mother.

With a loud sigh, Karen raised her eyes to the string of starry lights that ran along the edge of the ceiling. "If you must know, it's from Daddy."

Lily closed the door, not that the neighbors would be surprised if they heard Elaine and Karen argue.

"Your father gave you money?"

"I told him we were going today. He wanted me to have fun."

"You can have fun without spending money," Elaine replied. Of all of her kids, Karen knew that. What had changed?

The eyes traveled from the ceiling back to Elaine. "Is that what you're going to do? Refrain from spending?"

Elaine looked out the window at the modest house she'd been awarded in the divorce because it was their home: hers, the kids'. It had been home; it had never been about the money.

Karen took out her portable CD player—from Lloyd on her last birthday—and hooked the wires to her ears. Elaine gave Lily a grim look, as Lily said, "Okay, driver. Take us to New York."

Jo and Jack Allen went in separate vehicles to the luncheonette on Main Street near Second Chances. On the way there, Jo called and left a message where Andrew could find her if there was a crisis.

The last booth at the back was available. Jo ordered coffee and juice; Jack, a BLT. "My body's on Belgium time," he explained. "It thinks it's lunch."

"How do you handle jet lag?" Jo asked.

"Ah, the most frequently asked question. The answer is simple: I don't handle it well. For quick trips, I don't change my watch. I pretend I'm still on whatever time it was when I left. Other times I just let myself sleep for days."

The image of Jack Allen stretched out on a bed was not without appeal. Jo sipped her juice as if it were Chardonnay.

"I don't suppose that I'll do this indefinitely. Sooner or later I'll need a break."

She hoped his break wouldn't come before they'd gotten to know each other better, certainly not before she'd experienced another of his kisses. "Tell me about Belgium," she said, "about Brussels."

Jack launched into a travelogue of the Grand'Place and the market square and its gothic architecture and guild houses. He asked if she knew about "Mannequin Pis," the peeing-boy statue.

She diverted a comment about the statue's stone penis. Instead she said yes, that she'd heard it peed beer at certain times of the year.

He said he was impressed with her worldliness.

She realized his hand had, at some point, moved over to hers, and his fingertips now rested on hers. She raised her eyes to look at him. He laced his fingers with hers. She wondered if eight o'clock in the morning was too early for sex with a stranger.

"Jo!"

The sound of her name rose over the clatter of dishes and chatter of patrons. She looked up to see Andrew fast approaching their booth. She pulled her hand quickly from Jack's.

"Andrew," she said.

His cheeks were red and he seemed out of breath. "It's Irene Benson. She's on the phone. She insists on talking to one of 'the girls.' "

Jo looked at Jack, who patiently waited. "Oh," she said, "I'm afraid I'll have to go."

"We could have dinner," he said. "Tomorrow, perhaps?"

She stood up. "Tomorrow would be fine."

"Seven o'clock? My place?"

His place? She hoped that Andrew didn't see her shiver. "Fine," she replied. "I know where it is."

She smiled and he smiled back.

She followed Andrew from the coffee shop knowing that the next day, she and Jack would have sex.

He supposed he'd go to hell for what he'd done.

Andrew didn't feel guilty, however, for having called Irene, woken her up, and insisted she talk to Jo to keep her away from this new boyfriend of hers.

"Tell her you must decide immediately about a reception venue, that your husband wants the name and details included in an article for his magazine and he has a deadline."

"Andrew," Irene had said, "you're really a romantic."

He didn't care if he was romantic or nuts. He only knew that Cassie's distress the night before had reminded him about pain, about how he'd lost a woman he'd loved to another man.

He damned well didn't want to lose another, at least not before he was ready.

15

"It's awful," Karen said to her mother as Elaine emerged from the dressing room in Ann Taylor wool pants and a beige cashmere sweater. Elaine supposed she should at least be happy that her daughter was there, and that she was speaking.

"It's not awful at all," Elaine responded. "It's soft and it's elegant and it's tailored to look good for any occasion." The salesclerk had said so, though Elaine didn't add that.

"It's awful," Karen repeated. She stood next to the triple-view, full-length mirror. "It's as bad as your hair." It was the first time Karen had acknowledged her mother as a blonde.

Elaine bit her lip and tried to smile. "It's just different for me, that's all."

"You're trying to look like Lily, Mom. Forget it. Look like yourself."

"I am myself. My new self, not Lily." Each caustic remark of Karen's only reinforced Elaine's resolve. Karen's judgment was skewed. She was still the girl who wanted her mother to get back with her father, despite the things that her father had said and had done. Elaine had shielded her from most of the details, except for one night when he'd shouted that Beatrix had given him head. "*Mind-blowing head*, Elaine. Do you know what that means?" Neither of them had known that the then-thirteen-year-old Karen was home. Neither of them had known she was standing outside of their room until she let out a wail and raced down the stairs and out the front door.

No wonder Lloyd gave her CD players now, and suede jackets and hundred-dollar bills.

Karen sighed. "Try this," she said, handing her mother a pink-and-orange shirt with a beaded fringe hem. "It came from another department."

"It came from Mars, dear," Lily interjected as she approached them. "Quick, put it back before it multiplies!" She laughed, then eyed the garment more closely. "On second thought, you try it on. It might be perfect with your coloring."

Having won a form of approval from her mother's friend, Karen skipped off to a dressing room. Lily turned to Elaine and surveyed her slowly. "You look marvelous," she said. "The Ann Taylor is very becoming on you."

"Karen doesn't like it."

"Good taste is acquired," she said, her voice a small whisper. "For Greek olives and malt scotch and good clothes, as well. Karen is still young. She can get away with lots of fashion faux pas. Especially in West Hope." Lily fussed with the roll collar of the sweater.

Elaine shrugged. "She thinks my hair looks ridiculous, that these clothes are awful, and that I'm trying to look like you."

Lily's nose wrinkled. "Like me? Heavens, no. I don't wear Ann Taylor. I'd look absurd in such conventional pieces." She stepped back and surveyed her again. "But you really do look marvelous. That sweater shows off your slim waist and those pants drape so softly they camouflage other parts."

The lumps and bumps under my white cotton briefs, Elaine knew, but didn't add.

"I like them, too," Elaine said. "Can I find others in different colors? If I can just get a couple of outfits, then we can have lunch and get back... before Karen totally depletes my Laurel Lake Spa glow."

"Not spend the whole day shopping? Good heavens, dear, what will my credit card think?"

Elaine laughed. "You've been so wonderful, Lily, but I'm not going to exploit your generosity. Besides, I think maybe the less time Karen has to watch my transformation, the better for everyone."

She strolled to the rack where the pants were hung, and picked out a pair in chocolate and one in black. Lily handed her a black blazer, an off-white tank, and a long chocolate cardigan. "Toute suite," she commanded, and Elaine dashed into the dressing room, grateful that Lily had the patience for the delicate mother-daughter dynamics.

Lily suggested lunch at Patsy's, knowing it had purportedly been Frank Sinatra's favorite hangout; unaware, however, that Sinatra's number one fan in Saratoga had been Bob McNulty.

The maître d' escorted them into the long, narrow room that was filled with delightful sounds of laughter and delectable aromas of Italian secrets. Elaine knew her father would have loved the place. Like the walls of McNulty's, Patsy's featured rows of eight-by-ten black-and-white photos, photos autographed *To Patsy.* They were mostly of celebrities, famous singers, movie stars. In Saratoga, the photos had been signed *To Bob McNulty* and were of horses and jockeys and horses' owners.

Elaine ordered the Tortellini Bolognese; Lily and Karen, the veal special.

"Reginald and I were here once for a wedding reception," Lily said, "in the private facilities upstairs." She laughed. "They had a five-thousand-dollar cake. Can you imagine? The woman who made it lives right here in Manhattan." She took a sip of Chianti, then said, "Oh no! Why didn't I think of that earlier! We could have invited her to lunch."

As usual, Lily was way ahead of Elaine. "Seems a little pricey for a cake," Elaine responded. Her wedding to Lloyd had cost less than five hundred dollars in its entirety.

"That's not the point. Some of our brides might want the option."

Elaine couldn't argue. She had, after all, never given her father a chance to throw a lavish restaurant wedding, though McNulty's had been famous for making special events more special.

"Even the old ones?" Karen asked.

"Every bride wants her wedding to be unique, no matter if it's her first or her hundred and first."

It was not the only time Lily had claimed that, and having had three of her own, Elaine supposed she qualified as an expert. "My father always said that," Elaine said.

"He had weddings at the restaurant?" Lily asked.

"Sure. They were so society-like at the time. By today's standards they were pretty simple. Elegant, but simple." She smiled, remembering. "We had one for a Reisling. They owned one Derby and two Preakness winners."

"Your father had *weddings*?" Lily asked again. "Why didn't you say so before this? What were they like? What did he do for them?"

"The Reisling one had lots of flowers. And everything was horseshoe-shaped. The bride's bouquet, the cake, even the arch they walked through to get into the reception."

"See?" Lily asked, moving forward on her chair and dipping a slice of bread into herbed olive oil. "The wedding was unique to them. Do you have pictures?"

"Not me. My father might, unless he's thrown them out."

"Can you get them?"

"What?"

"The pictures! Anything and everything he did for weddings. We might find all kinds of gems hidden in the past." Lily poured a glass of wine for Elaine and a half a glass for Karen before Elaine could protest. "Your father must have archives with all kinds of ideas."

Elaine blinked. "Well," she said, "I suppose he does. He has recipes, anyway."

"Recipes? Well, don't you see? There must be *something* we can use."

Elaine might have wanted to see her father more often, but did she want him involved in the business? Did she want him involved with her life? "We'll see him at Christmas," she said before dwelling on it any longer. "I'll ask him then."

"*Christmas?*" Lily shrieked. "We have a huge event for New Year's Eve! Your father might have what we need to make it fabulous. To make Irene Benson—and the world—sit up and take notice of Second Chances."

Elaine doubted that the world would notice, but Lily might be right about Irene Benson. "I'll call him this weekend."

They saved room for dessert, something chocolate and decadent. On the way out, Lily said, "Here you go, Lainey. In lieu of your cooking class."

In a glass case by the door were several colorful cookbooks.

"For Christmas," Elaine said without hesitation. "For my father."

As the cashier rang up the purchase, Elaine smiled. It was a much better gift than another cardigan or handmade socks from the church fair.

And maybe, just maybe, it might be a good year to celebrate Christmas in Saratoga: a holiday makeover for her whole family. With or without the archives of the past.

16

Andrew decided to ask Jo out for a drink after work, because Cassie was right, he needed a girlfriend, and Cassie needed a mother and he couldn't bear it if she wasted any of her years pining for Patty the way he had wasted too many of his. Tonight would be the last chance to spend time alone with Jo before chaos (translation: Lily, Sarah, Elaine) reconvened next week; the last chance to see her alone before her next date with the jerk who ate BLTs for breakfast and planned to make dinner (ha!) for her at his place.

Tonight Andrew would take her out and he would tell her the truth about who he really was and what he was doing and how he could have gone this way forever except that he was crazy about her.

He would tell her, and they would get on with things,

or not, but at least he'd know, at least he would have tried for Cassie's sake, if not his own.

The phone had been ringing all day. Inns and B&Bs looking for guests, DJs looking for a job, even a pet-grooming service for those lucky enough to be included in the nuptials.

Andrew waited until the phones, at last, stopped ringing and the sun, at last, had set. He put his feet up on his desk and said, "I need a glass of wine. Are you interested?" The asking was easier than he'd expected, as if he were tired of his game and simply wanted it over.

Jo closed her eyes and let her soft, narrow shoulders relax. "A glass of wine. After a day like today, you certainly deserve it. But I'm afraid you'll have to count me out. I'm going to my mother's, to go through some things."

He resisted the urge to suggest she could do that the following night instead of going to her neighbor's. "But your mother and Ted won't be back from their honeymoon for a while."

Jo stood up wearily. "If I decide not to move there," Jo said, "she'll put the house on the market. I have to sort through what belongs to me, and start figuring out what I should get rid of."

Why was that more important than a drink with him?

"Would you like some help? I move boxes with much more efficiency than the way I row boats."

"You're a dear," she said, "but no, thanks. I'm afraid I have to do this on my own." She took her large leather bag from the bottom drawer of her desk, shut off her computer, and straightened pens and papers. Then she went to the coatrack and put on her cashmere jacket.

"But Cassie is spending the night canning pumpkins with Mrs. Connor." He made what he thought was a comical face. "All in the name of pie for Thanksgiving."

Jo laughed and said, "I'm sure you'll survive. I'll see you Monday. Enjoy the wine." She closed the door behind her and it took Andrew a second to understand what it meant when she'd said "Enjoy the wine."

What it meant was she'd rejected him. Clark Kent foiled again.

Jo stepped outside and noticed it was already dark. She buttoned her jacket and inhaled the autumn air, trying to compose herself. She'd brushed Andrew off, and she'd upset him. But there was no way she could go hang out with him. Work was one thing, but social time quite another. His invitation, after all, had been friend-to-friend. She did not want to risk him figuring out that she'd started thinking it was too bad he was gay.

17

On Saturday morning, back home on Cornflower Drive, Elaine poured herself a giant cup of coffee, took not one credit card but two, and went into Kory's room, which once had been the sunroom, but which Lloyd and his brother Russell had converted to a bedroom when Kandie became a teenager and started pleading for her own room. The garrison-style home in the subdivision had only three bedrooms on the second floor, so Lloyd bought a Time/Life How-To-Remodel manual and he and Russell got to work.

Kory had been thrilled to be relegated far from his sisters and his parents. It had provided him with a haven in which to stockpile his sports gear at age eleven and his girlie magazines at twelve. It had also provided the unfortunate privacy for Kory to smoke marijuana at fifteen, and blow the smoke out the jalousied sunroom windows. It never had occurred to him that smoke rises, and after only two or three nights, Elaine and Lloyd had figured out that the sweet smell drifting in to their second-floor master-bedroom window was not honeysuckle. Kory was caught, grounded, and dragged off by his Uncle Russell, who also happened to be a cop, and shown firsthand what happened to addicts who ended up in doorways or crack houses and never played sports again.

Elaine had always credited Uncle Russell and basketball for saving Kory. She was reminded of it every time she cleaned his room or went in to use the computer, and looked up at the jalousied windows that had, for years now, acted as a backdrop for an orange basketball hoop instead of as a means to another kind of life.

She wondered if her father would have approved of how they'd handled the situation.

Plopping herself at the computer, Elaine knew she had to call him. But first, she would "go" shopping!

With a shudder of anticipation, she logged on and Googled "women's fashions." She would spend the day—the weekend if she had to—shopping online for more clothes: Elaine had been frugal too long. She would shop and she would put it all on her credit card, which she could max out like most of the rest of the world.

"Some color might be nice," Karen had said over breakfast that morning, just before she'd left to spend the day with her father because it was the "other" of the "every *other* weekend," as per Lloyd's visitation rights. "You've gone from looking like Mr. Brighton's garden to the CNN coverage in Iraq."

Mr. Brighton lived over on Third Street and was renowned for his summer wildflower collections, none of which had roots that could be traced to the Middle East.

"Leapin' lizards," Elaine said when Google brought about a zillion shopping sites right into the sunroom.

She settled back and went to work, blissfully knowing she'd have no interruptions, not even from the doorbell. It was Saturday, after all, and the roses wouldn't be there until tomorrow.

Jo didn't know what to wear.

Jack would no doubt have on jeans, so she probably should, too, but in her years in the city she'd grown more accustomed to nice fabrics, sleek styles.

You won't need that many clothes, her mother had said when Jo had been in the process of returning to West Hope. *You won't be in Boston.* It had hurt, that reference to her former life, when she'd thought she'd had it all, when she'd thought she'd been in control, before money and success resulted in heartbreak.

"And a closet full of clothes," she said now, as she pulled out a black silk jumpsuit that, like the suits and the dresses and the pants and the shirts stuffed in her closet, had once seemed a perfect façade for her emotionally empty shell.

Tonight, however, she'd wear the jumpsuit. She'd save the jeans for a day or a night when she felt less vulnerable, less in need of looking her sexy, she-devil best.

His living room/dining room was sparse. There was a brown futon, a card table, two folding chairs, a floor lamp, and a fake ficus tree that stood in the corner and could have used a good cleaning. A wobbly-looking bookcase was next to that, and held a stack of what appeared to be old magazines and a few books. On the top shelf were two five-by-seven frames with photos that might have been of people, but Jo couldn't tell from the doorway.

"I never did get the hang of decorating," Jack said. His accent was charming, his charisma alluring. He took the thirty-dollar bottle of wine that Jo could ill afford but had nonetheless brought, set it on the counter, and scooped her into his arms. "You look fabulous," he said.

It was the first time his arms had encircled her, the first time she'd felt his full embrace. His arms were strong, his dark eyes as probing as they'd been before. She'd promised herself no sex until after dinner, until she felt justified in believing this had been a third date.

But then he kissed her.

It was a soft, full-mouth kiss that started gentle and slow, then turned more eager, more wanting, with small nibbles on her lips and ready touches of his tongue.

Her body moved more closely to his. Her breasts merged into his chest, his penis pressed against her thigh. It was hard. It was good.

The last time she'd been this close to a man . . . well, it had actually been just the other day, when she and Andrew had toppled all over each other, and she'd had the strange feeling that they'd been about to kiss.

Andrew.

God, why was she thinking about him? Andrew was gay. Jack Allen was not.

Still, she gently pushed Jack away. "Well," she said, "if we keep doing that, your dinner will be ruined."

He half smiled back. He placed his index finger on her lower lip. He kept his gaze on it as he drew it down in a straight line, over her chin, down her throat, into the small hollow that rested beneath, then continued down her chest and between the V where the tops of her breasts were exposed. He stopped at the zipper; he played with the tab.

"Later," she said. If the foreplay could linger, the sex would be great. She'd read that somewhere, most likely in a self-help book on a Saturday night when she'd been alone and wondering why.

Jack laughed. "Okay," he said. "Later. First, the wine. And the pasta." He opened the bottle, poured two glasses, while Jo reclaimed her wits.

"Pasta?" she asked with a smile as she took a glass. "I didn't know pasta was a tradition in Belgium."

"What can I say? I cook as well as I decorate." He turned to an old aluminum pot that sat on the stove. "Make yourself comfortable," he said. "This will only take a minute."

Jo strolled into the living area, toward the window. "Your view is the Dumpster," she said, relaxing with every deep inhale and every slow exhale, with every small sip from her glass. "My view is the courtyard."

"Ah, the Dumpster," he said. "But sooner or later, if I sat by the window, I'd get to see all our neighbors." He laughed with a good-natured laugh, then Jo heard him shake dry pasta into the water.

She moved to the bookcase and picked up one of the pictures. It was of two children, a boy and a girl, swinging on swings. "Who are the kids?" she asked.

"Gretchen and Pierre. You must say they're beautiful, because they're mine."

His?

She took another drink, this time a long one.

Well, she thought, of course he had two kids. Unlike her, most people in their forties had had kids, stability, permanence of some kind. "They are beautiful," she said, because they were. She set the frame back on the bookcase and hesitated before looking at the one next to it. With another sip of wine, she dared a glance.

Gretchen and Pierre again. This time, each holding the hand of a woman. A pretty woman, with blond hair and a fresh, cheerful smile.

Jo didn't want to ask, but knew that she must.

"And is this their mother?"

"Yes," Jack called from the kitchen. "That's Mavie. She is my wife."

18

Monday morning the bell over the front door jingled. Sarah looked up. Her eyes fell back quickly to the papers spread across the desk. "Andrew, will you take care of this woman?" She scooped up the papers and disappeared into her studio in the back room.

When she was safely out of earshot, Andrew winked at Elaine. "She didn't know you," he whispered. "You look terrific."

A crooked smile crossed Elaine's coral-colored mouth. Had she always worn lipstick or was that part of the "new" Elaine?

Unbuttoning a dark brown cardigan, she lightly fluffed her shoulder-cropped blond hair. " 'Not too much fluff,' Lily told me. 'Fluff is out; flat is in.' "

Andrew nodded as if he knew what the heck she meant.

And then she beamed. "I spent a fortune this weekend buying clothes online."

She seemed excited, so he said, "That's great."

"I used to get depressed on weekends when Lloyd had the kids. But this," she added, pointing to herself, "this is the new me. The new, energetic me." She laughed, then looked around. "Where's Jo?" she asked.

Andrew shrugged. "Not here yet," he said. "She had a date Saturday night. Maybe the guy swooped her off to Brussels."

Elaine hesitated a moment, then ambled to one of the mirrors on the wall. "Brussels," she said. "How romantic."

Romantic. Romantic, his ass. He shifted on his chair. There was only one reason a guy would take Jo to Brussels, and it didn't have anything to do with romance.

"I can't believe Jo's seeing a guy she met in the garage where she lives." Elaine fixed her hair again, then added, "It used to make me sad every time I heard about a woman over forty who'd started dating again. I mean, true, I'd dated Martin 'late in life,' but I'd known the man for years. We were on several of the same town committees, did you know that?"

Andrew admitted he hadn't.

"Then, gosh, it seemed more than sad—it seemed a little scary—that someone as smart and beautiful as Jo had resorted to picking up a stranger in a parking garage. Do you know what I mean?"

Yes, well, that he definitely could relate to.

Elaine giggled and turned back to him. “Of course, when I thought those things, I was still a brunette. Now it all seems exciting! Erotic! It seems like so much fun!”

Andrew crumpled a paper, flung it in the basket.

Elaine turned from the mirror and sank into the French provincial chair behind Jo’s desk. “Maybe I’ll go to Belgium, someday. Or London. I’m forty-three years old and I’ve never been to London!”

“Make it a priority,” Andrew replied.

“Okay. Right after the Benson wedding.” She touched the lipstick at the corner of her mouth as if it felt like something foreign. “Do you think I’ll ever meet a handsome prince the way Jo has?”

“I think any man would be a fool to pass you by,” he said. Elaine stood up and laughed a sweet, innocent laugh.

“Oh, Andrew,” she said, “you’re such good medicine for this bunch of middle-aged, dowager women.”

“ ‘Dowager’?” It was Andrew’s turn to laugh; Andrew’s turn to remember that his job at Second Chances truly was one of the good parts of his life. “I can think of many words. ‘Dowager’ is not one of them.”

Elaine laughed, too, then simulated a haughty prance. “I think I’ll go tell Ms. Sarah she must pay better attention when a potential customer sashays through our door,” she said, then winked at Andrew and strutted toward Sarah’s workroom.

Andrew looked back to the door and wondered when—if—Jo was going to show up.

"Sarah!" she called. "It's me. Elaine!"

Sarah was hunched over her drawing table, scraps of fabric at her elbow, spray-painted white-and-silver twigs standing upright in tall, clear glass vases filled not with water but cranberries. Elaine supposed they were decorating ideas for the Benson wedding.

Sarah turned toward Elaine's voice, then gathered her long, shining ebony hair and knotted it into a bun. She stared at Elaine. She blinked.

"It's me!" Elaine repeated. She twirled around as if she were four or five again, spinning in front of the full-length, oval mirror in her parents' bedroom, watching as her dress and its layers of petticoats twirled straight out. "Do I look divine?" It was a Lily-word, but Lily wouldn't mind.

"Good God, Elaine. What have you done?"

Elaine abruptly stopped spinning.

"She has completed steps one and two of her fabulous makeover," Lily announced as she made her way down the stairs that went from her apartment on the second floor straight into Sarah's studio. "A week at the spa and a new wardrobe."

Elaine stepped back and let Lily into the room.

Sarah made no comment. She looked from Lily back to Elaine, then back to Lily again.

"Well?" Lily inquired. "It's quite amazing, isn't it?"

"Personally, I've never wanted to be a blonde." Sarah turned back to her work.

"It's not about being a blonde. It's about total transformation. It's about all of us helping Elaine reach her full potential by teaching her about the finer things in life."

Elaine felt as if she weren't in the room.

"It looks blond to me," Sarah said.

"If changing what's on the outside helps her look at herself in a more positive way, then that's all that matters," Lily continued. Her hands were on her narrow hips now, the blush in her cheeks rising to an anger-pinkness. "We're all going to help, Sarah. You included."

"Swell. I'll show her how to make jewelry. She ought to have it mastered by Thursday."

Of all the roommates, Sarah had sometimes been the moody one. Lily had excused it with comments about "creative" and "artistic." But right then, Lily didn't look as if she cared about excuses.

"Sarcasm does not become you," Lily said.

"Right. I keep forgetting you're our in-house expert on everything."

Lily and Sarah had gone at it two or three times over the years, head-to-head, fisticuffs, as Elaine's father would have called it. This time, Elaine stepped forward.

"Please," she said, "stop arguing. It's not that important."

"Yes, it is," Lily said.

"I'm with Elaine," Sarah said. "It's not that important."

She said it without lifting her head; she said it in a way that made Elaine feel as if she was the one that wasn't important, that her desire to better herself plainly didn't matter.

"Just forget it," Elaine said quietly, leaving the studio, walking through the showroom where Andrew sat, bewildered, and out the front door. The last thing she heard was the small bell announcing her exit.

Jo hadn't wanted to go to work Monday. She would have preferred to stay home, burrow under her blankets, and continue to nurse her Jack Allen wounds as she'd been doing since Saturday night.

Upon his announcement that "Mavie" was indeed his wife, Jo had allowed herself only a brief moment for introspection, then she'd headed for the door. She ignored his remark about narrow-minded Americans, told him to drop dead, and retrieved her thirty-dollar bottle of wine on her way out.

He had the audacity to look insulted.

But that had been then and now it was a new week, and Jo knew she had to collect the pieces of her ego and resume her life. She pulled two suitcases from the closet: They should hold enough clothes to last a week or two. There was no way she would risk running into Jack in the garage of the secretaries' building. Not until she was certain he could not charm her again with his clever notes and his crooked smile and his liquidy eyes.

As Andrew had reminded her, her mother and Ted would not return from their honeymoon for a while. Which meant Jo could stay at her mother's house, and not have to answer anyone's questions.

The gazebo on the town green was used to hawk tourist information and as a minibandstand Wednesday nights in summer. Funded by the arts council, the concerts were eclectic: big-band music one week, Dixieland another week, then a sing-along with a barbershop quartet. When he wasn't doing Shakespeare, Martin liked to go. He was older than Elaine and it was always more his kind of music.

She had gone with him because that's what a wife-to-be did, not that it was a sacrifice. After the divorce, she'd felt disconnected from the community; Martin had helped her feel she belonged again. It was nice to share cans of soda and crackers and cheese and town gossip. It had reminded Elaine of Saratoga, back when she'd been a young girl.

For no special reason, Elaine walked to the gazebo now. She sat on a bench next to the rack of maps and brochures of area attractions. She didn't care about getting dirt on her Ann Taylor pants.

Leaning forward a little, Elaine clenched her jaw. She gazed around the town common. Most of the maples had already lost their red and gold leaves; the amber oak leaves would soon add a topcoat to the ground and the sidewalks that meandered through the grass.

She thought about Martin. It was nice that he enjoyed simple, easy things like town concerts and holding hands and making her feel special even when she did not. He'd been eons away from Lloyd when it had come to that. She missed Martin sometimes.

She thought about Lloyd. Was it sadder that he was pursuing her, or sadder that she didn't care?

She thought about Sarah. Why had her approval seemed so important, her disapproval so earth-shattering?

Elaine had never handled unhappiness well, especially in autumn, when the horse people had left and then the leaf peepers had, too, and all that was left was the bleak promise of winter and its gray skies and cold.

Autumn was when her mother had died. October twenty-third, ten years ago.

She lowered her head, hating that Sarah had snuffed out her good mood and dredged up the uglies again. The memories, the losses, the season.

"Mind if I join you?"

19

Elaine flicked away her tears so Andrew wouldn't see. She patted the bench beside her. "This part is clean."

He sat down and picked up a brochure for Six Flags New England. "As if life isn't enough of a roller coaster," he said, pointing to the brochure. "This place has eight of them."

Elaine smiled. "Sarah thinks my makeover is foolish."

"One person's opinion."

"Two. Counting my daughter." She swept away a maple leaf with the toe of her shoe. "Karen is pulling away from me. She's moving closer to her father, and I hate that."

"It's the newness," Andrew said. "Kids feel threatened when something is new. They worry about how it's going to shake up their lives." He put the brochure back in the rack, picked up another for the Norman Rockwell Muscum.

"What's Sarah's excuse?"

"She's a woman. You know how they are."

Elaine appreciated that he was trying to make her laugh. "All my life I've wanted to please everyone," she said. "First my mother and father, then the customers at our restaurant, then Lloyd and the kids, then Martin. Now I feel as if I'm supposed to please Lily, Sarah, and Jo. And you."

Andrew laughed. "Me?" He returned the brochure and put his hand on hers. "Lainey, before you change too much more of your life, you need to learn what you really want. Not what other people want. Or what you *think* they want."

"I want to be here. I want to work at Second Chances. And I do want my life to change. Really I do."

"Good. Then to hell with what anyone else thinks."

"Lily is supportive. And you are," she added. "Thanks."

He smiled. "Jo is, too," he said. "She even said so on our weird trip to the spa."

"That was quite an escapade."

"Yes, well, it's the story of my life."

Elaine smiled, then drew in an uncertain breath. "Speaking of life stories," she said, "my father had a restaurant, a very nice restaurant. Lily thinks I should find out what he did for weddings and banquets. She thinks he might have some clever things we can offer our brides."

"Such as?"

"I don't know, but he was quite a chef. He had some wonderful recipes." She pictured her mother at the kitchen table late at night, her hair teased into a perfect sixties-bubble, her flowered shirtwaist dress covered by a neat apron, her feet in penny loafers, crossed at the ankles. She listened to the radio, to Frank Sinatra and Dean Martin, while she carefully pasted the recipes into large, three-ring binders.

"You could ask," Andrew said. "It wouldn't hurt."

She hadn't called him over the weekend. She'd thought of it once, twice, maybe three times. But she was so *busy* with her online shopping. And procrastinating was always so much easier, like with car oil changes and dental appointments. "I suppose it would help me contribute something worthwhile to the business."

Andrew let out a laugh. "You already contribute, Elaine. You know people in this town it would take the others decades to get to meet."

She ignored the compliment. "My father lives in Saratoga Springs. I'd have to go there and see what he has."

"What are you waiting for?"

She buttoned and unbuttoned the bottom button of her new sweater. "Bob McNulty always seemed larger-than-life. I was a disappointment to him. Over the years we've kind of drifted apart."

A pigeon flew under the gazebo. It looked at Elaine, then Andrew, then flew away. "I guess I could drive up Saturday," Elaine continued. "The visit could be part of my makeover. The new me. No more skeletons—or polyester— hidden in my closet."

Andrew laughed again. "Conflict happens, Lainey. It's

part of life." Then he gestured back toward the shop. "Believe me, it's better to face it than let it get the better of you."

He meant, of course, Sarah.

Elaine went back to work because she knew Andrew was right. No sense turning a small difference of opinion into a major disaster.

She settled in at her desk and took out a fistful of menus they'd already collected from caterers from West Hope to the New York State border. Nine-fifty each for Shrimp Cocktail Diablo—which was merely four shrimp with a cheap jalapeño sauce; twenty-four ninety-five for a platter of a dozen Beef Teriyaki with hot honey mustard; Asian Lettuce Wraps, which sounded like a diet version of egg rolls, at twice the price. And those were just appetizers. All very expensive; nothing terribly exciting. Surely her father's files had more imaginative, less costly items to offer.

All she needed to do was call him.

Just before lunch, she finally did.

He answered the phone.

"Dad," Elaine said cheerfully, if not a bit awkwardly. "How would you like a visitor Saturday?"

She was not surprised when he hesitated.

Then suddenly he said yes, it would be good to see her, he could make a nice Crab Creole for lunch. He sounded as if they'd spoken—perhaps seen each other—only yesterday, as if Elaine were the attentive daughter that she was not.

Before hanging up, she added, "Oh, and Dad, don't be too shocked, but I'm a blonde now."

He said he didn't care if her hair were purple.

She felt the tears start to well up in her eyes, so she said good-bye. She wondered how many weeks, months, or years it would take for her guilt to subside, and if she would ever relax.

Jo meandered into the shop as if she didn't start work until noon every day.

"Sorry I'm late," she said. "I had somewhere to go." She went to the coatrack to hang up her jacket. Her head hurt: for someone who'd spent thirty-six hours in bed, she was achingly tired.

"We thought you went to Brussels," Elaine said.

Jo didn't make eye contact with Elaine, Lily, or Andrew. "No," she replied. "I won't be going to Brussels. It turns out the man is very married."

The moment of silence that followed perhaps was not as long as it seemed.

"Married?" Elaine asked, as if hoping it wasn't true.

"Hell's bells," Lily added.

Andrew had no comment. He simply put his elbow on his desk, his chin on his palm, and quietly shook his head. Commiseration, Jo supposed.

"And I'm sure you'll understand that I don't want to talk about it," she said, moving back to her desk, pulling out her chair, and sitting down. She turned on her computer as if this were just another day.

"But..." Elaine began.

"No 'buts,'" Lily interrupted. "The man lost his chance the day he said 'I do.' Over and done with. Kaput." She snapped her fingers, then smiled at Jo. "But as you know, my dear, there are plenty of fish in the sea—or, in your case, the parking garage. Of course, in today's world, there's always the Internet. Not that you'd ever stoop to that."

Silence again. Then Jo shook her head and focused on her screen. "I'm going to forget about men for a while," she said. "We have a grand wedding to plan. Between now and then, my energy will be spent only on the Bensons."

He would have jumped up from his chair and shouted *Hoo-freaking-ray!* but Andrew thought it best to restrain himself.

Elaine wondered how it happened that a woman as beautiful and as smart as Jo had so much trouble with men.

Maybe she was too beautiful. Maybe she was too smart.

For the first time since her makeover began, Elaine questioned her goal. Would she be better off to stay as she was? Was an "average" woman more appealing to a regular guy?

There are plenty of fish, Lily had said. *In today's world, they're on the Internet.*

Elaine smiled.

Jo wouldn't dare. She was too beautiful. She was too smart.

But what about Elaine? At least she was blond now, so that might make it easier to attract men in the first place. The right kind of men. Not weirdos or losers or married men.

She waited until Jo went out with Lily for lunch, then she turned to her computer.

Maybe she could shop for a man the same way that she'd bought new clothes.

"I meant it when I said I don't want to talk about it," Jo cautioned Lily. They'd both ordered the special, a turkey-and-boursin wrap, though Lily doubted the luncheonette two doors down from the shop would make it as good as Café d'Claire on the Upper East Side in Manhattan.

She was right, she announced, when the plates were delivered.

"Irene gave me the go-ahead to work up the contracts with The Stone Castle," Jo said, determined to keep the conversation on work. "It's Scottish, as is John Benson."

"I know the place," Lily replied, as she nibbled the edge of her sandwich. "Frank helped them decorate. The place is loaded with authentic antiques. Several from Dryburgh Abbey, near the river Tweed. The burial place of Sir Walter Scott."

It amazed Jo that Lily had learned so many things from her suitors: art history from poor, dead Reginald; orchid-growing from husband number one; competitive sailing from number two. It amazed Jo because, while they were in college, Lily had not cared much for studying. Apparently it was more appealing when a man was involved.

"I still think there's more we can do," Jo said. "There must be unique things that say something about the Bensons, about their lives."

"Well," Lily replied, "Irene Benson never worked, to my knowledge. Only for society. Charitable events."

"They never had children?"

"Not that I know of."

"Do they travel?"

"Not in the circles Reginald and I were in. I think John Benson works most of the time."

Jo took a bite of her sandwich, which tasted fine. She chewed slowly, thinking about John and Irene Benson, wondering what their lives were like. She swallowed and said, "So he's a workaholic." She could relate to that, though his reasons would be different.

"I suppose," Lily said.

Drinking her tea, Jo glanced around the restaurant, the place where only days before she had eaten breakfast with Jack Allen, where she'd nearly been swept away by a complete stranger.

As with the Bensons, she'd known nothing about him. She supposed there really had been no way she could have learned the truth except from the source.

What source could she use for the Bensons? They wouldn't meet Irene for another two weeks. On the other hand, John . . .

Jo stood up quickly. "I have to go to the bookstore."

Lily pointed to her plate. "You haven't finished your entrée."

"I had enough. Before I forget, I have to run to the bookstore. If we're ever to learn about the Bensons—or at least about John—I know where there are plenty of clues."

Lily looked up without speaking.

"I have nothing to do with my evenings right now," Jo said with a shrug. "I might as well study the latest issue of *Buzz*."

20

Who knew there were so many available men within a fifty-mile radius of West Hope, so many who were unattached and well educated and had a hefty income range?

Find your Mate, one site beckoned. *Only $19.95 per month*. Elaine had spent more than that on add-ons to her cable TV at home, pay channels that she thought would fill the void between Lloyd and Martin, and now, after Martin. The prospect of a man, however (unattached, well educated, with a hefty income range), seemed suddenly more exciting than a rerun of another Tom Hanks, Michael Douglas, or Julia Roberts film.

And, after all, she might not be Jo, but she was a blonde now.

And her new clothes were being shipped in ten to twelve business days.

Hopefully she'd be made over enough for West Hope and the surrounding fifty-mile match radius.

SIGN UP NOW. The button was enticing, a Hershey's Bar to a Weight Watcher, a nip of gin to Darryl, the village "drinker."

It was after lunch and Elaine had not eaten because she'd been too busy scanning the web. She glanced around the shop to see if anyone was watching: Jo had returned and was directing new energy to someone on the phone; Andrew was typing something on his laptop. Sarah was in her workroom, and Lily announced she was going somewhere with Frank to check out a bagpiper he knew who might be an amusing addition to the Benson nuptials.

Elaine turned back to her computer, dug her credit card from her purse, and wondered if she truly dared.

I met him online, she could hear herself tell her daughter Karen.

I'm having you arrested, Karen might retort. *For impersonating my mother.*

Then her daughter would call her Uncle Russell, *Detective Sergeant* Russell Thomas, or worse, she would call Lloyd, and soon all of West Hope would know that Elaine McNulty Thomas had resorted to the Internet to find a date.

Poor Elaine. What had happened to the nice girl she once was?

She clicked back to her selections.

WAYNE, age 46. 5'11", brown hair, blue eyes. *I love museums and the theater and the Indian casinos. I love thunderstorms and cuddling. I own three businesses.*

NICK, age 49. 6'1", gray hair, blue eyes. *Cooking is my passion! I'm a gourmet chef at night, a successful investment counselor in the day. I have a yacht at Old Lyme, CT, and a second home in Naples—Italy, not Florida.*

GERARD, age 36. 5'10", blond hair, brown eyes. *I do some modeling for TV and magazine ads. I prefer older women. I workout every day because it keeps me in perfect shape.*

It did not escape Elaine that Gerard had spelled "workout" as one word, as if it were a noun. Nor did he mention what his profession was. But in his picture, all he wore was a Speed-O and a smile.

She went back to the order form and typed in her credit card number. Not that she'd submit it.

She stared at the little SIGN UP NOW button.

Did she dare? Did she really?

"Elaine!" Andrew called from across the room.

She must have jumped a foot or more. She jerked her hand that rested on the mouse and inadvertently clicked the button.

She sucked in a sharp breath. "Yes?" she asked meekly, her eyes glued to the pixels on which big, bold type appeared.

"*Congratulations!*" the type read. "*Thanks for joining mates.com.*"

She turned to Andrew. "Have you decided about going to Saratoga?" he asked.

She supposed her father would side with Karen on having her arrested if he knew what she was up to.

"Yes," she said, "I'm going Saturday."

Jo was off the phone now. She looked at Andrew and

Andrew smiled. Jo asked what was up and he mentioned Elaine's father and the restaurant, but Elaine quickly flicked her attention back to her computer and the new line that crawled across the screen that said the mates she'd selected should be in touch soon.

Andrew told Jo about Lily's idea for Elaine to loot her father's archives.

"That's great," Jo said. "We need all the help we can get." She stood up and stretched. "Speaking of which . . . I need help. Here." She reached across her desk and placed a pile of papers on his. "If Elaine works on the food, maybe you can do the media."

The media?

The media? As in newspaper, radio, and . . . television?

He might have swallowed his tongue if one really could do that.

"We need to get them revved for the Benson wedding," Jo continued. "Let them know this will be an outstanding photo op. Tell them we'll help with their accommodations. The bigger a deal they think this wedding is, the greater the chances they'll show up. And the more media that come, well, the better for us, right? Not to mention it will make us look good to the Bensons."

Andrew blinked. Moisture spread across his face.

"Could you start by calling the networks?" she asked. "Then the cable shows. You know, that TV journalism stuff. It would be a big help."

He supposed he'd asked for it.

He narrowed his eyes and tried to grasp what the top

page read. It was information about the network he'd last worked for, the place he'd been an up-and-coming star on the program, *The Edge.* To make things more alarming, the contact person—Betsy Gardner—had been a college intern the last year he was there, the last year *Andrew David* had worked. Betsy had been eager, sometimes too eager. And she often ate glazed donuts that left sticky marks on the sheets of copy. Perhaps she'd been too busy eating and angsting to have given Andrew David much notice.

He felt a sudden tightening around his sweaty head, as if he'd put on a hat that was way too small. "Can I start on it tomorrow?" he asked. He knew that to pull this off, he must be at his best, at the top of his game. He sighed with the knowledge that this, indeed, was a game.

"Tomorrow's fine," Jo said. "And if anyone's looking for me tonight, I'm staying at my mother's house for a few days."

Andrew left work early and drove out to the stables to watch Cassie put Big Bailey through his paces. It bothered him that his daughter hadn't bounced back from the funk she'd been in since she'd seen the picture of her mother romping on the beach with her new family and a smile.

He wondered if Cassie had the same tight head that Andrew now had.

Maybe a visit from old Dad would help cheer her up. Wasn't that what fathers were supposed to do?

He thought about Elaine's father. He hoped they could

reconcile. Fathers were important, weren't they? Or was Andrew confusing fantasy with truth?

After all, he'd never had the father he'd dreamed of. Oh, sure, Dr. David Kennedy had been brilliant and in demand, and, for godssake, he saved lives. But he wasn't the kind of father who'd played ball with Andrew or rode bikes with him or who'd taught him how to swim.

It was too late for Andrew and his father, but it wasn't too late for Elaine, and it wasn't too late for Cassie to know how much her father loved her and wanted her to have the best life in the world.

He was, however, too late for the lesson. Cassie was in the barn, rubbing Big Bailey down.

"Hey," he said, approaching the stall, "I was hoping to see you in action."

"We were fast today. Bailey was hungry."

"And Cassie was distracted," Mary Delaney said as she pitched a clump of hay from the next stall. Mary was a West Hope townie who was majoring in mathematics at Winston College and taught equestrian skills to cover her tuition.

"'Distracted'?" Andrew asked, and Cassie rolled her eyes. She reached into her pocket and gave Bailey an apple.

"Long day at school," Cassie said. "I forgot to study for an English test."

He wanted to ask Mary if she could confirm Cassie's excuse, but the girl had left the area. He looked back to the horse: It gnashed its top teeth against its bottom ones; bits of apple sprayed from the sides of Bailey's mouth.

"So," he said, "any homework tonight?" He wished he

had someone to talk to, specifically, a woman. He sensed he and Cassie had entered that dark territory of the Men/Mars, Women/Venus thing.

"Just studying," Cassie replied. "Mrs. Donovan is going to let me make up the test tomorrow."

"What's it on?" he asked. Andrew knew there were four women he could ask about raising a girl. But how could he do that when the problem seemed to lie with Patty, and none of his friends at Second Chances knew the connection?

"Oh, it's just stuff," Cassie said, then brushed the front of her jeans.

"Maybe we should pick up a pizza tonight. Save time once we get home-on-the-ranch." It was a ha-ha phrase he'd coined when Cassie first took riding lessons. It almost made her smile now.

"Sure, Dad," she said and walked out of the barn.

Andrew followed close behind. Irene would be coming to West Hope soon to review the wedding plans: Irene would talk to Cassie, would make her feel better.

Then Andrew thought about Jo. Cassie liked her a lot. Jo said she'd be at her mother's—would she enjoy a visit from the Kennedys? They couldn't talk about Patty, but they could talk about, well, stuff. Besides, as much as Andrew hated to admit it, Jo was probably bummed about what had happened with that guy from her building.

Maybe Jo and Cassie would be good medicine for each other. Maybe they'd be good medicine for him.

21

Jo forgot that her mother had cleaned out the refrigerator before the wedding and what food remained had either been transferred to the condo over by Tanglewood or thrown out in the trash. Not that it mattered; she had no appetite anyway.

She went in the back door and tossed her pocketbook and the *Buzz* magazine on the kitchen table. She'd start perusing the *Buzz* pages after her shoes were off, after she rested a few minutes, after she answered the phone that suddenly started ringing.

"Pizza?" It was Andrew. "Cassie and I ordered a large veggie thin crust, and we can't possibly eat it alone."

"Oh, Andrew, thanks for the thought, but I just got home and I'm too beat to go out again."

"No problem," he said. "We'll bring it to you. We'll be there in ten minutes. Five if the traffic light is green."

"You didn't have to do this," Jo said as she took plates down from the cabinet, the same pale yellow plates with tiny painted bluebirds that she'd eaten most every meal off of for as long as she could remember: her mother's Sunday pot roasts, her grandmother's tuna casseroles, her grandfather's fresh-caught trout from the Housatonic River.

"It was Cassie's idea," Andrew said, peeling back the corrugated cardboard box lid.

"No, it wasn't," Jo said with a smile. "You thought I was depressed. You thought I needed friends." She winked at Cassie. "Right?"

"I know nothing," Cassie said, rolling her eyes. "I am innocent. I am only eleven."

Andrew tossed a stack of napkins at her. "You are incorrigible," he said, and Jo and Cassie laughed.

Jo told them both to sit. Curiously, Andrew went to the far end of the table, the place tucked under the corner of the ceiling that was slightly slanted to accommodate the flight of stairs around the corner that led to the second floor. It had been her grandfather's chair. He'd said the slanted ceiling was because of a design flaw for which he took full responsibility because he'd changed the architect's basic design. "I don't want a straight-up staircase," he'd supposedly told the man. "I want a fancy one that has a few stairs, then stops for a window seat, then turns and climbs the rest of the way." Grandma often said that Grandpa had "grandiose ideas" for a man who worked in a paper mill.

Andrew ducked his head and sat down. He moved Jo's

pocketbook from the place in front of him. He picked up the magazine. He hesitated. "*Buzz?*" he asked.

Cassie leaned over the rock maple table and peered at the cover.

"Don't be shocked, Andrew," Jo said, sitting across from him and swiping a lock of hair from her forehead. "It's only for research. I thought I might learn something about John Benson that we could use in the wedding." She looked at Cassie. "Mr. Benson runs the magazine," she explained.

Cassie nodded as if she already knew that.

"But it's a men's magazine," Andrew said. "I can't believe anything in here might help. . . ."

"You never know," she said, serving veggie thin-slice pieces onto the pale yellow plates. "Don't worry, I won't look at the pictures."

The dimple in Andrew's right cheek showed its boyish curve. "Nonetheless," he said, "it sounds like man's work to me." He slid the magazine onto his lap. "I'll take it home with me. You have enough to do."

Jo shook her head. "Absolutely not. You are our receptionist. Not a slave required to donate thankless hours."

He shrugged. "I'll enjoy the reading. I'll get to see how the other side lives."

Of course it was a joke, because *Buzz* was a straight-man's periodical. "No," Jo repeated. "Leave it here." She looked at Cassie. "I doubt that it's required reading in the West Hope sixth grade."

This time, Cassie shrugged. "I've seen it before," she said. "It's helped me pick out Uncle Andrew's clothes. It might be straight, but it has a great take on fashions for every kind of man."

Andrew laughed, as did Jo, then Andrew said, "It's fine, Jo. Honest." He picked up his pizza slice and took a big, assertive bite. "One of these days you'll have to come watch Cassie ride Big Bailey. Do you like horses, Jo?"

She knew when a subject had been changed, and she was too tired to argue over something as ridiculous as a glorified, sex-selling magazine.

It would have been worse if she'd taken the down payment she'd saved for a new minivan and spent it on a dating service for professional people, or at least that's what Elaine told herself when she crept downstairs after Karen had gone to bed, sneaked into Kory's room, and logged on to the web site for a fast peek.

At least it was only $19.95 a month—less than the cost of twelve Beef Teriyaki with hot mustard sauce.

She had mail.

Playing with the drawstring of what once had been Kory's college sweatpants that she'd recently commandeered as her at-home-when-no-one-is-watching attire, Elaine wasn't sure if she had the courage to open the mail.

Was it from Wayne the Business Owner? Nick the Investment Broker? Gerard the Young Hunk?

She put her finger on the button, closed her eyes and whispered, "Gerard, please." If she were going to be daring, she might as well go all the way.

Ha! Ha! She laughed at her own little pun, then clicked twice and waited for strength.

She opened her eyes. The subject of the e-mail was *Nick*. She went back to his profile to see what she'd landed. The chef... like her father! And the yacht and the house in Italy. Well, she'd been saying she'd never been to Europe. "Way to go," she whispered.

And then her heart began to race. A date. A real date! Her breath began to stutter small bursts of excitement, as if she were in the waiting area of DiNardo's or Judie's or Bubba's Bar-B-Cue, waiting for her man.

Six one. Gray hair. Blue eyes.

Elaine smiled and sucked air through her teeth. Then she quick-clicked the button to open her mail.

Sorry, the type read. *This mate is currently unavailable.*

She stared at the screen. Unavailable? How could he be unavailable? He was supposed to take her to Europe, like Jack Allen was supposed to have taken Jo.

"Damn," Elaine said. "Damn, damn."

Her eyes traveled the screen.

Want more mates? A large link summoned. *Post your Profile.*

Well, she wouldn't do that. She would never put her story up on the web for West Hope, or the world, to see. She would never post her story, her likes and her dislikes, and she would certainly not put up a picture.

For one thing, she wouldn't know what to say.

For another, she didn't have a recent photo of her as a blonde, in her makeover clothes, except the snapshot for her ID badge at Laurel Lake.

No. She wouldn't post her profile or her picture.

Elaine McNulty Thomas was not that desperate. Yet.

Age, 43.

5'5".

Blond hair.

Brown eyes.

Well, Elaine thought as she drew her feet up in the chair and sipped a cup of tea, it was a beginning.

After all, why not? Why the heck not?

She'd sat there for an hour or maybe it had been two, perusing other profiles and potential mates. Surely those people had family and friends and coworkers who might embarrass them if they saw their profile online. Surely they hadn't been afraid. It was the new millennium, had been the new millennium for a few years now.

Besides, she hadn't seen anyone she recognized. Maybe the existence of *mates.com* hadn't yet reached West Hope.

Weight, Average. She deleted "Average." *Slender,* she checked. After all, Lily had implied that the new pants made her hips look less bulky. And Elaine was so tired of being "Average."

Likes. I like sunsets and thunderstorms and traveling. (She'd borrowed that line from the profile of a particularly lovely woman who was half her age.) *I like cooking* (for Nick's benefit) *and museums and the theater* (for Wayne's), *and I really like younger men.*

She smiled. Would she dare to post this? Her mother would turn over in her unassuming grave, but it was Elaine's life, wasn't it? Elaine's chance to take or leave?

She took another sip of tea and glanced at the clock in the shape of a basketball that Kory had bought at the Hall of Fame in Springfield. It was two-fifteen. Somehow the night had crawled into the morning. But now that she'd started, Elaine couldn't stop. She took another sip of tea.

Dislikes.

That one was easy.

Anger. Betrayal. Not taking risks.

She stared at the last line, surprised she'd written it. Maybe the makeover was beginning to take shape on the inside as well as the out.

She smiled another smile, this one a little braver. Then she got up from the chair and went to the kitchen where her purse hung on the doorknob. She opened the zipper compartment and reached inside and slowly took out her Laurel Lake Spa ID, the one with the picture of a blonde named Elaine.

Wasn't it ironic that Lloyd had bought Kory a scanner last year for Christmas and now here was Elaine about to use it to find herself another man?

"Betsy Gardner, please," Andrew said into the phone the next morning. He'd decided to begin with the toughest call—the young woman who'd once worked for him. If she didn't catch on that it was him, chances were the others wouldn't. "I'm calling about the Benson wedding."

Jo looked at him oddly from across the desk.

He touched his throat. "Allergies," he mouthed, as an explanation for why his voice sounded like sandpaper on the banister of the old West Hope Town Hall. He could not, of course, admit that he was trying to sound like someone else, anyone else. It was bad enough he'd practically stolen *Buzz*—hell, he'd practically dropped it into the pizza box, he'd been that stunned when he'd seen it—from Jo last night. Who'd have thought she would have bought a copy? Someone else might read the issue from one cover to the other and not get it that he was the clandestine author of the "Real Women" column. But Jo wasn't someone else. She was way too smart.

"This is Andrew," he said now, carefully omitting a last name in case Betsy Gardner had ever heard that Andrew David's real last name was Kennedy. Not one of *the* Kennedys.

"Ms. Gardner," he said, while doodling very bad doodles of squiggles and flowers and anything to keep his hand racing as quickly as his brain. "I'm with Second Chances, the wedding planners for the Benson nuptials."

Ms. Gardner replied, "Yes?" in a tone that revealed she'd become network acclimated, poised for the defense, ready to say, "No, we're not interested."

But Andrew gave Jo a thumbs-up signal because, after all, the intern hadn't hung up on him. Besides, he needed Jo to get back to her own work and not watch him with those green eyes while he sat there, stuck between his two worlds like an elevator between floors.

"We've decided to assist the media by blocking several rooms. New Year's is a busy time in the Berkshires, and accommodations aren't only hard to find, they're at a premium. I'm calling to see if we can help with your arrangements."

Ms. Gardner paused a moment. Andrew pictured her in the PR office, the glass-walled cubicle just off the newsroom that would be stacked with heaps of binders filled with press clippings (hard copies always backed up online archives). Lining the perimeter, TV monitors would be set to every network and many cable stations, and no less than three computers would be present, though Andrew had never determined why the lowest-funded department needed three computers.

He wanted to ask if she were nibbling on a glazed donut or if she'd rid herself of them.

"I suppose we'll send someone," Ms. Gardner at last replied. "At least a photog."

"Three rooms, then?" As soon as he said it, Andrew gulped. Only someone in the business would know that every network "photog"—aka videographer—came complete with a soundperson and a field producer. Larry and Curly didn't venture out sans Moe.

"What's your name again?" Betsy said. "I'll have to get back to you."

At least she was still green enough to have missed his slip. However, if she hung up now, she might never call him back. "I can reserve three rooms in our block," he said. "It won't cost the network anything to hold them."

She sighed a little, well, why not? She no doubt had at least a week's worth of work to do today, and another week's tomorrow. By now Ms. Gardner probably had learned that the glamour of television was limited to precious few on-air personalities, while the other staff members were relegated to the heap of underappreciated grunts.

"We're only trying to help," Andrew added, "so no one is turned away. I can reserve the rooms, then e-mail you confirmation. Just let us know for sure a week ahead."

"When is it, again?"

This was, Andrew knew, a ploy to feign disinterest, to

make it appear that "network" was a word and a concept superior to "tabloid."

"New Year's Eve," he said.

"Oh. Right. Well, yes, then, go ahead and do what you said. I appreciate the help." She hung up and Andrew felt deserving of a wide smile.

"She bought it," he said to Jo. "Now I can call the others and tell them we're holding rooms for the other networks."

Jo nodded, but her green eyes narrowed. "Good. It's good about your voice, too. You sound like yourself again."

Andrew cleared his throat. "Well, yes. Damn. I hate those allergies." He turned back to the next media victim on his list and chuckled to himself that he had talked with Betsy Gardner and that he had pulled it off.

And then paralysis overtook him the way it had overtaken him when he'd seen *Buzz* on Jo's mother's kitchen table. His jaw went slack, his pulse and respiration stopped. He suddenly realized that the game was almost done, history, finis. Because though Andrew might be able to fake allergies on the phone and steal magazines from Jo, what the hell was he going to do when the wedding actually was there and so were the photogs, the soundpeople, the field producers—some of whom he no doubt would have worked with over the years?

And, *OhMyGod*, he thought with heightened panic, *what about the guests?* He'd know most of them, wouldn't he? And they would know him, too!

Why the hell hadn't he thought of this before?

And worse, why hadn't John?

22

Men lie.

Andrew typed the words without hesitation, knowing it was true, that even the kindest, most well-intentioned male was not above telling a fib or two if he felt it was for his own good.

Men lie to women. They lie to other men. They even lie to kids if they have to, like when he told Cassie that Patty had left because she didn't love him anymore, not because she didn't want to be a mother, *her* mother.

He supposed women lied, too.

I think it's harder for most women to lie, he added, *because they hate keeping secrets. Especially from one another.* He thought about the honesty Jo shared when she'd said she learned her new boyfriend was married. She could have made up a lie to cover her embarrassment.

Now, however, Andrew had no time to worry about Jo

or what she might or might not figure out based on browsing through a magazine. He had no time for self-indulgent thoughts right now: He needed to figure out what he was going to do.

The phone rang: It was John Benson, returning Andrew's call. Andrew quickly told him about the mess he realized they'd created.

"Unless we can be sure that every photog and reporter and their cast-of-thousands crew has only been in the business for the past five years, I'm screwed," he said to John. "And unless you dump all your friends who know me, too."

"You'll have to find a way to hide," John replied.

" 'Hide'?"

"Wait until the day before everyone is to arrive, then tell the women your mother died. And that she lived out in Seattle."

"They know my mother's already dead."

"Okay, your father, then."

"They know about him, too."

"Okay, then, say you're sick."

"They'll never fall for that."

"What about Cassie? You can say her mother needs to see her and you must take her to Australia."

"They think Cassie is my niece, remember? That her real mother is dead, too." His exasperation mounted. Was his mentor growing senile, now that he'd passed sixty?

"Well, Jesus, Andrew. I don't know what to tell you." At least he didn't add that this whole fiasco had been Andrew's idea from the start, to write his column under cover, to . . . *lie* to the four women. "I only know you have to think of something. The column has become too important to the magazine."

Ah, yes. The magazine. The ratings. The money.

"I can always quit."

"You can always hang yourself, too," John said. "Either way, you're screwed. Lose your jobs or lose your life. Not much of a choice."

He said "Lose your jobs" in the plural form, because if Andrew left Second Chances, he'd lose the best fodder any reporter could ever imagine for his column. John knew it, and so did Andrew.

Andrew laughed. "I can always come clean," he said. "Tell the truth. That would be a novelty."

Silence hung like wet socks on a clothesline. Then John said, "Don't be so quick to discount that."

"Excuse me?"

"You don't have to fess up to all of them. But what about one? If you took one into your confidence . . . told one of the women what was really going on . . . she could be your decoy."

Andrew laughed more loudly. John really was growing senile.

"I'm serious, Andrew. We do it all the time in the media, you know that. Make one of your sources your new best friend. Your chosen informant. My bet is she'll stick by you just for the fun of it."

"For the fun of betraying her practically-lifelong friends?"

"Don't position it as betrayal. Position it as protection. That you're trying to protect the others from being hurt."

"Hurt from what?"

"I have no idea. Surely you can think of something."

He tried. "I could say I was trying to help Second Chances be a huge success, but what reason could I give for why I even cared?"

"Tell her you're in love with one of them, that you loved her from afar long before you applied for the job at Second Chances."

John knew how Andrew felt about Jo because Andrew had been stupid enough to tell him, the way that he'd told Cassie.

"Well, then I'd have to tell all my secrets."

"I don't see that you have much of a choice." He'd said that twice now.

Andrew sighed. "So which one should I pick?"

"The one who's the least likely to think she'd be your favorite, out of all the rest. The one who'd be picked last in dodgeball."

"Elaine," Andrew said.

"Whomever," John replied. "I only know that you promised me six months' of columns. Just do your job, my boy."

23

"How about lunch?" Sarah asked Elaine. It was Friday already: Lily, Jo, and Andrew had gone to The Stone Castle and nearby inns and motels to coordinate the Bensons' guest list to the available rooms, and make a preliminary plan of who would stay where.

Elaine had brought in egg salad, and was about to decline when Sarah added, "I'm sorry, Elaine. For the way I was the other day. Let's have lunch. My treat. A peace offering."

A peace offering? It was odd, but sometimes so was Sarah.

They went to Le Fusion, which Elaine hadn't been to since the day the roommates had decided to open Second Chances.

"I've been hideous lately," Sarah said after they'd ordered salad greens and cheese soufflés.

Elaine could have agreed, but she did not. Instead she wondered if she and Sarah had ever gone out for lunch together, just the two of them. Despite that their group was four—five now, counting Andrew—even back in college, Sarah had preferred to stay on an invisible periphery, the loner who would occasionally join in, usually when Jo or Lily had prompted her.

All the years since college, though Sarah only lived in the next town, the only time she and Elaine got together was when they went to New York to meet Lily and Jo. They never just "did lunch," the way they were doing now. They never even said they would. She'd only been to Sarah's house once or twice, and had never met Sarah's lover, but then, he was a rock star and always on the road.

It was indeed odd, this peace offering. Just as it had been odd this morning when Andrew asked if Elaine would like company on her trip to Saratoga on Saturday. He said that Cassie had been in a blue mood and he thought a visit to the racetrack, maybe to the horseracing museum, might give her a boost.

Elaine had said okay, just like lunch with Sarah. She wondered if her makeover was responsible for people wanting to be with her, that maybe people thought her attitude had changed for the better, like her hair.

Of course, that wouldn't be the case with Sarah.

"I know you think I'm being silly," Elaine said, "for wanting to change my life."

Sarah's black eyes flashed with sparks of silver, like the silver she crafted into such beautiful jewelry. She shook her head; her long hair swayed like sheets of satin. "It isn't you," she said. "Besides, have you ever known anyone more tolerant of other people than me?"

Well, that was true, Sarah was tolerant. She'd had friends back in college who were Buddhists and friends who were capitalists and friends who wore a mass of tattoos before tattoos were cool. She'd had her three roommates who each heard her own muse. Sarah didn't criticize; she just did her own thing.

"You're pretty tolerant," Elaine agreed. "You don't make fun of people. Especially your friends."

Sarah covered her face with her long artist's fingers. Unlike the sheen of her hair, her hands were dull and dry. They looked made of clay, as if she were a potter. "Oh, God, Elaine. I'm sorry. I'm having a hard time at home right now and I'm taking it out on everyone."

As long as Elaine had known her, she'd never known Sarah to complain of anything about her personal life. She never bitched about men (much to Lily's chagrin), never complained about any frustrations regarding her son. She'd grumbled about the price of gas, unnecessary pesticides, the Bush administration. Never anything personal.

"Jason wants to move into the city."

"New York City?"

She nodded and sipped her tonic water.

Elaine wasn't sure if Jason was leaving Sarah or if Sarah would go with him, so she simply asked, "And?"

"And I don't want to go. I love my life here. I had my doubts about Second Chances in the beginning, but now I feel as if we might just make it. I'd hate to walk away from that."

"You can't leave us, Sarah. You're too important to the business." She supposed she shouldn't have said that; she recognized emotional blackmail when she heard it. But, gosh, Lily had the money and Jo had the brains, and if it weren't for Sarah, there would be no creativity, no *real* creativity, the kind that turned an ordinary room into the Taj Mahal. "The last time I decorated anything was for homecoming weekend," Elaine said. "Remember the red-and-yellow crepe paper? Everyone hated it."

Sarah laughed. "It was pretty ugly."

"And what about Burch? Where would he go to school?"

"Oh," Sarah groaned. "That's another problem. He really wants to move. He'd see more of Jason. Half the time when Jason is on the road it's because he's in the city."

They talked back and forth throughout the lunch, Elaine trying to help Sarah come up with a solution, Sarah relating pros and cons and not coming up with any answers.

But by the time the crème brûlée arrived, Elaine wondered if her makeover had indeed helped make her more approachable to Sarah and to Andrew, or if it was simply that, as people got older, they realized how important their friends really were.

Elaine had said she'd pick Andrew and Cassie up at ten, but she got there at nine-thirty because she was ready and she didn't want to wait around. She'd told Andrew she'd drive her minivan so there would be "room for my father's archives," or at least, that's what she'd said. The truth was, Elaine wanted to drive so she'd have something to do to keep busy, something to focus on other than wandering thoughts about her father and how she would feel when she saw him. And when she saw the house, her home, the place she'd been avoiding since her mother had died, because it wasn't the same, it would never be the same again.

She knew she'd be nervous. Excited. Not unlike the seven-year-old girl she'd once been, who'd tried so hard to make her father's favorite angel cake and present it to him for his birthday. She'd somehow been aware that hers didn't stand quite as tall as when he made it for the restaurant, and it leaned slightly to one side. He'd said it was perfect, but Elaine had known it wasn't.

She hoped her father hadn't let the house go, let the pewter-colored paint start to chip and peel, let the floorboards of the wide front veranda begin to buckle and crumble. She could not take that guilt, if she was forced to see that he'd been suffering, that he'd become despondent, an old, unhappy man.

"Saratoga isn't just a county," Cassie interrupted, reading from the pages she'd downloaded off the Internet. "It's like a country all its own." She sat in the backseat next to a cooler that Elaine had loaded with root beer, Macintosh apples (the sweetest in the fall), and packets of string cheese because those were the things her kids had loved whenever they'd gone on a road trip, usually to Saratoga when her mother was still alive.

It had been a long time since any of her kids were Cassie's age, and Elaine felt envious of Andrew, who rode shotgun beside her, and wasn't saying much of anything since he'd gotten in the van.

"Hey!" Cassie said. "It has the oldest thoroughbred racecourse in the nation!"

"And the most beautiful," Elaine added. She waited for a rebuttal from Andrew, but his head was turned out the window, and he seemed more interested in the trees that had long since lost their leaves and now stood naked in the margins of the Massachusetts Turnpike.

"Dad, can we go to a mineral bath?"

It was heart-wrenching the way that Cassie sometimes called him "Dad." It was wonderful that Andrew had taken Cassie in when her mother, his sister, died. Elaine remembered he'd said the woman had been killed in a car accident.

Andrew cleared his throat. "I thought you wanted to see the horse track. And the museum."

"I do. But after that?"

Kory had been like that—the energetic child, the one eager to see and do it all, as long as "it" did not involve anything that hinted of schoolwork.

"We'll only be here a few hours," Andrew said, "not a month or two."

In the rearview mirror, Elaine saw Cassie set down the papers. She wanted to tell Andrew not to be so hard on the girl, but he was not her husband and Cassie was not one of her kids.

"You'll have to excuse my Uncle Andrew," Cassie said. "He's having some personal problems."

Andrew didn't speak: He just chuckled and shook his head.

"Andrew?" Elaine asked. "Is it something I can help with?" He'd been so kind to her, so patient to endure all the female silliness at Second Chances.

"Maybe we can talk about it on the way back," he said. "Right now you need to think about your father's recipes, and Cassie and I need to think about having fun. Right, Cassie?"

The girl rolled her eyes and said, "Sure thing, Uncle Andrew."

24

Andrew didn't recall being as glad to get somewhere as when Elaine finally pulled to a stop at a big Victorian and said, "This is it." Between the breakneck speed at which Elaine had driven, the fact that he'd been unable to unload his secrets as yet, and Cassie dying to wisecrack from the backseat because he'd told her of his intention to confide in Elaine, Andrew was more than ready for the trip to be over. He already decided that he would do the driving on the way back.

"Come in and meet my father," Elaine said. "Then you two can take the van and explore the area. Don't forget the snacks in the cooler in the back."

He must remember to take some soda from the cooler she'd been so thoughtful to bring. If nothing else, they could give the apples to a horse or two and Elaine would never know. Just as she'd never know if they ditched the plastic, tasteless cheese ("Gross and disgusting" were Cassie's sentiments, he knew). Surely they'd find a trash container along the road.

Andrew and Cassie followed Elaine onto the front porch. She rang the bell.

"What a great old place," Andrew said.

"My parents bought it not long after they were married, the first year they had the restaurant. My father often said he'd been afraid they'd never have another good year like the first."

"He was wrong?" Andrew asked.

"Very." Her hand rubbed the woodwork. "It looks freshly painted. I am so glad."

They stood a moment, then Elaine rang again. She checked her watch. "We're about an hour early," she said, which was easy to account for since she'd come to get them half an hour before she'd said, and they'd practically hydroplaned across the Mass Pike and the New York State Thruway up to Route 87. "I suppose we can go in the back way. I know where there's a key."

Andrew felt a little weird sneaking around the concrete walk to the back of the house, where the same porch had stretched itself around the sides and to more steps that led to another door. That one was solid wood, not decorated like the one in front.

In the yard, next to a garage that had been painted to match the house, was an old-fashioned clothesline and a giant grape arbor. Elaine walked to the arbor, reached up, and produced a key that dangled from a bright green plastic tag.

"Bingo," she said, then smiled. "Of course, Lily

wouldn't say that. She'd say something like 'Aha, here we are, then!' "

Cassie frowned and said she liked "Bingo" better, and Elaine lead the three of them up the back stairs.

As Elaine began to turn the key, the door opened. If the person on the inside was Elaine's long-lost father, he looked a little strange wearing a flowered dress and a long-sleeved cardigan, not to mention that his blue-white hair looked recently bouffanted and hair-sprayed to death.

"Elaine?" the person asked.

"Mrs. Tuttle?"

Then a man appeared behind the alleged Mrs. Tuttle.

"Dad?"

"Elaine?"

Andrew resisted an urge to pipe up with his name, too. He decided the drama unfolding was more entertaining.

"Well," Daddy said.

"Well," Mrs. Tuttle said.

"Well what?" Elaine's eyes fell to a clothes basket that Mrs. Tuttle held. All eyes followed accordingly. "Are you helping Dad around the house? How nice."

Mrs. Tuttle smiled and looked to Elaine's father.

Slightly stooped, the man hiked up the edges of his flannel shirt and shoved his hands into the pockets of his flannel pants. "She lives here, Elaine," he said. "She's been here, what is it, Larry, two or three months now?"

Elaine stood there, still holding out the key with the bright green tag as if she were about to insert it into something, perhaps Mrs. Tuttle's throat. "Well," she finally said, "we didn't mean to interrupt."

Her father excused himself, stepped past Mrs. Tuttle, and came out onto the porch. "I've been meaning to tell you, but we don't talk too often anymore." Even Andrew—grown-up, orphan Andrew—knew a zap of guilt when one flew past him.

"Well," Elaine responded, finally lowering the key. "You've been keeping busy, or so it seems."

"When you called and said you were coming, I knew I'd tell you today. But you're early. We aren't ready. Larry was going to go to the market. She planned to come back after you'd been here a while and I'd had the chance to tell you."

Andrew wished he'd stop calling the woman "Larry." It was confusing.

"Well," Elaine said, "it didn't work out that way."

"No," he said, "I'm sorry." He withdrew his right hand from his pocket and gestured to the woman with the basket. "This is Laurene Tuttle," he said, then held out his hand to Andrew. "Bob McNulty. The embarrassed father."

Andrew shook his hand. "Andrew Kennedy," he said. "And this is Cassie. We're friends of Elaine's. We came up to see Saratoga." He did not add "and to meet you," because that subject seemed to have been covered. He turned to Elaine. "So we'll run along, if you'll give me the car keys." There was a bit of back and forth while Elaine mistakenly handed Andrew the back-door house key, then corrected herself. Andrew and Cassie said good-bye, that they'd be back later, and made it down the stairs as Bob McNulty said, "Well, come inside, Elaine. It's chilly out here."

"Chilly" wasn't the word for it.

And though he felt a little guilty at leaving Elaine behind, Andrew quickly guided Cassie back to the minivan, where they jumped inside, looked at each other, and Cassie asked, "Geez, Dad, what the heck was that about?"

25

It was agonizing. As soon as Elaine stepped inside the back hall she knew that this was one of those forever moments that gets locked up in your heart and hurts too much to let it out.

Mrs. Tuttle was everywhere.

A pair of gardening boots was parked beneath the coatrack. Next to them were an umbrella with pink and yellow flowers and a frayed straw hat that Elaine's mother never would have worn.

"Coffee?" Mrs. Tuttle asked. "Your father's Crab Creole won't be ready for a while."

Elaine said okay and sat down at the boothlike kitchen table—our "dinette," her mother used to call it. She waited for the numbness to wear off. This did not feel like the right atmosphere in which to rebuild the family.

Her father sat across from her. Mrs. Tuttle went behind

the counter where Elaine's mother should have been in her shirtwaist and loafers.

"So," Bob McNulty said, "this is some surprise."

He could say that again.

"I worried when I first heard your voice. Is something wrong? Are the kids okay?"

Elaine realized that the "surprise" to which her father referred was her phone call to him, not that Mrs. Tuttle was now sleeping in his bed.

"Nothing's wrong, Dad. The kids are fine." Her voice was clear and unwavering, as if she were not at all in shock. She tried to take a deep breath. She tried to smile. She tried to act as if this was no big goddamn deal. "Remember Lily, Dad? And Sarah and Jo, my old college roommates?"

He laughed. Time had not changed the wondrous chortle of his laugh, a chortle that was honest and sincere, as if he always got the joke. "You girls were something. And that Lily. How many times is she married now?"

"Three times. But her last husband died."

"Too bad," he said.

Mrs. Tuttle put a plate of shortbread biscuits on the table. It was an unfamiliar plate with a gold scalloped rim, not a white plate with green ivy like the ones that belonged here, in her mother's kitchen.

"We have a shop now, all of the roommates," she continued. "We're planning second weddings. It's a big business these days." She blinked at the irony. She wondered if her father would surprise her with that next: "Mrs. Tuttle's my wife now. Isn't that great?"

Instead he said, "Do you need money?"

It was not the first time he'd asked if Elaine needed money. He'd asked in different ways, but the offer had been there.

When he learned she'd gotten married: *You need money, I suppose.*

Then when she was divorced: *You'll be needing money now.*

She hadn't accepted any, ever. It just hadn't seemed right.

"No money," Elaine said now, picking up a biscuit to be polite. "A little moral support would be great. And maybe a few ideas for receptions. And some old recipes."

"Recipes? What? You're going to give brides a recipe collection?"

She bit into the biscuit, expecting it to be tasteless and dry, disheartened that it was good.

Mrs. Tuttle set two mugs of coffee on the table and abruptly said she'd be off to do her errands. She asked if there was anything Bob or Elaine might need. Both of them shook their heads.

When the back door was closed behind her, Elaine's father said, "She's a good woman, Elaine. She helps fill up the lonely days and nights. We're going on a cruise this winter. I always wanted to go on a cruise. Your mother was afraid of the water."

Elaine nodded. It was the closest thing she could come to approval.

"Anyway, Dad," she tried to continue, "if you still have anything—especially your recipes—would you be willing to let us have them?"

"Who's doing the cooking?"

"We'll look for a caterer."

Bob scratched his chin. Elaine realized that the gray-white stubble that she'd seen in recent years now was shaved clean. Perhaps for Mrs. Tuttle. Then he chuckled. "I was going to give my old restaurant scrapbooks to the museum. But if you girls could use them . . . oh! Remember the Ashton wedding that they canceled only an hour before the guests were to arrive? We ate prime rib for months."

Elaine smiled. She remembered.

"And the time we had Dover sole flown over from the Bering Sea . . . it *had* to be from the Bering Sea, as if the guests would know . . . and how about the Blakely wedding? It was so hoity-toity."

"Caroline Blakely," Elaine said.

"It was her first wedding. She had half a dozen more. Ha! She could dance wedding rings around your friend Lily."

Elaine smiled. "What do you think, Dad?"

Slowly he nodded. "The recipes? Sure. You can have them. They're upstairs in the attic. You want me to go with you?"

She said "No, thanks," that she'd be fine. Then she left the table, her coffee untouched.

Mrs. Tuttle had lived three streets over and had been married to Mr. Tuttle, head of the Department of Streets and Engineering when Elaine was growing up. They lived in a house not unlike the McNultys', and had twin sons in the third grade when Elaine was in the eighth.

They were good customers at the restaurant, and often called to place orders for Filo Mushroom Pies, which Elaine delivered because Bob believed in going out of your way for good customers.

Elaine climbed to the second floor, bypassed the bedrooms without looking in, then took the narrow stairs up to the next level.

It was dimly lit, dusty, a typical attic. She glanced around quickly, pleased that all the boxes and storage cabinets seemed as she remembered . . . that no new ones had been added by the other woman.

Elaine suddenly wondered what the twins—Dennis and Danny—thought about Bob McNulty and their mother's new life. Sons accepted those things far more easily than daughters, didn't they?

With a deep sigh, Elaine decided she'd worry about all that later.

She popped the lid on a cedar chest—Elaine's mother's "hope chest," she remembered they had called it—the place where young women put linens and china and kept them until the day they were married, or "hoped" they were married. A pungent scent of cedar exhaled from inside.

She coughed. She pulled out one afghan, then another, and a third, dragged them in front of a pile of sealed boxes and made a comfortable nest. She sat down on the top afghan: It had been her favorite.

Lily would have died if she saw the multicolored yarn in browns and rust and harvest gold. But though the colors were garish, the blanket reminded Elaine of one snowy winter when the yarns spilled down her mother's lap, the *click-click* of the knitting needles keeping time with the *crack-crack* of the fire, all synced with the melodies from the grand piano that her father created across the big room. Elaine remembered sitting and reading, as if they were a family of a century ago, before television and radio and the Internet. They'd been a family as tightly knit as the brown and rust and gold afghan.

It was, of course, her fault that they'd drifted apart. She should have tried harder, especially after her mother died. But she had been brokenhearted—she'd loved her mother so much. Still, if Elaine had tried harder, maybe her father would not have needed Mrs. Tuttle.

She dug through the cedar chest; she lingered over photo albums with pictures of her mother—young, happy, absurdly in love with her father; and of her father—robust, smiling, Mr. Personality of Saratoga Springs.

There were also photos of people Elaine didn't know: rich people, horse people, dressed in their finery (fashions and hairstyles and heavy black eyeliner on the ladies that Lily would have laughed at), posed at "their" table in the restaurant, as if they were important, which they had been, at least to Bob McNulty, whose livelihood depended on them having a good day at the track.

Elaine pored through box after box, sorting the pictures of her parents away from the rest.

And then she found the recipes.

"Oh," Elaine cried when she opened a metal storage chest that had been tucked under a dormer behind a few thousand cobwebs and an old dress form. "Oh."

The recipes were in neat binders, the way Elaine's

mother had carefully organized them late at night, hand-printing the labels, the way Bob had liked. Appetizers, Soups, Salads, Entrées. And Bob's special favorites, Decadent Desserts.

"Women love desserts," he always maintained. "Give a man a good brandy, give a lady a dessert."

And because he felt women often were the ones who selected the restaurant, Bob made sure they had plenty of sweets.

She thumbed through yellowed pages.

Velvet Mousse.

Crème Fraîche.

A White Chocolate Lace Bridal Veil. She stopped. She remembered he had made the first one for Caroline Blakely's wedding. She thought it was the most beautiful creation that she had ever seen.

And then, *Tiramisu à la Saratoga* (layers of custard on raspberry sauce, made from the finest New York State wild raspberries, picked by, of course, Elaine).

"Why are New York wild raspberries better than others?" Elaine had once asked her father, but he'd simply winked and hadn't offered any answer.

One by one the memories collected in little puddles in her eyes. Then quietly they overflowed and ran down to her chin.

They were exhausted. Andrew and Cassie had hoofed around the racecourse, not once, but twice, examined the back track and the paddocks and the cooling-down fields. Then they'd visited the museum—the National Museum of Racing *and* Hall of Fame—followed by a drive to the Saratoga Performing Arts Center where they saw an awesome sunset reflected in the mineral baths between the huge cathedral pines. They even ate some of the string cheese and drank the root beer because they didn't want to waste time having lunch.

As always, Andrew had the most fun when he was with his daughter. Just hearing her laughter, watching her delight at experiencing new things, made his heart ache with love and his problems seem nil.

It wasn't until they went back to pick up Elaine that Andrew thought about what he would say.

I am not gay.

I am not a receptionist.

I am Cassie's father.

He was glad Cassie was there. If things became too tense, she would make them laugh.

In the Stop 'n' Shop on the outskirts of West Hope, Jo reasoned that no matter how good Andrew's intentions were, the fact was he would glean less insight into John Benson's character from reading a magazine than Jo could if she'd read his palm.

She dropped another copy of the latest issue of *Buzz* into the half-filled supermarket cart. *Some things*, she thought, *need to be left to the professionals.* Twenty years in public relations certainly qualified her for that title.

Then she headed for the checkout, determined not to dwell on the fact that it was Saturday, and that, unlike last week, she didn't have a date.

"Your friends are here."

Elaine stirred at the sound of the familiar—yet unfamiliar—voice. She opened her eyes. "Dad?"

He crossed the floor toward her.

She blinked and looked around. The attic. She looked down. She had curled up on her mother's afghan and fallen asleep.

He squatted by her side. In the dim light he looked softer than he had last Easter, less wrinkled, if that were possible. His gray eyes looked brighter, more at peace. "Did you find what you wanted?"

Nodding, she sat up. She smoothed the afghan, straightened the fringe.

"Would you like to take the blanket?" her father asked. "There's a whole stack of her things in your bedroom, too. I was hoping some day you'd want them." He said *your bedroom* as if Elaine still lived there, as if it hadn't been more than two decades since she'd moved away.

She knew it wasn't realistic to think that if her mother's things stayed there life wouldn't have to change, the house would remain "Bob and Alice McNulty's," and not become "Bob and Larry's place."

She knew it wasn't realistic, but her father's recipes were one thing, her mother's belongings—things her mother had touched, jewelry she'd worn, trinkets she'd cherished—were quite another. Those would stay in Saratoga, where they belonged.

Elaine rubbed a spot of hurt that had formed over her heart. Then she folded the afghan and replaced it in the hope chest. "Maybe another time," she said.

"You slept through the Crab Creole," he said.

Elaine nodded. "Another time," she repeated. Then she reached up and touched her father's cheek. "I love you, Dad," she said, and wondered how many years it had been since she'd spoken those words.

26

They loaded the minivan with cartons from the attic, said awkward good-byes, then hit the road. Gratefully, Elaine didn't hesitate when Andrew asked to drive. It wasn't long, however, before he pulled off Route 87 and stopped for pizza. (He supposed that he and Cassie ate too much pizza, but he'd deal with that another day.) He'd decided that if he were going to tell Elaine the truth, he'd rather do it across a table, eye-to-eye. Cassie sat next to Elaine on one side of the booth, so he faced them both.

"What a day," Elaine said after they'd ordered a large cheese pizza, half with broccoli and mushrooms for his daughter, who continued her seeming quest to become a vegetarian since she'd met Sarah's son. He'd deal with that later, too, he supposed.

"The Mrs. Tuttle experience was rather unexpected,"

Elaine continued. "I'm sorry if that was uncomfortable for you."

"For us?" Andrew asked. "No problem here. You didn't know about his . . . about the woman?"

"Who would think a seventy-five-year-old man would suddenly start living with someone?"

"I hope when I'm seventy-five, a woman out there will want me." It wasn't until he'd said it that Andrew realized he had opened the door. "Of course," he added, "I can't even get one to want me now."

Elaine said nothing for a second, as if she were trying to determine whether or not Andrew's comment should be taken at face value.

"He's trying to tell you something," Cassie said.

The waitress came and set down their sodas and their napkins. When she had left, Elaine asked, "He's trying to tell me what?"

Andrew would have answered for himself, but he'd just sipped his soda when Cassie piped up with, "He isn't gay, you know. Or, wait, I guess you didn't." She giggled.

He could have refuted his daughter, called her a little wishful-thinker, and Andrew knew Cassie would have gone along with it. But there it was, laid out on the small Formica table with the chrome strip around the edge and white paper placemats printed with a map of Italy in red.

"She's right," he said. "Someone other than your father leads a secret life."

Elaine cocked her head to the right, as if trying to hear something that was just out of range. "What on earth do you mean?"

And so he told her. While they waited for the pizza, while they ate the pizza, while they lingered over what remained of their sodas, Andrew told Elaine the truth. Everything. From the day John Benson had called him to New York to suggest that Andrew write the column, to when he applied for the job at Second Chances and pretended to be gay so they wouldn't be afraid to share their secrets and their thoughts, especially about their relationships with men. He even told her that he'd been married and about how Cassie was his daughter and that he had a crush on Jo. "A wicked crush," Cassie interjected, and he didn't refute that, either.

When he was done, Elaine stared with eyes that rivaled deer-in-the-headlights as the all-time look of shock. "Well," she said.

"Well," Andrew replied.

"Well," Cassie asked, "can we get dessert?"

The fact that Andrew had confided in her was almost as confusing as his story. But when they were back in Elaine's van (that time, she said she'd drive), she glanced at him every so often, and decided that, yes, he indeed resembled the young Andrew David she had seen on TV.

"This is Andrew David in Jerusalem."

"This is Andrew David in London."

"This is Andrew David on the road with the presidential campaign in Tuscaloosa, Alabama."

Yes, Elaine supposed it was him. His hair was longer

now, his demeanor more casual. And he was older by a few years, five, almost six, he'd said. She wondered what Lloyd would think if he knew she'd become such good friends with a celebrity. It would surely be a tidbit that might afford an edge of intrigue to her profile on *mates.com*.

As for Jo, it was no surprise that Andrew was in love with her. What man wouldn't be?

She turned her eyes back to the road. "I don't know how I can help you."

"First, you must promise you won't breathe a word of this to the others. Or to anyone. It will only hurt everyone. It will only hurt the business." He'd beseeched her about this already, when he'd first begun his tale. Now that Elaine knew the facts, she knew it was important that she agree.

"I promise, Andrew." She supposed she'd be good at keeping a promise. She wasn't sure anyone had ever asked her to.

"Wait. Better than that . . . you must promise *Cassie* you won't tell a soul."

"Oh, for goodness' sake, Andrew, I won't. I promise." So much for building up her intrigue on *mates.com*. She turned to Cassie in the backseat. "And I promise you, Cassie, that I won't tell anyone your father's secrets."

"Good," Cassie replied, "because someone might hurt him. And I really need my dad."

Elaine turned back to Andrew. "What are we going to do? How are we going to keep you out of the Benson wedding?"

"I have no idea," he said. "But I'm hoping you will cover for me."

She smiled. "We can always send you to Shavonne. You can have a makeover like I did."

"No, thanks. It's bad enough Cassie has spent the last few months scanning magazines looking for clothes that she hopes will help me look gay."

Elaine laughed, because laughing was easier than trying to absorb all this.

She supposed his intentions had been harmless: a former journalist trying to earn extra money by getting close to women, to earn their emotional trust.

It had been harmless, depending on the things he'd said about them.

She fiddled with the seat belt; she moved her hands from ten-to-two to twenty-after-eight on the steering wheel. Before she passed judgment—good or bad—she knew she'd have to find the back issues of *Buzz*.

Had he made fun of Lily, Sarah, and Jo?

Had he made fun of her?

She was reminded that people really didn't know one another, not friends, not family, not anyone.

She fastened her eyes on to the road and laughed again and said, "Well, this day has surely been full of surprises."

She couldn't breathe.

Jo sat in her mother's living room, in the old rocker by the fireplace, a glass of wine in one hand, a copy of *Buzz* in the other.

The magazine was open on her lap. The masthead at the top of the right-facing page read "Real Women."

She tried to tell herself she was imagining things.

But her brain said otherwise.

Olivia.

Eileen.

Sadie.

Jacquelin.

How could they have been so stupid?

How could they have been so . . . used?

"I lived with you nearly twenty years. I thought I knew you."

It was a fine welcome home from Saratoga when Elaine walked through her front door and into her family room and there was Lloyd sitting on the sofa that he had paid for the year Kandie graduated from high school and they had planned a party for which Elaine had wanted the house to look its best.

He must have parked on the next street and walked over. He would have known better than to park his minivan—the twin to hers—in plain sight on Cornflower Drive.

She closed her eyes a moment, thinking this was so unfair. Her mind still spun with images of Mrs. Tuttle and her father and Andrew as a straight man. She opened her eyes again. Lloyd was still there.

"Who let you in?" she asked. It was, of course, a stupid question, because Karen would have done that. Elaine might have changed the locks after Lloyd had moved out to be with Beatrix, but there was no law against one of his children opening the door to him, and Elaine had never threatened a restraining order.

He'd reminded her of those facts more than once: It had been her luck that she'd married an attorney.

"What happened to your hair?" He answered her question with a question, because he was good at that.

"You'd better leave, Lloyd. It's late, and I've had a long day." She dropped her bag in the doorway. She stared at her former husband: He seemed somber, almost lifeless. His hair seemed thinner, grayer; his long-sleeved oxford shirt (blue, he always wore blue shirts) seemed more wrinkled, like his face.

She thought about the cartons from Saratoga that sat out in the van. She could ask Lloyd to make himself useful, but he might misconstrue it as an invitation to stick around.

She pushed a shock of hair behind one ear. "Lloyd," she said, "please. I'm not in the mood for games." What she'd been in the mood for was going on the Internet to find copies of *Buzz*. And to check her e-mail, of course.

"You weren't so difficult when you were a brunette."

She sighed. "I was, however, 'tedious.' " That had been his word, not hers. The word he'd used when trying to define his reason for taking up with Beatrix, the judge, who, he'd said, was far more interesting, energetic, "more *alive*, for godssake" than Elaine.

He ignored her reference. "Karen is worried about you." He stood up and walked too close to where she stood. She stepped back two steps.

"Karen has had a lot of changes in the last few years. She'll adapt."

"She's afraid of what you might do next."

His words floated on a scent of gin, evidence of one or two martinis, the courage to have come. He'd often done that before a trial, though no one but Elaine had known.

She turned from him and crossed to the fireplace. "I had my hair highlighted. I bought a few new clothes. I have a job. I haven't exactly gone from Dr. Jekyll to Mr. Hyde."

"She's more concerned about the men."

Elaine turned on her heel. "Men?" She asked with a laugh. "What men?"

"The men you'll be attracting on *mates.com.*"

She stared at him. She hardened her eyes into slits. "Get out," she said.

He stared back a moment, then stood up and stomped toward the door.

"And stop wasting your money on those goddamn roses," she shouted after him.

His gnarly face whipped back at her. "Excuse me?"

"You heard me. Stop sending roses every Sunday. They won't get you anywhere."

Frown lines trenched across his forehead. "What the hell are you talking about?"

She decided she hated him, the man she'd once loved, the man she had slept with and had kids with and all that other crap. She stepped in front of him and opened up the door. "Call West Hope Florist," she said. "Cancel the order. We're through, Lloyd. Finished. Kaput." She shoved him out. She closed the door, then snapped on the dead bolt.

From the other side his stupid voice resounded, "I haven't sent you any goddamn flowers, Elaine. I wouldn't waste my time, let alone my money."

27

The half moon spilled a dim, foreboding light into Jo's mother's living room. The embers in the fireplace had lost their glow, the wine was finished long ago. Yet Jo remained seated, motionless, not turning on a lamp, not wanting anything but for this day to not have happened.

It was over, she supposed. Their new business, her new life, the safety net of friends.

It was over unless she could come up with a solution. A perfect, foolproof way to make the bastard, Andrew, pay.

Andrew thought he'd done fine with Elaine.

When he climbed into bed (an old-fashioned double bed that had come with the cottage because the queen size that he'd wanted wouldn't have fit up the narrow, low-ceilinged staircase—not that it mattered, because the bed was just for him), Andrew felt relieved. With his confession had gone the weight of the world as Andrew David Kennedy had known it, evaporated like the morning mist off his meager pumpkin patch.

The room glowed from the half moon that splayed its light through the window that Andrew had never covered, not with a curtain or a shade or one of those fancy blinds. After too many years choking in the city, he'd wanted to grab as much real fresh air and light and even darkness as possible.

He stared at the shadows of the branches of the trees as they lightly danced upon the slanted ceiling.

How long had it been since he'd enjoyed their nightly recital? Since he'd said his first lie, no doubt. Since he'd been encumbered by trying to be two people living in the same skin.

He'd never known that lies could feel so heavy.

A large limb with many twigs shuddered a little, then went still. He wondered if Patty had ever felt this kind of heavy, and if she'd figured out that all the bulimic behavior in the world could not have unclogged her soul, could not have compensated for a heart weighted by lies.

You're the only man I'll ever love.

We will grow old together.

Trust me.

He turned onto his side and tried to listen in the darkness for the sound of Cassie's breathing in her room across the hall. But Cassie slept with her door closed now: some time in the last year she'd lost her fear of darkness.

He supposed that fear could burden a heart the same way as a lie.

He settled his head against one pillow and pulled the other close beside him as if it were a woman, then smiled with the thought that he and Cassie both, at last, were free.

Elaine wasn't going to let him wreck her life, not when she had come this far in changing it. She wasn't going to let him intimidate her about meeting someone new just because he was embarrassed about sending all those roses, now that he learned she didn't want him anymore.

She'd show him who was in charge of her life, and that it wasn't him.

Angry, determined, no longer exhausted, Elaine plopped in front of the computer in Kory's room. Sure enough, Karen had left the page open to *mates.com*. Apparently her daughter was smart enough to figure out Elaine's password was "makeover."

There were two (two!) e-mails for her.

"Okay, my lovely daughter and my most annoying ex-husband," she said. "Let's see the kind of men I've snagged."

The first was from someone whose screen name was GrnHnt62.

Dear Pretty Lady, he wrote. *I am 47, 5'8. I have brown hair and brown eyes. I love reading, antiquing, and traveling. I work in a bank in Pittsfield. I am divorced, with two kids who live down near Boston, so they wouldn't get in the way of a relationship. Shall we get together?*

The picture he attached was a little small, but his looks were okay. His letter was certainly brief and unimaginative, but Elaine smiled when she reread "Dear Pretty Lady." That was nice.

She checked the other response.

And then her heart stopped. It was from Gerard. The thirty-six-year-old who, God help him—and her—preferred older women.

He must be a gigolo.

Dear Elaine, he wrote. Her heart, which had stopped, now started to race. *Before you get the wrong idea, I am not a gigolo.*

She sat up straight in her son's desk chair.

I've always been mature for my age. And when I say I prefer older women, I don't mean women twice my age. But I do find it exciting to be with a woman who has experienced things that she can teach me.

She smiled.

She read on.

I'd like to meet you. I live in Brattleboro, but I'll be in Pittsfield soon. Call me anytime. Then he left his number.

Of course she wouldn't call him. What would Lloyd and Karen say? She really wouldn't be so daring... would she?

It took about thirty seconds for her to pick up the telephone. She reached his voice mail.

"Hi, this is Gerard. I'm not available right now. Leave your name. And number. Thanks."

He sounded nice. Normal. Even a little sexy. Not like a man who might destroy her life.

Of course she wouldn't leave a message.

Quickly, Elaine hung up.

She stared at the phone. She decided that hadn't been much fun; that had been the old Elaine.

Taking a deep breath, she redialed. This time she said, "Hello, this is Elaine. Call me when you have a chance. I'd love to get to know you." Then she hung up, surprised she didn't even tremble like she might have thought she would.

Just for good, I'll-show-you-Lloyd measure, she went back to the computer, and replied to GrnHnt62.

28

Elaine's phone rang Sunday morning.

She squinted at the alarm clock. It might have said six-thirty.

Between rings two and three, she felt a sudden rush.

Gerard?

She fumbled for the receiver.

It was not Gerard, but Jo.

"We have a crisis," Jo shouted. "Be at the shop in twenty minutes."

"The bastard lied to us," Jo said.

Sarah sneered. "And we thought he was a journalism professor. Do you think the theme of his dissertation is 'gullible women'?"

"Oh, it's not to be believed," Lily wailed, though it was

hard to take her seriously when she was dressed in pink marabou pajamas sprayed with silver sparkles.

Elaine made no comment. How could she?

"We need to decide what to do," Jo continued. "Obviously the Benson wedding has been a setup, though I can't imagine why."

"My guess is the Benson wedding is why we're in business," Sarah speculated. "Otherwise, where would Andrew get material for his precious column?"

In the silence that followed, Elaine could have sworn she heard anger churning, like smoothies in a blender on a hot summer day.

"We'll have to fire him, of course," Lily said. "We can't have the hired help spying on the employers, no matter how much we adore him and the little girl."

Elaine didn't know if protocol was the same for lying receptionists as for domestic staff, which undoubtedly had been Lily's only experience with such matters.

"No," Jo said. "If we get rid of Andrew, we will lose the Bensons. Everyone is excited about what the wedding means to the town: the money, the prestige, the media hype. Without the buzz the wedding's going to bring, we can kiss Second Chances good-bye."

"You're right," Sarah said, then looked at the others. "She's right," she repeated.

"Oh," Lily moaned.

Still Elaine said nothing. If they knew that she knew... if they knew *everything* that she knew... they'd be angry with her, wouldn't they? They'd be angry that she hadn't called them last night, that instead she'd been online trying to find a new man, when she should have been warning the others what she'd learned. Shouldn't she have?

She slid down in the deep navy chair.

"I do, however, have a plan," Jo said. "We need the Benson wedding. So let's take advantage of it—of the opportunity, the publicity, the money. Once the wedding's over—and we've been paid in full—we'll tell the worldwide media what a lowlife 'A.K.' really is. He wants to know about real women? We'll show him the wrath of real women when they've been betrayed."

"He'll be stunned," Sarah said.

"As was I," Jo replied. She held up the magazine. Her cheeks were as pink as the brightest shade on the palette that belonged to the makeup lady at Laurel Lake Spa. Jo looked at Elaine. "You need to read this," she said. "I'm going online to read every damn back issue where this column appears. We need to know exactly what Mr. Andrew Kennedy—whoever he is—has shared with the world."

Lily stood up and went to the window. She looked out onto Main Street; she played with the gold tassel that softly bunched the elegant drapes. Then she turned back to the others. "I suppose there's also a good chance our Andrew isn't gay."

Well, Elaine couldn't stand it another minute. Maybe she'd promised Andrew, maybe she'd promised Cassie, but Elaine had to leak something to her friends. After all, they'd been there for her first, long before Andrew. "I bet he isn't, too," she said. "I bet he made that up, so we'd trust him with our secrets and our thoughts—especially about our relationships with men." They had been his words, so she knew they were true.

The others gaped as if she were brilliant.

"Well, if that's the case," Lily said with a mischievous twinkle of her impish blue eyes, "our Andrew is in for a surprise."

Women call it a makeover.

I call it an act of not-so-divine desperation, a misguided adventure destined for chaos.

Elaine sucked in her breath. She'd carried the magazine over to her corner where her small desk sat apart from the others. She'd been the last to join them, after all. The last, the least important. The one no one would expect to know the things that she knew.

She wondered if she should warn Andrew.

But Jo had called him "bastard," so Elaine decided she'd better not say anything to anyone, not until she'd read the column for herself, not until she'd judged and juried him, too.

She held the magazine close to her eyes.

Guys, after all, don't do makeovers, he'd written. *When a guy wants to change his life, he buys a new car or a Harley, or changes from beer to vodka martinis, extra dry.*

Her eyes scanned the rest of the not-so-clever disguise: he mentioned a "women's shop," not a second-wedding planning business; he said that the women had been childhood friends, not college roommates; he claimed they lived "somewhere in the country," not in West Hope, Massachusetts.

And then there were the names:

Olivia.

Eileen.

Sadie.

Jacquelin.

Well, of course Jo had figured out it was about them, and that the makeover was about Elaine.

She twisted in her chair. It wasn't an ache that she felt, or even a gut-wrenching pain. Instead, tiny, needlelike pricks perforated her skin as if she'd become the pincushion in her mother's old sewing basket, sentenced to endure a thousand small hurts.

Oh, Andrew, she thought, *did you ridicule us to the whole world?*

She forced herself to keep reading.

Four middle-aged women, Andrew—A.K.—had written, *only two of whom once were married, now all of whom are single.*

Elaine knew, of course, that they all were single. But somehow seeing it in print was jarring, as if they were second class, as if they were losers.

She didn't know if she was more upset by that or by the fact he'd called them "middle-aged."

As I've said in earlier columns, the women are very different. Interestingly, not one of them appears to have her life driven by a man. Not even Olivia, who is enamored by romantic notions, but no doubt holds her own.

Jacquelin's lovers have offered little and taken much; Sadie's have remained as mysterious as she has, and there's nothing wrong with that.

They are all doing well, hanging in, building new goals and new dreams.

Which apparently has been the stimulus for Eileen's sudden need for a makeover.

There they were again, the thousand tiny needles. "Andrew, you scoundrel," she said under her breath. Would his next column be about her father and Mrs. Tuttle?

Between her teeth she sucked in a narrow strip of air.

Eileen is the typical divorcée, Andrew continued. *Not quite sure what has happened to her life, not quite sure where to go from here, though it's been two or three years. She has a few kids, so that must add to her confusion.*

Ha! Elaine thought, as if he knew the half of it.

She almost got married again.

If train tracks traveled through the middle of Second Chances, surely one had just arrived and knocked her flat down. She looked around the shop to see if there was any evidence that she'd uttered a deep and woeful cry. Then she turned back to the magazine, masochist that she was.

She must have thought that getting married was what she was supposed to do. Lucky for her, she came to her senses before the damage had been done, before she'd learned that too many women—and, yes, too many men—marry again too quickly because single life is so damn awkward, especially in a town and a society where couples rule.

She stared at the page. Was he now praising her?

She took another breath, this one bigger than the last.

And now, Eileen wants to change it all.

Across the room, Jo uttered something unpleasant. She must have found more of Andrew's writing.

Elaine went back to *Buzz*. And then she read:

I applaud Eileen for her heroic attempt to make her life over.

She read the last sentence again. And again. Then she went on. A small, shy smile grew on the right side of her mouth.

I applaud any woman for not settling for a new car or a Harley, but for standing up and saying, "I hate my life, but I'm not going to sit around and whine. I'm going to do something about it. Something constructive. Something fun."

So, Andrew concluded, *these women-friends of mine continue to amaze me. And I, as a man, can sheepishly admit I wish I could be more like them.*

Smarter.

Stronger.

Less afraid of life.

The initials—A.K.—signified the end.

Less afraid of life, he'd written, and he had been right. *Smarter. Stronger.* He'd said those things about her.

A small tear slid down her cheek and landed on the page that was opened on her lap. She wanted to tell Jo that Andrew wasn't their enemy, that he truly was their friend. But Elaine didn't know how to do that without wrecking everything, without having them think that she'd betrayed them, too.

29

Jo found several months of "Real Women" columns, proof that the one lousy man she'd let herself trust had turned out to be no better than the rest. She hated to think she'd become one of those women who hated men, and yet, there she was.

Men lie, Andrew had written.

In another column: *Never underestimate the mood swings of a woman.*

Other comments were equally insulting: *Women have no penises with which to think.*

I've found the perfect ruse that will let us go behind the scenes.

Don't play games . . . at least, not with a woman you might care about. What did that mean?

Then there was the big one: *Why . . . do I have to pretend that I am gay?* Lily would love that one.

While she read, Jo realized it wasn't Andrew's words that had fueled her anger. It was his deception. Plain-and-simple deception.

She tried to imagine how he had landed such a journalistic coup. Oh, he was good-looking and smart, but he and Cassie had been in West Hope for years. What was his connection to John Benson? Not that it mattered. Not that anything to do with Andrew Kennedy mattered.

She rubbed the muscles that climbed from her shoulders to her neck. They felt like rubber bands, pulled too taut, ready to snap. It occurred to her that not even Brian had made her feel so incensed. Perhaps because, with Andrew, it was such a shock.

"All set," Lily said as she came back into the shop, though Jo hadn't realized she'd left.

"What's 'all set'?" Jo had seen that cocky little grin on Lily before, like when they went looking for the U.S. Men's Olympic Hockey Team when they'd been in college.

"Friday we'll be going to lunch. You. Me. Elaine. Sarah. And Andrew."

"And?"

"We'll be trying a new place called The Bear Claw Tavern, outside of town. Don't ask any questions. Just put it on the calendar."

Jo leaned back in her chair. "Lily, what are you up to?"

The cocky little grin faded to a sad smile. "You're right that we can't fire Andrew. But we can damn well make him regret that he underestimated us."

30

Monday morning Elaine carried the binders with her father's recipes into the shop, hoping to get right to work, hoping Andrew would be there so the others wouldn't start bitching again, wouldn't waste more time and energy cooking up a scheme to get back at him.

It had bothered Elaine all day yesterday. She knew that Andrew had lied, but she worried that the payback would be too uncomfortable. Elaine hated conflict and the dis-ease it often wrought.

Juggling the binders from one hip to the other, she let herself in the back door of the shop. She wondered if she should tell them her exciting bit of news—the fact that Elaine McNulty Thomas was going to have a date Saturday night. She decided it was doubtful that today they'd be happy about anything positive if it involved a man, Sarah's Jason or Lily's Frank notwithstanding.

But, gee, she was feeling kind of giddy about the prospect.

GrnHnt62. His e-mail had been there yesterday when she'd arrived home from the anti-Andrew madness at Second Chances.

She'd answered the message quickly, not wanting to criticize men too readily. "Saturday is fine," she typed.

About an hour later, up popped the logistics: Seven o'clock? Geraldine's?

Seven o'clock was fine, too, but Elaine hesitated about Geraldine's. She didn't do bars, and Geraldine's was notorious.

After about two seconds of contemplation, she decided what the heck. If Lloyd ever found out, maybe he'd have a stroke.

"Elaine," Andrew said now as he jumped from his chair and took a carton from her arms. "Irene Benson just called. She'll be here next week."

"Oh," Elaine said. "That's great." She wanted to give him a huge heads-up. She wanted to hug him and say, "Oh, Andrew, I don't care what the others say. Those were beautiful things you wrote about me—about all of us." But Jo, Lily, and Sarah were all standing in the showroom. Plotting their next move, Elaine feared.

"Next week is practically tomorrow," Jo replied. "We have a ton of work to do before Irene arrives. And the phone keeps ringing with other brides-to-be wanting other bookings."

It was what Elaine had been missing from her life: the

crazy chaos, the nonstop spin-cycle of working with her friends. Second Chances was on its way to becoming a success and Elaine was now part of it. As long as the business didn't lose its luster. As long as the others didn't ruin everything.

"These are my father's recipes," she said, patting the carton as Andrew set it on the desk. "I'll start going through them this morning."

"Sorry," Sarah said, "but I need your help today. We have to go to The Stone Castle and measure for table centerpieces and room decorations. Lily is bringing my concepts to florists for price quotes, Jo's covering the phone, and Andrew's working the media. Jo's right: Next week leaves us no time. We have to do this fast."

Elaine stopped herself from saluting. Instead, she turned to Andrew and said almost apologetically, "We can get the other cartons later."

The next thing Elaine knew, she was off in Sarah's truck and Monday had started and she needed to pretend that nothing was amuck.

Besides, she had a date for Saturday night. She'd concentrate on that and forget about Andrew and all the things she wished she didn't know.

Of the four of them, Elaine had been the one who'd had the normal family when they were young: the mother who stayed at home and took care of their needs, the father who went off to work each day and came home every night.

Jo had been envious.

In the house where she'd slept (or tried to sleep) for several nights, where in between naps she'd wandered from room to room, she now foraged through the kitchen cabinets, sorting her mother's old yellow plates, trying to make herself useful, when all she really wanted was to call Elaine and say, "For godssake, be good to your father. Be grateful you have him."

It saddened Jo that Elaine had grown so detached from her father when he'd been such a nice man.

Sometimes the girls had piled into Lily's new Camaro and gone to Saratoga for a weekend. They went shopping and took long walks and went to the empty racetrack where they shared a pack of cigarettes and a six-pack of beer.

At night, tucked into an old twin bed in Elaine's house, sharing a room with Lily or with Sarah, Jo lay awake and pretended that this big place was hers, that she and Brian were married and they lived there with their half a dozen kids. It didn't matter that Jo was in college and should be too old for make-believe.

In the spring before graduation, they went for the last time.

"Jo." Elaine's father had greeted them one Saturday when they returned with shopping bags and smoky breaths. "Your mother called this afternoon," he said. "Please, come into the music room. Elaine, take Lily and Sarah upstairs to your room."

Jo went into the music room with Mr. McNulty, where a grand piano was covered with a golden, velvet shawl.

"My wife is out doing errands," Mr. McNulty said, "or she would join us."

"Something's wrong," Jo said, and Elaine's father asked her to sit down.

She sat on a sofa that had curly legs. Mr. McNulty sat on a needlepointed footstool in front of the sofa.

"It's your father," he said.

"My father?"

"I'm so sorry to tell you, Jo, but your mother called to say she heard that he has died."

Jo stood up. "You must mean my grandfather. Oh no. I must get home."

But Bob McNulty shook his head and touched her hand. "No, dear, your grandfather is fine. It's your father, Sam Lyons, who has died."

Jo sat back down and stared at Mr. McNulty.

Her father died? How had her mother found out, and why should she really care? It had been a dozen or more years since he'd abandoned them. Even when she tried, Jo could not recall his face.

"Am I supposed to do anything?" she asked. "I mean, is there a funeral?"

Mr. McNulty shrugged. "I think your mother only wanted you to know." He was trying to be so nice, like the kind of father Jo would have wanted. Not like the father that now was dead.

She stood up again. "Thank you for the information," she said. "I guess I'll go find the others."

"Would you like to call your mother?"

Jo said, no, that she'd stop by when they returned to West Hope.

Mr. McNulty stood up, too. "Will you be staying for dinner?" he asked.

Jo remembered that she'd frowned and said, yes, of course. Why would she go home just because her father died? And why had her mother called and left the message, anyway?

Yes, Jo thought now, as she packed the butter dish into a box because no one in the family used butter anymore, it really was a shame that Elaine had grown detached from her father when he'd been such a nice man.

Elaine held out until Thursday before she told Sarah about her date. They were driving from the florist to the fabric shop so Sarah could buy white velvet to line the bridal sleigh.

She said Elaine was nuts—*certifiable.* "Who is this man?" she asked.

Elaine ran through the bio.

"He's into antiquing?" Sarah continued. "Are you sure he isn't Lily's boyfriend? How do you know you can trust him?" "Trust," of course, was the word du jour, what with Andrew's deceit foremost in their thoughts.

"He isn't Lily's boyfriend. And he must be trustworthy. He works in a bank."

"Ha!" Sarah chuckled, then asked, "What's his name?"

"I don't know."

"You don't know?"

"Well. No."

Sarah hissed. "Come on, Elaine. Are you really that desperate?"

Elaine felt she'd been pinched. She didn't mention that no one had thought Jo had been desperate when she'd met that man in her garage. That man who ended up being married. "I'm not desperate, Sarah. I decided it's time for some fun. For the new me."

"The world is different now than when we were in college."

"I know that."

The black/silver eyes darted sideways to her. "Bull," she said.

They rode in silence, Elaine's wonderful mood sliding away.

"I'm going, too," Sarah suddenly said.

"Where?"

"Geraldine's. Saturday night. I'll be there watching. Just in case."

"In case what?"

"In case you need help, Elaine. In case he's a wacko."

"No," Elaine protested. "I would be so embarrassed. If you show up I'll never speak to you again."

Sarah paused for a moment, then said, "Suit yourself. But it's not as if I'll be around to protect you forever. I've decided that once the Benson wedding is over, Burch and I will move to New York with Jason. But don't mention it to the others just yet, okay?"

It occurred to Elaine that she might have missed being with her friends all these years, but she surely hadn't missed the up-and-down roller-coaster ride that came with having friends. With her friends, anyway.

Nor was she happy that she now had another secret she'd been asked to keep. Before her makeover, Elaine would have taken on the problems of the world and everyone in it. But right now she didn't want to have to worry about Andrew or Sarah or anyone but her.

This was *her* time.

This was *her* chance.

This was supposed to finally be about *her, her, her.*

The perfect distraction came late in the day when they returned to the shop.

Andrew handed her a small slip of pink paper. "From the post office," he said. "They tried to deliver something while we were out to lunch."

Elaine didn't ask where they'd gone or if Lily had pulled any pranks or if she were saving that for Friday. She pushed those thoughts from her mind and focused on the delivery. Then the light dawned.

"My clothes!" she shrieked. The note reported that the packages could be picked up after four o'clock, but must be collected before five.

She glanced at the clock: four-fifty-two.

"If you hurry you'll make it," Andrew said. She blew the dear, sweet man a kiss and raced out the door, not caring if the others thought she was Benedict Arnold-ette.

31

The post office was housed in what was called the "new building," even though it had been built in 1978. But Elaine supposed it was a fact that the beige brick, one-floor building had replaced the white clapboard structure that had sat there since the mid-1800s, so compared to that, 1978 was indeed new.

She ran across the town green and dashed into the main lobby at four-fifty-seven. She scooted up to the counter. Catching her breath quickly, she said hello to Margaret Birdy, and nodded at Mr. Clawson (Elaine never could remember his first name, though they'd served together on two parent-teacher committees), then set her pink piece of paper on the counter. Yvonne asked how she could help her.

"I have a few packages," Elaine said.

The woman in the dark blue pants and light blue shirt

with the red, white, and blue eagle on the breast pocket disappeared behind a wall. While Elaine waited, she wondered which outfit she should wear on her date Saturday night. She thought there was a pants set in pale gray: that might be nice.

Yvonne returned, carrying three large bundles. "Looks like you've been spending time online," the woman commented and Elaine blushed, then glanced around to see if anyone had heard.

"There's not much time for shopping these days, what with the new business." It was certain Yvonne knew about Second Chances. Because Yvonne worked at the post office, she was privy to all the gossip in town.

"I like your hair," Yvonne added.

Elaine gathered the bulky packages, said thank you, and maneuvered her way back to the front door, wishing she hadn't scampered across the common when she might have still arrived before five if she'd driven the van.

"Let me give you a hand with those," a familiar voice said. From the corner of her eye she'd seen a man approach from the annex where the post office boxes were; she hadn't expected it to be Martin.

"Oh," Elaine said. "Martin. Well, thanks."

He took the packages from her, seemed to realize they were heavy, then laughed and handed one of them back. "Guess there was a reason I was late getting the mail today," he said.

Elaine remembered that Martin picked up the mail for his car dealership every afternoon at two. It was one of those predictable qualities of his that had made a future with him seem humdrum compared with the ever-changing maelstrom of her former college roommates.

They walked outside and Elaine explained that her car was in the lot at Second Chances.

"No problem," Martin said. "It's a nice evening for a walk."

She fell into step beside him. Two years of dating had left a layer of familiarity, a comfort zone of sorts.

"How are the kids?" he asked. Martin had given Kory a summer job to help out with college expenses. He'd offered Kandie an office job, but she'd curled her lip and made it quite clear that a pre-law student did not "do well" around the scents of oil and grease. Karen had liked Martin, though sometimes she seemed to feel guilty about it, as if she were cheating on her dad.

"They're fine," Elaine said and nodded. "Yes, they're all fine." They walked a bit farther. "How did you make out with the zoning board?" she asked. It had been the last big event in Martin's life, or rather, in Martin and Elaine's life as a couple. He'd been trying to get a variance for a lot to offer Jeeps, a complement to the Chevys he already sold.

"Good. Fine. We'll break ground in the spring."

Elaine nodded. They crossed the green, now lit only by the lampposts.

"How's the business going?" Martin asked.

"Good," she answered. "Fine."

He gestured to the packages. "Bought yourself some new clothes for the new job?"

He didn't say it to be mean; Martin wouldn't know how to be mean.

"Yes," she said. "A working woman's wardrobe isn't the same as someone who stays home."

Martin nodded. "I like your hair," he said. The words were the same Yvonne had said, yet somehow they meant more.

"Thanks," Elaine replied.

"So," he said, "it's going well?"

"Yes," she said again.

They walked the rest of the way in silence. When they reached Elaine's minivan, she opened the back door, set the package that she'd carried on the seat, then took the others from Martin and arranged them there, as well.

"Thank you, Martin," she said, and he responded with "You're welcome, anytime." Then he raised his hand as if tipping his hat and said good night and turned to walk away.

"Martin?" Elaine asked. "Can I give you a lift to your car?"

"No, thanks," he said with a smile. "It's a nice evening for a walk." She wondered if he knew that he'd said that already.

She smiled back and waved and wondered why—with a new date to think about and a pile of new clothes—she felt disappointed.

32

Ceremony.

Gowns.

Tuxedos.

Flowers.

Minister.

Music.

Attendants.

There hadn't been time to figure out the damn food.

Just before Lily's "surprise" lunch at The Bear Claw Tavern Friday, they reviewed the list to make ready for Irene. Monday, after all, would arrive in a flash.

By some minor miracle, the women kept straight faces when Andrew offered to be Irene's chauffeur while she was in town. He said he'd start by picking her up at the train station Sunday night. Jo thanked him and said she hoped it wouldn't interfere with his weekend plans.

No, he'd said, it would be fine.

Jo knew she'd be able to remain composed as long as she didn't make eye contact with him. She had, after all, been well trained at keeping her chin up, stiffening her upper lip. She'd learned to cope by pushing down her feelings, hadn't she? She'd learned to cope by attending to her work.

This week, however, had been a challenge. The disappointment of Jack Allen, then Andrew's lies, compounded by the complicated emotions of being in the house all alone at night, with no one to talk to except the memories, and nothing to focus on except fathers and daughters, had simply been too much. She'd tried to work in the evenings, but the distant voices stole her attention.

I'm sure your father meant to visit on your birthday.

Grandpa will take you to the father-daughter dance.

That's all, honey. There are no more gifts.

The last remark came one Christmas morning when Jo had gone behind the twinkling tree, not out of greed, but because she just knew there must be a gift there from her father, the man who had left them all. But her mother had been right, there were no more gifts.

Years ago Jo had scoured the house, looking for evidence of her father's existence: a photo, a love letter, something. But Marion had wiped the house clean, as if a crime had been committed and the evidence skillfully destroyed.

The way Andrew had tried to camouflage any evidence of a prior life, too. She suddenly wondered if Cassie were his niece, or if she were really his daughter.

Clenching her jaw and wishing for a way to make the

hurt just go away, Jo decided to pretend that Andrew wasn't in the room.

"Let's focus on the ceremony with Irene on Monday," she said. "Tuesday and Wednesday we can do the reception. That will leave Thursday for anything we've left out, or anything she wants to change." Irene needed to be back in the city Thursday night. "We'll give her a few options, then our recommendations. As long as she's okay with the major things—the castle, the white-and-silver theme—we should be all set."

The room was silent for a moment, then Lily let out a sigh. "I'm worried about the food," she said. "She's going to hate the food."

All eyes traveled to Elaine's desk, where her father's binders sat untouched. Elaine had been so busy—they all had been so busy—there hadn't been time.

"I'm sorry," Elaine said. "I can take them home this weekend... but I don't know how to convince a caterer to make something that isn't theirs... and I'm not sure it would be fair to give away the secrets of my father's creations."

"Don't worry, Elaine," Jo said. "We have menus from the best caterers between here and Boston. I'll bet we can get them to drive out here with samples. It's the Benson wedding, after all."

Lily stood up and paced the room. "And I say the menus are all too ordinary, too predictable. I have friends like Irene Benson. Believe me, *predictable* is not a word she'd want to equate with anything, let alone the food. I think Elaine should cook for her."

For a moment no one, Elaine included, said anything.

The full thrust of Lily's words began to slowly take some kind of shape.

"Me?" she asked.

Lily rubbed her small hands together, her eyes lit up. "It's perfect," she said, gesturing toward the cartons. "They're *your* father's recipes. You cook them, we serve them, we claim a link to the famous McNulty's of thirty and forty years ago. Irene will be charmed." She spoke a bit maniacally, as if she'd been ignited by another spark of payback against Andrew.

"But my father was the chef, not me."

"At least give it a chance, Elaine. We can present it as another option."

"And if she likes it?" Sarah asked.

"Then Elaine will become a caterer."

"No," Elaine replied. "I only know how to wait on tables."

"Oh, come on," Lily joked. "You're the one who's wanted a new life. And the restaurant business is in your blood. Besides, how far wrong can you go with your father living only a hundred miles or so up the road?"

Jo supposed that Lily had a point.

"We'll make Irene wait until Wednesday night," Lily continued. "Then we can all go to Elaine's house for dinner!"

No one objected, not even Jo, who was too tired from pushing down feelings to argue.

Lily slapped the desk. "Consider us done for the day." She circled the room. "Ladies? Andrew? I believe we have a date for a well-deserved lunch. I understand the tavern makes a roasted veggie gumbo that's totally divine."

The Bear Claw Tavern was out by Sarah's log cabin, in a village on the outskirts of West Hope, a universe from civilization. The dark interior was wood, wood that ran along the walls, wood that ascended to the peak of the cathedral ceiling. Symbols of the Berkshires were hung all around: cross-country skis, buck and bear heads, snowshoes.

It didn't seem to Andrew like a place Lily would have selected. There was no maître d'; there was no linen.

"Now," Lily announced, after the waiter had taken their order and gone to fetch the Chardonnay, "I wanted to have this little celebration because we've been working so hard."

Yes, well, Andrew supposed they had been working hard. Including Elaine, who'd chosen not to join them, but had gone home to plunder her father's recipes because Lily had pretty much backed her into that corner.

Jo smiled.

Sarah smiled.

"And," Lily added, "I thought it was time for Andrew to have more in his life than a bunch of niggling women and a little girl, sweet though she is."

Andrew wasn't sure if he should smile in return, or if he should excuse himself and leave. There was something unsettling about Lily's demeanor. He placed his palms on top of the pine table and lightly drummed his fingers and his thumbs.

A tall man—not the waiter—suddenly appeared with four large-bowled wine glasses. "Good afternoon," he said to them all, then his eyes landed on Lily. "It's nice to see you again, Lily. Thanks for bringing your friends." He was a handsome man. He looked about forty, give or take, with slick black hair and light gray eyes. He wore a black turtleneck and tight black jeans.

He poured the wine for Lily to taste.

She tasted. She nodded. He half filled the other glasses while she introduced him to Sarah and Jo. Then she turned to Andrew.

"And most important of all, this is our Andrew," Lily said. "Andrew, this is Damien, who has simply been dying to meet you, haven't you, dear?"

Andrew supposed he should have known that sooner or later it would happen, that one of the women for whom he worked (of course it would be Lily) would have thought it *such a hoot* to set him up. With a man.

He extended his hand to the wine steward named Damien, reminding himself that he was neither born nor raised into prejudice of any race, color, religion, or sexual orientation. Still, when Damien's broad hand met his, Andrew tried to pump it like Gunter at Laurel Lake.

His eyes moved to Lily, then Jo, then Sarah, all of whom, he expected, thought this had been a great idea. "Oh," was all he said. Then, "Well." One uncomfortable moment led to two. He wondered if the warmth in his cheeks meant they had turned scarlet.

"You must order the gumbo, Andrew," Lily said. "If you find it as delicious as Frank and I have, I'm sure Damien will be delighted to bring some to your house. Say, Sunday afternoon?"

Andrew's smile was as unmoving as if his lips were stuck to a metal flagpole in the middle of winter. "Sorry," he said, "but Sunday Cassie has a competition." He tried not to act impolite. He tried not to act pissed.

"Another time, perhaps," Damien said, and gave a slight bow.

Andrew nodded and quickly ordered the gumbo. The rest of the lunch went by in a blur. Andrew wished Cassie was there. He would have felt safer, though she might have said later that he deserved it, and she might have reminded him to end this charade before anyone was hurt.

Lily might have been happy with her bit of vengeance, but Jo was embarrassed watching Andrew be embarrassed. She wanted to fast-forward to the Benson wedding, when all truths would be told, when this finally would be over, and she wouldn't have to look at him or think of him, or wonder why he'd done it. To them. To her.

Cilantro Carrot Soup.

Grilled Romaine Salad.

Veal Medallions.

Toasted Basil Pasta.

Elaine sat at the small desk in the kitchen Friday night, clad in the Springfield College sweats, digging through her father's recipes, perusing a cross section of temptations that might please Lily, which would then be good enough for the bride-to-be. She was beginning to think that the strength of a second-wedding planning business—or, she supposed, any wedding-planning business—hinged on a bunch of lists.

She would work until midnight. Then she would stop worrying about this, take a hot bath, and go to bed.

Tomorrow she'd start shopping. She'd go to the gourmet shop in Pittsfield where she'd find the freshest ingredients, the finest-quality selections. Then she'd race home and get ready for a date with a man whose name she didn't know.

Hopefully, she'd have enough time.

Thumbing through more glassine-covered pages, Elaine studied the ingredients. She wrote out more lists. Through it all, she thought between-the-lines thoughts about Andrew and what had happened at the lunch she couldn't bring herself to attend. She thought about her date, and tried to summon some excitement about the potential for love. And with each page she turned, she thought about her father.

Was he truly happy with Mrs. Tuttle? Or was she better than nothing, a loneliness cure? Whatever the reason, he had a new life.

But so did she, or at least she almost did.

Why did she find his so disturbing?

"Kids don't like change," she remembered Andrew had said about Karen.

"No kidding," she said out loud and hauled another fat binder onto the desk. The small square of paper tucked into the spine read "Decadent Desserts," her mother's hand-lettered title for her father's favorites.

Elaine inhaled a deep breath and opened the notebook. Then she remembered the White Chocolate Lace

Bridal Veil, the pièce de résistance her father had crafted for Caroline Blakely's "hoity-toity" first wedding.

Elaine turned the pages. Was the recipe there? If it was, could she possibly make it as good as her father had? As delicate, as original, as melt-in-your-mouth?

She remembered that first time he'd made it, and how she had stood, barely tall enough to peek over the counter, holding her breath as he peeled back the first layer of lacey chocolate and sculpted it into a delicate creation that looked just like a bride's veil with gentle folds and scalloped edges.

"Daddy, it's so pretty," Elaine had whispered.

Her father had smiled. "It's all in the proper balance of the ingredients," he said. "And a touch of my magic."

She sighed with the memory, then turned another page. Praline Pie, Pear Custard, Orange Meringue Cookies.

Then Elaine had another idea. Why not have Sarah create a tiara...a duplicate of the one Irene would wear...or to the one she had worn at the first Benson wedding?

The glittering tiara could top the wedding cake; the white-chocolate veil could cascade along the sides and down the back. Guests could break off small pieces of chocolate throughout the reception. Talk about a photo op. The media would love it.

Elaine wondered if she was becoming a wedding planner after all. If only she could find the damn recipe.

And then, there it was.

White Chocolate Lace Bridal Veil, her mother's penmanship read. *Created by Robert McNulty of McNulty's Restau-*

rant, Saratoga Springs, New York. August 23, 1967, for the wedding reception of Miss Caroline Blakely and Mr. Howard MacBride.

He had created dozens of "veils" after that. And now, Elaine could revive the tradition, with a new twist, a crowning glory that would turn an ordinary wedding cake into a truly decadent dessert.

There was only one problem: the proper balance of the ingredients—the right amount of butter, the right amount of cocoa and sugar . . . and, of course, the magic. Could Elaine recapture it? And, if it was possible, did she have the time?

She glanced at the clock. Seven-twenty-five. If she hurried, she might make it to the gourmet shop in Pittsfield. If she hurried, she might just pull this off. Wouldn't Lily and the others be ecstatic?

Unsnapping the three rings, Elaine pulled out the recipe and tucked it into her bag. Then she grabbed her keys and headed out the front door, just as her thoughts settled on another idea: Should she—could she—possibly ask her father to help?

33

The West Hope train station looked the way it might have looked fifty or a hundred years ago: a small, redbrick building; slatted, wooden benches; a stack of morning newspapers propped up in a corner. Even the man behind the lone caged ticket window wore a stiff, round, short-brimmed hat and a charcoal-gray vest whose buttons were connected by several gold links no doubt attached to a pocket watch. Andrew could have sworn he'd seen the man in movies from the forties.

The man said yes, the ten-twenty-six from Manhattan was on time, which meant Irene would arrive in seven minutes. It was Saturday morning: the women at Second Chances thought she wasn't arriving until Sunday night. They did not know she was coming early to spend time with Andrew and Cassie.

He shivered in the cold brick building. How he was growing to hate every one of his lies! He walked outside to the quiet platform and stood facing south, trying to forget that he'd quietly told Lily after their lunch that he was not interested in Damien, or anyone right now, thanks anyway... trying to forget that she'd *tut-tut*ted him and said perhaps he might at least give Damien a chance.

Lily hated taking "no" for an answer, which left him only with the hope that Irene's visit might sidetrack her.

He stared at the horizon capped by the gray November sky, at the path of steely railroad ties bordered by barren, between-season trees. Even in its bleakness the Berkshires held a certain beauty, as if lying in repose, awaiting the shroud of winter whites and the crackle of applewood in big stone fireplaces.

And this year, awaiting the New Year's gala of the Benson nuptials, the *Re-Wedding*, as Andrew liked to think of it, the event that couldn't get there quickly enough, so the lying would finally be done.

He put his hands into the pockets of his denim jacket and he waited. He looked forward to seeing Irene.

She had, after all, been his first lover.

It had happened quite by accident one spring break night when Andrew was seventeen and John and Irene had secretly been separated several months.

Andrew was finishing his junior year at Avon Old Farms in Connecticut. He'd not been home since Christmas; he hadn't known that John had moved out of the penthouse across the hall.

"I got a letter from him last month," Andrew said to Irene as they walked along Park Avenue in the evening. She'd taken Andrew out for Chinese food; he'd mistakenly assumed that John would join them. "He lined up a summer intern job for me at NBC."

Irene nodded and slipped her slender arm around Andrew's. "I'm sure it will be fine," she said. "We'll call and check tomorrow."

There had been many prior nights they'd eaten Chinese food together, then walked along the avenue. There had been many prior nights, but John had always been there, pointing out new storefronts that had materialized, new investment brokerage offices, new residential buildings for which he'd speculate the cost of new apartments. The void of his absence hung between the high-rise buildings like deep, unwanted chasms.

"He's always been like a father to me," Andrew said. "More than my own father."

Irene adjusted the long, silk scarf that flowed around her neck. "I wonder if that's what his new girlfriend thinks. That he's like a father to her."

Andrew hadn't answered because he'd not known what to say.

Then Irene said John's girlfriend was only twenty. "A model from California. One of *those.* With a fake tan and no tits and too many teeth."

Andrew had laughed.

Irene had laughed, too.

The next day Andrew went across the hall and they

called the man at NBC and learned, indeed, they were expecting Andrew sometime in mid-June. Irene said he was home on spring break and asked if he could drop by for a visit.

Later that afternoon, he did.

After which, he went to see Irene, to thank her for her help in John's absence.

She'd offered him coffee.

She'd offered him tea.

Slowly, the hole he'd felt in the Benson penthouse began to dissipate. And for the first time since he had known her, Andrew saw Irene as a beautiful, enchanting woman, with a long, golden neck and slender, ballet dancer's arms, and a way of looking at him that made him believe he was the most important boy—man—on earth.

The rest of the week, he made frequent excuses to stop by. On the last night, Irene fixed him a drink. A martini, the precursor to another, more important first.

It could have been the lights that shimmered over Manhattan. It could have been the comfort that he felt in the sprawling living room that was a mirror image of his own. It could have been the soft scent that Irene wore, or the elegant chiffon caftan she had on. It could have been that the housekeeper and the cook were both off that night.

Or it could have been because Andrew was seventeen, with more testosterone than a bull in mating season.

Whatever the reason, one of them (later, he could never be sure which one it was) made the first move, touched the first touch, encouraged the first sweet, gentle kiss.

He remembered that he slid the chiffon from her shoulders. He remembered that these were the first full breasts of a woman that he'd seen in person, not on magazine pages or in R-rated movies, the first breasts he'd caressed or, God, the first he'd kissed.

He remembered she unzipped the zipper of his jeans; she removed his man-boy manhood from its confined space; she sucked it with her mouth until he thought that he'd explode. Then she guided him to mount her, and they did what they'd done.

It had been sweet.

It had been wondrous.

It hadn't seemed wrong, despite that she was—eighteen? twenty?—years older. It hadn't seemed wrong because, though John had been a father figure, Irene had never been like a mother. She'd always been John's wife, untouchable because of that. Until John had left.

It had, sadly for a seventeen-year-old boy, been the one and only time. He'd gone back to school; by the time the school year was over, John had moved back into the penthouse and the model apparently was gone.

They'd spoken about it only once, when Irene let Andrew know she had not told John. It was best that way, she'd said. It was best for all of them.

And now, Irene was on a train rumbling toward Andrew. She was his friend and mentor's wife, his daughter's beloved godmother, and just another one of Andrew's secrets, though he'd take this one to his grave.

34

GrnHnt" meant the *Green Hornet* and "62" referred to the number of original Green Hornet radio scripts that Elaine's date possessed. So far.

Niles Hockinsworth was shorter than the five feet eight inches he'd mentioned to Elaine, and stood almost eye-to-eye with her five feet five. He wore small glasses over his small eyes, and had on a button-down shirt and a tie. When he spoke, the left edge of his mouth twitched. But he seemed nice enough in a dull sort of way.

All things considered, she'd rather be home starting to experiment with her father's recipes. She'd spent the whole day shopping: She had everything she needed now except for time.

As soon as her eyes had adjusted to the dim light of the beer signs, Elaine realized she was way overdressed in her five-hundred-dollar gray pants set. She'd never been inside Geraldine's, never experienced the moans of the seventies country music from the jukebox or the brouhahas from the denim crowd perched on the stools. She ordered a glass of wine and was grateful that Niles had found a booth, though the split vinyl threatened to make tiny pulls in her pants—not a good enough reason, she supposed, to say that she must leave. Every few minutes Elaine squinted and scanned, hoping Sarah had ignored her threats and was seated there, at the corner of the bar, maybe, or at the booth in the back. So far, she was not.

"George Trendle," Niles was saying. "He wrote the first scripts. Most people don't know he also created the Lone Ranger for radio. In fact, even fewer know that the Green Hornet was actually the great-nephew of the Lone Ranger."

Elaine smiled and said she hadn't known it. Then she asked if he had any children. He said some people thought Kato was his son, but he was really his Filipino valet.

She stared at him with wonder. Wonder at what she was doing there, wonder at how soon would be impolite to leave.

"Oh," he said, "you mean me. Do *I* have any children. I thought you meant the Green Hornet."

She didn't reply. What could she say?

"I'm sorry," he said, lowering his small eyes to his beer glass. "I am so nervous. You're so pretty."

Now, of course, Elaine felt horrible, wedged in that place between reality and pity, where no matter how weird the guy was, she felt sorry for him. Did other women feel this way on dates?

"Niles," she said softly, just above the refrains of Merle Haggard. "I'm sorry if I'm not paying attention. It's just that I'm involved in a new project at work and I'm terribly preoccupied tonight." She sipped her wine. She considered knocking the glass over—perhaps onto herself—then declaring she must go home now, that it had been nice to meet him. Later, when she was alone, under the covers, she would probably feel the disenchantment that her first *mates.com* date had not been Mr. Right. At the moment, however, she simply wanted to flee.

"Maybe we should make it another time," Niles said. "Next week? Are you free Thursday night? Or Friday? There's a great place in Williamstown where we could go dancing . . ."

Her thoughts swirled with images of her dodging phone calls, making excuses, trying to shake Niles Hockinsworth from her life. *Are you really that desperate?* Sarah had asked. Suddenly Elaine held up her hand and said, "Wait."

Thankfully, he did.

She moved her glass to the center of the table and said, "Niles, it's been nice to meet you, but I don't think this will work. You're a very nice man, but we are way too different." With that she smiled, stood up, and said, "Thank you for the drink."

With confidence she didn't know that she possessed, Elaine threaded her way through the local debris and calmly departed Geraldine's.

Outside on the step, she took a deep breath of cool, refreshing, liberating evening air, admitting only then—and only to herself—that she'd feared she'd be *that desperate*; congratulating herself that she really, truly, was not.

"Good job," Elaine heard, then turned and saw Sarah. The sneak had on a cowboy hat that concealed her long hair, tinted, eighties glasses, and a big, ugly parka.

"You were there," Elaine said.

"In the booth right behind you. I'm proud of you, kid. You were right to the point, without being hurtful."

"When did you come in?"

"Before you. I recognized your date from the apprehension on his face."

"Hey," Elaine said, "thanks. I can't believe you did this. Now I can't talk to you for the rest of my life."

Sarah shrugged.

"But first, there's something I'd love to show you. I'm so excited. Can you come over to my house?"

"Only if you tell me one thing," Sarah said. She removed the hat and shook out her hair. "Did you really not know that the Green Hornet was the Lone Ranger's great-nephew?"

Elaine grabbed Sarah's hat and put it on her head and pressed her fingers against her eyes like a mask. She laughed, realizing it had been a pretty cool thing that Sarah had showed up.

Irene sat in silence in the kitchen, drinking tea. It had been a long day for her, of that Andrew was fairly certain, if the length of days could be measured by the quantities of shopping bags and the quickness with which she'd shed her heels and rubbed her feet when they got back to the cottage in the evening.

It wasn't until after pizza, after seven games of Sorry!, after Cassie went to bed, after Andrew rescued his extra bedding from the linen closet and began to make up the couch for himself (Irene would sleep in his room—he didn't dare bring her to The Stone Castle until tomorrow night, for fear someone would see them), he began to ponder what the heck was wrong with her.

She'd looked fine—lovely, actually—and she'd seemed fine when Andrew had met her at the station in the morning. She'd had on a classic camel coat, her black-and-silver hair tied back with a colorful red sash, her pale blue eyes set off by the light tan on her skin. She'd kissed his cheek as she always did, as if they were, had only ever been, the best of friends. Her scent was light, familiar, good. It had occurred to him she was past sixty now; no matter when he saw Irene, she'd always be beautiful to him.

"Are you looking forward to the wedding?" he'd small-talked once they were in the car. "The women are working hard."

She made a gesture with her hand as if it didn't matter. "Whatever they do will be fine," she said. "I'm not fussy, Andrew."

He laughed a hearty laugh. He could have reminded her of his college graduation, when she and John had been "more than happy" to handle the party arrangements because both of Andrew's parents had been on call. She'd alienated the caterer—"The lady don't stop hovering!" Nicholas Cantini screeched and fled the penthouse, leaving Irene to order takeout from the deli down the street. He could have reminded her of his mother's, then his father's funerals, when she'd orchestrated lavish affairs as if the two doctors had been heads of state. He could have reminded her of Cassie's christening, but there'd be no point in that because that would only bring up Patty, and the two had never seen eye-to-eye.

"They're working hard, but I don't think they'd mind a little challenge," he'd said. "Don't make this too easy on them, or they might guess you're a friend."

She'd smiled through closed lips. "Tell me the details of your little scheme." She winked a prankish wink.

He hated the word "scheme." He hated any reference to his wretched sham. "Elaine is the only one who knows anything. And everything. Lily has forged a new mission, of finding me a man."

Irene laughed, as he knew she would.

Andrew shook his head. "But let's not worry about them right now. I have a little girl who needs to see her Aunt Irene and who can't wait to go shopping. And to tell you the truth, I think she needs some woman-talk."

Irene had turned her head to look out the window of Andrew's old Volvo. She looked out of place when not seated in a limo. "I should see Cassie more often," she'd said.

He'd taken a left and then a right into his driveway and there was Cassie, standing in the front yard, waving at them like crazy.

That had pretty much been the extent of his one-on-

one with Irene. It wasn't as if he'd said anything to piss her off. Had he?

All day he'd thought about them at the mall. He pictured them leafing through clothes racks. He pictured them trying on horrible hats and gawdy costume jewelry, just for fun. He pictured them having lunch, with Irene showing Cassie all the niceties of manners. He said a thousand prayers that they wouldn't run into Lily, Elaine, Sarah, or Jo.

Mostly, Andrew pictured Cassie and Irene laughing. All of which was why Andrew had been so surprised when he picked them up and sensed a peculiar pall in the air, as if Cassie's mood had leaked into Irene.

You didn't raise your kid for ten years and not pick up on a bad vibration.

You didn't know a woman thirty years and not sense when something was wrong, though he wouldn't say that in his column.

What the heck had happened?

He stuffed the pillow into its slightly wrinkled case. And then, the way he'd sensed that something was indeed wrong, he knew Irene was standing behind him.

He turned around.

She smiled a little. "We need to talk," she said.

There it was; he'd hoped that he'd been wrong. "More tea?" he asked.

She shook her head. "No," she said. "Sit down."

He thought that later he'd describe it as a squeezing in his chest, a tightening of the big muscle called his heart, that inched its way down to his stomach, then his legs, then back up to his head and out to both his arms.

He sat down on the couch. She sat across from him, on the overstuffed armchair.

"I don't know how to tell you this," she said. "But someone must."

He wished the light in the living room was better. He wished he could see her eyes. "It's the wedding," he said. "Please don't say you want to call it off." He tried to say it with a touch of humor, tried lightening the mood.

"No," she said. "It isn't about me. It's Cassie. You said she needed woman-talk. She did."

His eyes darted to the fireplace, then back again. Should he light a fire? It was suddenly so cold.

Irene dropped her gaze. She inhaled a long breath, as if smoking a cigarette. Then she looked at Andrew and simply said, "Cassie wants to see her mother, Andrew. She wants to see Patty."

35

Sarah had been excited when Elaine showed her the concept of the White Chocolate Lace Bridal Veil. They'd discussed possibilities—"Can you really make it?" Sarah had asked. "It would be unbelievably awesome, much better than an ordinary ice sculpture or one of those chocolate fountains that were unique when they were first done, but have become tiresome. It would be a real showpiece."

Then Sarah said she'd love to stay and witness the outcome, but she must get home to Burch.

So Elaine had stayed up all night trying to make the damn thing.

She'd melted the white chocolate, added the shortening, and was careful not to get any water on top of the mixture. She'd used a fine writing tip on the pastry bag and slowly formed "lace" over the top of the foil, which she'd shaped into a small veil—for show-and-tell only, to give Irene the idea. She'd tried her damned best, but all Elaine managed was a big chocolate blob. Not exactly lace. Not exactly a replica of anything that remotely resembled a wedding veil.

At six-fifteen in the morning, Elaine concluded that she was no Bob McNulty; she was no gifted chef.

She waited until seven to call him. Mrs. Tuttle answered the phone.

Elaine pinched the deepening frown crease on her forehead. "Is my father awake?" she asked. "I'm having a chocolate-lace crisis."

To her credit, Mrs. Tuttle did not ask for further explanation. A sleepy-voiced Bob got on the phone.

"I'm trying to make the White Chocolate Lace Bridal Veil," she said. "I found your recipe, but I can't make it work, Daddy." The "Daddy" had slipped out. How long had it been since she'd called him that? She skipped over her embarrassment and quickly added, "Help. Please."

He was silent a moment, then said, "Did you stir the chocolate constantly?"

She wouldn't have remembered, but he'd made that notation on the recipe: *Unlike dark or milk chocolate, white chocolate must be stirred constantly while melting.*

"Yes," she replied. She wondered if Mrs. Tuttle was still in the room. Elaine bit her lip; she wanted to cry.

"Did you let it get wet?"

"No. No, of course not." Her temper grew short, as if this were his fault.

"Did you shape the foil into the form that you wanted?"

"Yes." She feared that she was hissing now.

"Did you shape the foil, then put it in the freezer to chill?"

She stared at the white-chocolate mess splayed across her counter. "What?" she asked.

"The foil. You must freeze the foil so the lace can adhere to the form and then be released without breaking apart."

Elaine stared at the mounds of foil. "No," she said. "I made the form, but I didn't freeze the foil." She grabbed the recipe. In the upper left corner, in unfaded black marker, Bob had printed *Freeze foil first*, then underlined it. The perfect instructions had been there all along. She sighed.

"Honey?" he asked. "Would you like some help?"

" 'Help'? No, Dad, I don't need any help." What she needed was sleep. What she needed was to not have been as foolish as to have agreed to do this.

"When is the wedding?" he asked.

Elaine shook her head. "Not yet. But the bride is coming. I have to cook for her Wednesday night. I have to make a lot of the recipes—"

"You do need help." His voice grew animated, no longer half asleep. "I can be there before lunch."

She pictured her father and Mrs. Tuttle swooping into her kitchen with pots and pans and merriment. Elaine was too tired to be civil, let alone to pretend that such togetherness would be normal or fun. "No, Dad," she said.

"I won't take 'no' for an answer," Bob retorted. "Larry won't mind, don't worry. It's been a while since I've cooked—really cooked—but we'll figure it out..."

He said a few more words that Elaine didn't hear. She just said good-bye and hung up the phone and hoped she'd be awake to hear the doorbell when he—or *they*—arrived.

He didn't sleep because he didn't want to dream of Patty. He feared such dreams would evoke a rage of violence, as they had right after she'd left. Worse, he was afraid he'd dream of them having sex. Either way, Andrew couldn't risk the emotion. It had taken too many years for the torrents to subside.

He didn't sleep because he was on the couch and the cushions were fairly lumpy.

He didn't sleep because Irene was upstairs in his bed and she had told him something that had just ripped his heart apart.

Irene, however, wouldn't lie to him. Irene wouldn't make light of Cassie's wishes, or of Andrew's pain.

They'd stayed up talking for a while, he and his first lover. She'd offered a few suggestions about how to handle this, but Andrew could only hear the words "*She wants to see Patty.*"

And now it was morning.

He hauled himself off the lumpy couch and made pancake batter using blueberries that Cassie had picked and frozen in September. He wondered if there were blueberries in Australia.

"Hi, Dad," Cassie said tentatively when she came downstairs, dressed for her Sunday riding lesson. She tossed her hair back from her freckled face. When had she stopped wearing it in a ponytail?

"Hi, honey," Andrew said, and fired up the griddle. "How did you sleep?" It was what he asked her every morning. *Normalcy*, he'd decided, might be the key to thwarting Cassie's plan. Or to keeping himself together in the meantime.

She shrugged.

"Is Irene awake?"

"She's in the shower. She wants to come out to the stables, is that okay?"

"Of course it's okay. She used to ride in Central Park, did she tell you that?" *Normalcy*, he repeated. Don't react. *Don't be hostile. Don't be negative.*

"She had her own horse," Cassie informed him.

He hadn't known that. But then, Irene had always been a member of the elite set, one of the social-register ladies who had not known what was appropriate to do when her husband cheated on her.

He flipped the pancakes over. He waited for a moment, wondering if he should fill the blank air in the kitchen with a few vowels, as if this were *Wheel of Fortune* and he needed more pointless words.

He checked the underside; the cakes were golden. He slid them onto a plate without his usual flair. He set the plate on the table in front of Cassie. So far, amazingly, he had not lost his cool.

"Mmm," she said. "Blueberries."

He sat in the chair across from her, propped his elbows on the table, and rested his chin in them. "So, you had fun with Irene yesterday?"

Cassie's eyes drifted to the right, then left, then down to her plate. "Yes."

One of the most unacclaimed talents of a parent, Andrew realized, was the ability to appear calm and collected on the outside, while on the inside feeling shredded like the beef and pork at Bubba's Bar-B-Cue. But because this knack, this skill, this *art form*, one could call it, tended to be fleeting (at least for him), he knew he'd better get things out there on the old oak table before he felt himself implode.

"You want to see your mother?" he asked with someone else's voice, someone older, meeker.

She drowned the blueberries in one-hundred-percent Vermont maple syrup, the best, or so Andrew had been told. She shrugged again.

He leaned across the table and touched her hand. "Honey," he said, "it's okay." He'd have won the parenting prize this time, if only someone had been around to watch his remarkable performance. If only his voice would return to its usual state.

With a slow lift of those long-lashed lids, she brought her Patty-eyes up to meet his. "It is?" she asked.

"Well, it's okay that you want to see her. But I didn't think you did. It was only a few weeks ago I mentioned taking you. You said it was a lame idea."

Cassie lowered her eyes. He remembered that, at age eleven, a few weeks could seem like months. "But it's okay if you changed your mind."

"I did."

He patted her hand. "Honey, it's just that she has a new life now, remember?"

"I remember, Dad. I saw the picture. The one of her with that new baby, Gilbert Grape."

It would not be an appropriate time to laugh, so Andrew didn't. "I think they only call him Gilbert."

"It's a dumb name."

He took his hand away from hers. "Maybe you should write your mom a letter," he said. "See what she thinks about you going for a visit." He didn't know what would hurt worse: Cassie going to Australia, or feeling her pain when Patty turned her down. But how could he deny her this?

"I was thinking I could call her," she said. "Or send an e-mail."

"I didn't know she had an e-mail address."

"Everybody has one, Dad. She sent it to me a while ago. I wrote her a couple of times."

He didn't ask if Cassie had ever received an answer. "Well, okay then, maybe an e-mail might be better. Calling might take her off guard, you know?" Just because Patty had left them didn't mean she'd take it out on Cassie, did it? Now that Patty was a mother again . . . now that she seemed, God help Andrew, settled?

He patted her hand. "Why don't you write to her tonight after we bring Irene to the inn? I'll tell your mother it's all right with me—if you want me to."

She seemed appeased. She poked a blueberry with her fork and stuck it in her mouth. "Okay, Dad. Thanks."

He stood up with a smile, ruffled her hair, then turned back to the sink so she couldn't see his face in case he began to cry.

Jo had driven the butcher-shop van to the airport in Hartford so there would be enough room for her mother, Ted, and their honeymoon suitcases. Originally—way back at her mother's wedding—she'd planned to ask Andrew if he and Cassie would like to go for the ride. But as the van had rumbled east on the turnpike toward Route 91, Jo had realized that, like most things in her life, she'd ended up going alone.

Marion and Ted walked through the gate laughing and holding hands; at first Jo felt awkward at the newness of that, then she felt envy. As with Elaine and her father, Jo wondered why she was so often left out.

She kissed each of them.

They'd had a wonderful time.

Ted had climbed into the back so "the girls" could catch up; he nonetheless talked from the airport north to Springfield about the olive groves and the prosciutto factories and the miles of vineyards they had visited. He must have tired himself out, for somewhere around Westfield, he rested his head and fell sound asleep.

Jo smiled at her mother. "You're happy, aren't you, Mom?"

Marion nodded. "Very happy."

Jo sighed.

"Have you been busy since we've been gone? How is the business? How is everyone?"

She told her that Irene was coming. She told her about all the bookings they had. She told her that she'd been staying at the house because of that stupid man she'd gone out with. Then, Jo told her about Andrew.

Marion listened. When Jo got to the part about Lily's prank, Marion held up her hand. "Not fair," she said.

"No kidding," Jo said. "I still can't believe I—we—trusted him."

But Marion shook her head. "No," she said. "What isn't fair is that you haven't given Andrew a chance. You haven't heard his side."

" 'His side'? What? We should hear more lies?"

"You're angry," she said.

"You bet I am."

Marion clutched a handsome leather handbag Jo hadn't seen before. Maybe she'd bought it in Florence, a symbol of her wonderful new life. "All men aren't bastards," Marion said.

It started to rain. Jo looked for the knob, then turned on the wipers. "I wonder sometimes," she replied.

The wipers squeaked for a moment, then Marion said, "It wasn't all his fault, you know. It wasn't only your father's fault he left."

Jo stared through the cellophane-like windshield. "We weren't talking about him. We were talking about Andrew."

But Marion persisted. "I was to blame, too, Josephine. I was certainly to blame that your father never saw you, that you hardly heard from him. I was a madwoman when he left. I never gave him a reason to stay. I never gave him a reason not to run off to Great Barrington with that woman."

Great Barrington? That was the first time Jo had heard where her father had gone . . . or that her mother even had known.

"When he died," Marion continued, "no one was more

shocked than I was. I always thought he'd come back to us. I always thought I'd get to hear his side of the story, and that we would make things right."

Jo shifted uncomfortably on the old leather seat. She did not want to be having this conversation right now, what with her mother just back from her honeymoon and Ted sleeping in the back.

"As for Andrew," Marion continued, "no matter what he has or hasn't done, he has been a good friend to you and your friends. My best advice is to give him a chance. Wait to hear his side of the story."

She seemed not to have noticed that Jo hadn't asked for her advice.

36

November was an odd month in the northeast. When the sun came out at all, as it did that day, it seemed pale, stripped of summer's intensity, not yet ready for the assault of winter's glare.

"It's resting," Elaine's father had often said. "We should be resting, too." The tourists, after all, were gone; it was intermission month before the ski bunnies arrived.

Bob McNulty, however, did not rest that day. He drove into Elaine's driveway at ten-forty-five.

She went out to greet him, determined to be grateful for his presence, with or without Mrs. Tuttle. Larry.

The woman was not there, which may have been because there was no room left in Bob's old town car: the passenger seat, the backseat, and the floors in both places were filled with storage cartons from Staples.

"Is Karen around?" Bob asked his daughter. "I could use some help."

"She's at her father's," Elaine replied with some annoyance. She'd wanted to keep this simple—simple and uncomplicated. She should have known that *simple* was not in Bob's nature. She supposed it was what had helped him become such a success.

"Well, give me a hand, then." He was dressed in the red-and-black buffalo-plaid shirt, the kind he'd favored every fall that Elaine could remember.

She ran her hands through her hair. She'd napped only an hour, then taken a quick shower. In three days Irene Benson would be at her house with the entire entourage from Second Chances. In three days Elaine had to present a full-blown catering sensation that would take most professionals weeks to plan and prepare. And she needed to do it in a way that would make Irene applaud and the others be grateful that they could check the potential problem of food off the list.

Three days. And her father wanted to waste time hauling cartons.

With grim reluctance, she reached into the backseat. "More recipes? I thought I'd found them all."

Her father shook his head. "Your mother's things," he said. "I decided it was time."

Elaine sucked in a startled breath. She jerked her hands from a carton as if it were hot-wired. "Dad!" she cried. "This is definitely not the time."

He looked at her, his smile soft, his gray eyes a little tired. "When, then?"

The sun drifted behind a murky cloud. The air turned

cool and damp, as if it were going to rain. "Dad," Elaine said, "I can't believe you've done this. That you lugged down all these things without asking permission."

" 'Permission'? She was your mother. I didn't think I'd need permission."

Sadness framed his words. Elaine slowly inhaled, exhaled. She thought of her sweet mother, now apparently removed from the Victorian in Saratoga, now resting on Bob's backseat and in his trunk, because Mrs. Tuttle had moved in.

"I miss her, too, Elaine," her father said. "She is with me all the time. Right here." He touched the pocket of his buffalo-plaid shirt, the one over his heart.

She turned her eyes from him, feeling a suspicious tug that she was being blackmailed, as if Bob's help had come with strings. Strings and boxes and God only knew what was inside them.

Her mother would have smiled and thought her husband had been awfully smart, because her mother forgave everyone. She'd even forgiven Elaine for getting married "on such short notice," for not inviting her family, for staying in West Hope, so far away. Her mother had said so one night before she had died. "It's you, Elaine," she had said. "It's you who have not forgiven yourself."

Elaine stared at the cartons, aware that her father stood, waiting. She supposed she should at least be happy that he'd come alone. "Well, all right, then," she said, then heaved out the first box. "But let's do this fast. We have work to do."

She should have been working. She should have been looking at last-minute lists in order to be certain Irene would be pleased.

But after Jo dropped her mother and Ted off at their new condo, swapped vehicles so she was back in her Honda, Jo somehow found herself on Route 7 headed south. South toward Stockbridge. South toward Great Barrington.

She hadn't been down there in years, not since she and Brian had gone to the fair one long-ago September. She couldn't remember if she'd been in college or still in high school. She was beginning to feel an odd sense of relief that the lines of the past no longer seemed rigid, but a blend of one yesterday into another.

She stopped at LeeAnn's Diner, which was chrome-colored and shiny and had been there for more decades than Jo had been alive.

A young waitress wore a crisp, white cropped shirt, black pants, and a belly-button ring that shone like the exterior siding of the place. Jo asked her for coffee and pumpkin pie and if there was a local phone book that she might see.

The waitress delivered the phone book first. Jo turned the pages with surprising nonchalance. He'd been dead and gone more than twenty years; chances were good his widow had moved on.

And then there it was: Lyons, Samuel. 45 Rabbit Run Road.

She tipped her head to one side, again surprised that she felt no real emotion. Curiosity, but no real emotion.

"Can you tell me how to get to Rabbit Run Road?" she asked, when the waitress returned with her coffee and pie.

The girl gave her directions; it wasn't far.

Then Jo ate her pie, drank most of her coffee, paid her check, said thank you, and left. Not with haste, not with anticipation, still with only curiosity, she left.

It was a small clapboard house painted beige with white trim. A few pumpkins were clustered around tall cornstalks that rested against a white pillar on the front porch. A trio of deep red and golden Indian corn hung festively on the front door. A mailbox stood on the tree belt. "Lyons" was printed above the number forty-two. She moved her eyes from the mailbox to the front door of the house. She tried to picture her father living here, going up and down the three concrete steps and in and out the door on his way to work and home again, in and out of life, while Jo had been sitting by her bedroom window, looking out onto the street, wondering where he was and when she'd see him and if she would at all.

She wondered if he'd brought the lunch pail to Great Barrington—the lunch pail that she'd bought him at Sears, Roebuck for his birthday the year before he left, the black metal thing that had an arch-shaped top for his Thermos filled with coffee, and two silver latches on the outside to keep his sandwich (bologna and cheese) and his cookies (three Oreos) and his apple or his pear (depending on the season) protected until each lunchtime, thanks to her, he'd said.

Staring at the small house, Jo realized that her heart was aching, and her eyes had welled with tears, over a foolish lunch pail that she'd not known she remembered.

She wondered what things he had remembered about her, and if they'd been foolish, too.

Jo stopped her car.

It wasn't all your father's fault that he left, her mother had said. *I was certainly to blame that he never saw you. I never gave him a reason to stay.*

Suddenly the front door opened. Jo's first instinct was to jam the shift into "Drive," to get out of there before she was caught. But the person who emerged was a tiny, gray-haired woman. She seemed pleasant and unthreatening in her too-large cotton sweater and old, faded jeans.

"Looking for something?" the woman asked, and Jo knew it was Doris Haines, the junior-high science teacher who'd run off with her father.

She blinked. She reminded herself that she'd done nothing wrong.

Then with more courage than Jo knew she had, she turned off the ignition and got out of the car.

"My father was Sam Lyons," she said as clearly as if she'd said his name just yesterday.

Doris Haines scooted her hands up into the big sleeves of her sweater. "Jo Lyons," she said. "My, you turned into a beauty."

They had tea in the kitchen of the tiny, four-room home where her father had gone after he'd left Marion. And Jo.

Doris told her that, yes, Sam had passed on more than twenty years ago; she'd had him cremated like he wanted; his ashes taken by the current of the Housatonic River. She was a nice, kindly woman who made no excuses for what she and Jo's father had done. They'd married soon after his divorce had been final; they'd never had kids.

Jo was surprised by that: in her quest to push everything down, out of sight, out of mind, she'd never considered that she might have half siblings somewhere in the world.

Then Doris abruptly said, "He talked about you sometimes. He hated that he hadn't been allowed to see you."

Jo nodded. "My mother said she was a madwoman when he left."

The woman smiled a gentle smile. "Your mother? Oh, it wasn't because of her. It was your grandfather who'd threatened Sam. Said he'd see him rot in hell before he'd let him see his girls."

"My grandfather?" Jo asked, then she laughed. "No. It couldn't have been him." He'd never been angry; he'd never been mean, not once right up until he had died, a dozen years ago.

"Oh, it was him, all right. He confronted your father right here one night. I sat in the kitchen, hearing it all."

"My grandfather?" Jo repeated.

"Sam said he was only being protective. Protective of you. Protective of your mother. Sam understood that; he didn't blame him."

Jo looked around the room, trying to picture her father, her grandfather there, doing battle.

Then Doris got up and went to a small built-in

cupboard in the corner of the room. She moved around some papers, a photo album, some tiny boxes. Then she pulled out a small box and handed it to Jo. Inside was a long silver chain with a charm in the shape of an oak tree.

"Your father bought this when he read in the paper that you'd be graduating college. He never sent it, though. Didn't want to 'upset your apple cart,' he said. He died before he changed his mind." The woman sighed. "It was his way of saying he wanted you to grow tall and strong, sturdy as an oak, in your body and your mind. I believe he'd feel you've done just that."

Jo studied the small gift. Her throat closed, her eyes swelled.

"Would you like a picture?" Doris Haines then asked. "A photo of Sam?" She offered a faded color snapshot of a young, laughing man with light-colored hair and a bright, wide smile. He sat on a rowboat, a bundle of trout at his feet. It was her father's face, exactly as she now remembered him. Exactly the way she hadn't been able to visualize him for so many years.

Tucking the photo into the jewelry box, Jo covered it with the necklace. Then she thanked Doris Haines and left the small house, wondering if her mother had ever learned the truth, or if she'd accepted the blame because of her guilt.

Outside in the car, Jo set the gift in the glove box. She'd keep it there until she could decide where she would put it—somewhere safe, somewhere close by so she could look at it whenever she needed to.

They'd spent the morning and into the afternoon at the stables. Cassie had her lesson, then she convinced Andrew and Irene to take a trail ride with her.

Andrew was given "Stormy," the most mild-mannered horse in the barn. Stormy had a hard time keeping up, but that was just fine with Andrew.

Then they drove into Boston.

They went to the aquarium and ate at Legal Seafood and did the Museum of Science and the iMax Theater. Andrew secretly hoped the fun they were having might help change Cassie's mind about contacting her mother, about wanting to see her.

He should have known that trying to manipulate your child often doesn't work.

Dear Mom, Cassie typed into Andrew's laptop. It was after eleven by the time they dropped Irene at the castle and went home to the cottage. It was after eleven and Cassie should be in bed, but she claimed she'd slept in the car. When he tried to argue she said, "Come on, Dad, you promised," which was true.

It was also true that he'd told Irene he'd promised and, the last he had known, two against one never worked. Especially when the two were women and the one was a guy.

So there they sat at the kitchen table. He'd pulled a chair close to Cassie's so he could read over her shoulder. *I saw your picture in* Buzz *and wanted to write to you.*

Andrew had no idea his daughter could type so well. She'd been asking for her own computer. Maybe he could buy one with his next paycheck from the magazine. He supposed he'd have to learn about parental controls and all that high-tech kind of crap.

She stopped typing and looked at him. "Well?" she asked.

He realized he'd been daydreaming, avoiding the task at hand. He reread what she'd typed. "Would you mind changing *Buzz* to read 'a magazine'? I don't want her to make any connection of the column to me."

Cassie highlighted, deleted, typed "a magazine." "Now what?"

"Say it's been a long time since you've seen her and that you were wondering if you could go there for a visit."

It's been a long time since I've seen you and I was wondering if I could go there for a visit.

Andrew smiled.

Then she added, *Dad said it's okay with him.*

He ruffled Cassie's hair. He wondered if she should add that Andrew could bring her out in the summer during school vacation. He'd have to check the schedule at Second Chances. The summer would no doubt be booked with wedding on top of wedding—he'd worry about that later. Besides, it was too soon to be specific, and it might not be a good idea to let Patty know that he'd be going, too. She might not agree that an eleven-year-old should not be going halfway around the globe unchaperoned.

"I think that's fine," Andrew said.

"Maybe I should tell her that I miss her."

He shifted on his chair. "Well, okay. Sure."

I miss you, Mom.

He stared at the words on the screen. He nodded, because what else could he do? Some days—most days—he'd forgotten that Cassie even had a mother. He thought she had, too. To see it in print was—well, it was disconcerting.

"Okay," he said. "That looks good to me. Are you happy with it?"

Cassie nodded, then hit the SEND button before she—or he—had a chance to change her mind.

37

Elaine's father stayed overnight Sunday, Monday, Tuesday. He slept in Kory's room; he said it gave him a chance to practice shooting hoops. During the day he was "all business" he said, though they laughed while they scrubbed vegetables, pounded veal, snipped parsley, and more, while they recounted stories, one after the other, of the "good old days" at the restaurant. Even Karen got in on the family act, reluctant at first, but won over by her grandfather.

For Elaine, it was so nice to be with her father, to work alongside him. How long had it been since they'd had time like this together, without Lloyd or then Martin and always a houseful of kids?

It was nice to be with him. Yet, the cartons of Elaine's mother's possessions sat in the back hall, unopened, undisturbed. She told herself all that mattered now was

Irene, and presenting her with a menu that she would simply be mad about, mad in the good way.

Andrew agreed to let Cassie go to Elaine's Wednesday night as long as Cassie promised not to let anyone think she knew Irene, and as long as Irene promised not to let on that she knew Cassie.

Even though Elaine knew otherwise, it was best to forget that, he'd warned.

So far, the week had gone fine. A glitch about the ceremony (Irene had slipped and suggested that Andrew walk her down the aisle. He had turned ruby red but she quickly covered her mistake. Everyone had laughed; they didn't know it wasn't funny); a gaffe with the flowers ("These were the ones at my mother's funeral," Andrew had said in a familiar way to Irene, because, after all, she'd chosen them. Lily had looked at them oddly, but Irene had said, "Oh. They must have been lovely"). Other than that, he and Irene had pulled off the wedding planning with his secrets intact.

The chaos, the tension, the hectic days, had accomplished something else: Andrew had had little time to think about Jo, who'd been acting standoffish, or about Lily, who seemed excessively syrupy, or Sarah, who was more introspective than usual. He supposed people acted differently when surrounded by fervor. *Women*, he thought, *and men*, *too*.

"Remember," he reminded Irene and Cassie sternly as he pulled into Elaine's driveway and turned off the ignition, "not a word. Not a hint. Neither of you knew the other one until tonight. No winking, no giggling."

"My lips are sealed," Irene said with a playful gesture of fingers across her mouth.

"Scout's honor," Cassie said, which was pretty funny because she'd never been a Girl Scout.

"Just be sure to point out Jo to me," Irene said.

With a gulp and a sigh Andrew shook his head, got out of the car, and feared he was doomed.

A sumptuous array of epicurean selections and a plethora of desserts. "Sumptuous" had been Lily's word; "plethora" had been Irene's.

Elaine surveyed the buffet table after her guests had served themselves and moved into the family room. She was glad she'd taken the extra time to use the good china and sterling; she'd even dressed in one of her new outfits that complemented the tiny, pale peach-colored flowers that rimmed the dinner plates. With the proper linen tablecloth, the chandelier dimmed, and a lovely, low floral arrangement—"Use neutral colors," Bob had instructed when he'd called the same florist where the Sunday roses had come from (funny how once she'd mentioned it to Lloyd, the roses had stopped coming)—the table resonated of McNulty's in Saratoga, of glamour, of elegance, of class. Without her father, she could never have done this.

She stood there a moment, savoring the background sounds of spirted conversation and *clink-clink*ing of utensils. She marveled at what stood next to the floral arrangement: a miniature White Chocolate Lace Bridal Veil that her father had crafted into an exceptional, edible, one-of-a-kind sculpture.

"So?" her father asked, stepping from the kitchen into the dining room. "Did the old man do okay?" In honor of the evening he'd worn a tall white chef's hat that Karen had laundered and ironed to crispness.

She smiled and hugged him. "I can't believe you pulled this off, Dad," she said. He had worked tirelessly.

"You helped. Karen did, too."

Yes, it had been fun. Good family fun, like in the old days when she and her father and her mother had been a team. She only hoped that she could find a caterer to faithfully re-create her father's recipes and present them as brilliantly as he had done here.

"I can do it again tomorrow if you want," her father added. "If Mrs. Benson doesn't find a recipe she likes."

"She'll love them all," Elaine whispered. She looped her arm through his, turned her eyes back to the table, and realized that if she'd married Martin, if she'd not had her makeover, none of this might have happened. She might have remained old Elaine, unhappy, but not knowing why.

Then her father smiled. He crooked his index finger at Elaine. She knew what they'd do next.

With footsteps like tiptoes, they moved toward the doorway, then bent their heads in unison to carefully eavesdrop. It was what they'd done when Elaine had been young: according to her father, it was the only way to know for certain that the guests were having a good time, that the food was acceptable.

"You simply have to have the veal," Lily commented.

"Did you try the eggplant, Irene?" From Sarah.

"And the salad," Jo said. "It's wonderful."

"Uncle Andrew, what's this?"

"Just eat it, it's good."

"I shredded the beets for the salad," Karen chimed in with a sparkle of pride that floated to Elaine and filled her, as well. "It wasn't as hard as I thought it would be."

"Well, I only know one thing, and that is it's all wonderful," said Irene. "My friends will be envious that I've managed to shanghai Bob McNulty's recipes from the attic. Where is that man, anyway?"

Elaine looked at her father. "Your public is calling, Dad." She kissed his cheek. "Thanks."

"No problem," he said. He adjusted his chef's hat and put on his best smile.

Elaine waited a few minutes before following him, because he deserved to receive his compliments alone, and because it wasn't the right time for her friends to see her get emotional.

Andrew had been right, something was different.

From the minute Lily had opened the door at Elaine's house and welcomed them in, he had sensed the shift in attitude even more strongly than he had the previous week. When she kiss-kissed his cheek, her lips didn't meet flesh. Then she quickly dismissed him and moved on to Irene.

Maybe he'd been studying the women so long that he had developed their intuition. Or maybe he'd become stupidly sensitive. Whatever it was, he really wished things would just get back to normal.

He took another bite of the veal, gave kudos to Elaine's father, and ignored the ring of the doorbell and the way Lily leaped from her chair to answer it.

He focused instead on watching his daughter. It was both neat and bittersweet to see her become caught up in the wedding plans, the laughter and the chatter of lively women-things. He was reminded that Cassie wouldn't be a kid forever, that she wouldn't always be only his.

"Well, look who's here," Lily announced and all heads turned to the doorway, and suddenly Andrew had confirmation that, yes, things were different. In black jeans, a black turtleneck, and a black leather jacket, stood the epitome of contrast to fair-haired, fair-skinned Lily. "I'm sure the girls remember Damien," she said. "He owns The Bear Claw Tavern. I thought he'd be a marvelous help in selecting the menu."

"Hello"s and "Nice to see you again"s were murmured as Lily led Damien into the room, around the table, and, of course, to the empty seat that just happened to be next to Andrew. If he didn't know better he'd swear his chair had suddenly been backed into the corner.

"Andrew," Lily cooed, as Damien sat down. "Say hello to our friend."

Andrew did as he was told and tried not to notice that both Cassie's and Irene's eyes were now fixed on him with wonderment. Or was it amusement?

He turned back to his plate, ate a few shredded beets, and knew there was only one way he could get this to stop.

They talked about the wedding all through the evening. Irene Benson was not at all like Elaine expected. She was warm and kind and exactly the kind of person Elaine would have expected Andrew would have as a friend. It was reassuring to think he wasn't such a cad. Andrew David, the celebrity, had apparently not been money-and-power hungry and surrounded by shallow, high-and-mighty people, at least not his friends, if Irene was an example. Elaine didn't care what the others thought about him, Elaine knew the truth, that he was a good man.

She really wished Lily hadn't invited that guy, Damien, the guy who was seated too close to Andrew and laughed too loudly at his nervous jokes. Lily had orchestrated the set-up as Andrew's penance: It was obvious, and it was uncomfortable. Elaine tried to forget about it and instead focus on Jo, who handed out forms for everyone to complete, to rate their favorite foods for the wedding menu. Between now and the end of December, hopefully the caterer could learn to prepare them with more success than she'd initially had with the veil.

Unless...

"Dad," she said as they went into the kitchen after everyone was finished. It was a long shot, she knew, and maybe a crazy one, but if Elaine didn't ask, she'd never know. "What are you doing New Year's Eve?"

Bob wiped his hands on a towel. "Why?"

"Because I think Irene would be honored—we'd all be honored—if you would come and cook for the Benson wedding. If you'd be our caterer. If you'd let me help." She turned her head, fussed with the dishwasher and added, "Mrs. Tuttle could come, too, if she wanted. She might enjoy watching the festivities."

Bob turned off the water. "Honey," he said, "I'd love to help you girls. But the truth is, that's when Larry and I are going on the cruise. I told you we are going on a cruise? It leaves the day after Christmas and comes back the seventh of January."

Disappointment folded itself over her like a wet, woolen shroud. She knew it shouldn't bother her. After all, it had just been a silly notion, a spur-of-the-moment, silly notion. It should not have triggered the small lump that swelled in her throat or the reminder that she was no longer the light of Bob McNulty's life.

Thankfully, just then, Lily appeared in the doorway.

"Elaine," she said, "we have another unexpected guest. Shall we get out another place setting?"

A guest? What other mischief was Lily up to? Or had Mrs. Tuttle driven down from Saratoga? Had she traveled to West Hope to restake her claim?

"A good-looking guest," Lily affirmed, with a Cheshire smile. "He says he's a friend and that his name is Gerard."

38

He looked like his picture on *mates.com*, except he was more of an Adonis in person. He had a head of thick hair, where Lloyd was going bald and Martin already went. He had mahogany-colored eyes—not hazel like Lloyd's or plain brown like Martin's. And he had cheekbones that Cher or Michael Jackson might have paid a fortune for.

She gulped. "Gerard. What are you doing here?" Her voice was a mere whisper, a surreptitious warning.

"Hello, Elaine. You didn't leave your number."

"Excuse me?" She touched the tiny row of pearls that encircled her throat. She hadn't realized when she'd dressed in the soft peach-colored ensemble that she'd need rosary beads, too.

"Your phone number. You left your name and I knew you lived in West Hope. But you didn't leave your number." When he spoke his teeth showed bright and white. Lloyd's teeth had dulled and become crooked over time; Martin's had all been crowned.

She was reminded of Gunter from the spa. She slowly crossed one leg in front of the other.

"Now isn't a good time," she said. From the room behind her, silence drifted on transparent clouds of full-term pregnant pauses, as if all her guests had left and no one breathed in the house. She wondered if her father would think she'd turned into a slut. She wondered if Karen would call Lloyd again.

Gerard held his eyes on her. He smiled. "You're very pretty," he said. "Just like your picture."

Elaine laughed and put her hand on the door. He was the second man to call her "pretty" in less than a week. She wondered if registration on *mates.com* came with rose-colored glasses. "I don't think so," she said. "Pretty," after all, was not a word that described her, even with her new hair. "Acceptable," perhaps. Or "not bad." But "pretty" was reserved for women like Jo. If he went into her family room, surely Gerard would see the difference. "I think you'd better leave," she said and began to close the door. "I'll call you. I have your number."

Suddenly Lily was beside her.

"We still have some dessert," she said. "Tiramisu or Crème Fraîche?"

A rush of heat simmered in Elaine's neck and face as if she were twenty-one again, the scandal of the town. It felt like her makeover had gone terribly awry.

Then Gerard smiled. "Actually, Crème Fraîche is one of my favorites."

Lily extended her arm to him.

In a reaction that Elaine might or might not regret for the rest of her life, she quickly stepped between them.

"I don't think so," she said. Neither Gerard nor Lily moved. "This is simply not a good time." She gently but firmly removed Lily's arm from Gerard's, tried to smile and look as if she were not about to burst into either tears or short bursts of primal shrieks, then promptly, assuredly, closed the door in Gerard's beautiful face.

"Who was that, Mom?" Karen's eyes had narrowed the way Bob's always did when he thought Elaine might be telling him a fib.

"He was a gorgeous man," Lily replied, "and your mother sent him on his way."

Elaine removed plates, clattering one atop another despite that they were twenty-four-carat gold-rimmed wedding gifts and should not be set together because the gold could flake or chip. "Lily, please..."

"Who was he, anyway?" That question from her daughter.

"No one. Just a guy..."

"Oh, no," Karen said. "He's not someone you met online is he, Mom? He's not one of those online dating creeps?" She stood up, poised for confrontation.

All eyes in the room rotated to her. Lily's eyes. Jo's, Sarah's, Irene Benson's. Even Andrew's and Cassie's. At least her father was still in the kitchen.

"Karen, please," she said. "We'll discuss this later." She

juggled the stack of plates with a bundle of embarrassment and moved toward the kitchen door.

"Well, Lainey," Lily said, "he's awfully cute. If you don't want him, maybe someone else does." She was, of course, trying to lighten the mood. But Elaine wished all eyes hadn't landed on Andrew.

Elaine forced a smile and backed into the kitchen where she stood, barely breathing, until the murmur of voices started again. Her father had often said that when more than one person is in a room, sooner or later someone will begin to talk.

She turned to see if he was interested in what was going on. But instead of being aware of the drama unfolding in the other part of the house, he had stretched out on the padded bench next to the back door and fallen asleep.

"I'm sorry," Andrew said as plainly as he could. He stood in Elaine's driveway, next to the old Volvo, hoping that Irene and Cassie, who were sitting inside, couldn't hear his words that were directed at Damien. "Lily meant well, but she didn't know I'm not interested in dating right now."

"You mean, you're not interested in me," Damien replied, turning his collar up to the wind of rejection.

Andrew shook his head. "It's not that. Really. I'm not dating right now." He toyed with the idea of telling the truth. But then Lily would find out and so would everyone else and it would be a big mess because it would be too soon. It was faster, cleaner, just to hurt Damien's feelings. And hate himself later.

"Well, you and your niece are welcome to come to The Bear Claw anytime," he responded with that awful lump-in-the-throat act designed to save face. "Lily is right, I do make a mean gumbo."

Andrew could have said, "Sure, we'll stop in some day." Another lie. Another layer of crap. So he just shook his head. "I'm sorry," he repeated, and looked away.

Damien stood there a moment, his hands in his pockets. Then he quietly said, "Well, go fuck yourself then," and turned and marched off toward his car.

By Thursday, the only decision Irene had left to make was about the gowns. Jo and Sarah decided to drive her to Chestnut Hill in Boston. Andrew didn't think that was a good idea.

"No," he said to Irene when he picked her up at The Stone Castle in the morning. Three days of playing stealth bomber, traveling under the radar of three women who were too smart for their own good (Lily, Jo, and Sarah) and dodging Lily's persistent matchmaking bullet, had completely worn Andrew down. But he couldn't risk Irene being alone with the women. Once they got to yakking, there was no telling what would come out.

God, he was exhausted.

"Andrew, need I remind you this charade was your idea?"

He stopped at a traffic light, one of only three in town. "Which is also why I should get to say when enough's enough."

She turned in her seat to face him and smiled. She was

enjoying this, he realized. The attention, the power, the spending money with aplomb, all in the name of helping Andrew and his cause. "You are so uptight," Irene said with a smile.

"And you are so spoiled," he retorted with a quick chuckle.

She returned the laugh. "But, Andrew, the women have no inkling as to our relationship."

Relationship. He smiled at her choice of a word. He realized these past days held valuable fodder for his "Real Women" column. Too bad he couldn't use much of it. Especially the parts about the *Buzz* editor's wife. Behind them, a horn honked; the light had turned green.

"Speaking of relationships," Irene continued, "how do you suppose this little adventure of yours will end?"

Andrew didn't answer, because what could he say?

There was a lot, however, that he could have said when they reached Second Chances and went into the shop. Standing before him was the willowy back of a tall, svelte, dark-haired woman.

There was a lot he could have said, but he couldn't speak then, either.

Thank God Elaine was the only one in the shop.

"I found your house," the woman who once had been Andrew's wife said to him. "Your next-door neighbor told me where to find you."

His mouth went dry, his tongue stuck to the roof of it like the magnet of a butterfly that Cassie made in third grade and had stuck to the refrigerator.

Patty's eyes moved to his companion. "Irene," she said. "Well, this is interesting. I didn't expect to find you here, too." She'd always said that Andrew cared too much what the Bensons said and thought and did. He'd always known the real problem was that two dynamic women were predestined to clash.

Irene raised her head. At the hinges of her jaw, Irene's muscles fluttered, then went still. "I came to visit Cassie."

"How nice of you," Patty replied, "to spend time with my daughter."

"Someone has needed to."

Any moment now, acrylic fingernails would fly. Andrew should have stepped in, but he was as stuck to the floor as his tongue was to the roof of his mouth.

Elaine did the stepping. "Why don't you two run along?" she said with a gesture to Andrew and Patty. "Irene and I have business to finish. Then I believe she's going to Boston." Nobody breathed. Nobody moved. "Andrew," Elaine commanded. "Go. Now."

But still he didn't—couldn't—move.

Jesus, she was beautiful.

He surveyed her perfect porcelain face, her long, long neck, her—did he dare look?—yes, her breasts.

Shit.

It was in that dead moment he realized that once again it was not his brain that was working, but the parts much lower down. He forced his mind to rewind to the look on Cassie's face when she'd only been five and her mother had left. Once the image arrived, it was amazing how much less beautiful Patty became.

"What are you doing here?" he asked.

"Andrew," Elaine said, moving closer, "I really think it's best if you leave the shop right now."

That's when he heard footsteps descend the back stairs in the studio. The footsteps would be Lily's and there would be no stopping her from questioning the gorgeous woman in the shop as if she were Leslie Stahl and this were *60 Minutes.*

He pried his sneakers from the floor, grasped Patty by the arm, and hustled her out of there before his world imploded.

39

There were a million ways Andrew could use this in his column. There was just one that came to mind:

Never believe, not for one minute, that women don't know they're in control.

"Is this your car?" Patty asked, because she just couldn't, wouldn't, let it go once she'd seen the old Volvo that was in bad need of a wash and a small body job.

He didn't answer because he didn't want to.

It wasn't until they were in the car and he'd driven safely out of eye and earshot of Second Chances that he decided there was no way he'd take her to the cottage. Not until he knew what her agenda was.

He drove out to Laurel Lake. He pulled into the parking lot at the public beach and turned off the motor.

"Tell me what you want," he said.

"It's that easy? I just tell you what I want?" Her words hinted of flirtation, because Patty had always done that well.

"No," Andrew said. "First, you tell me. Then I'll tell you if it's possible."

The air grew late-autumn-chilled. She buttoned her leather jacket and said, "God, do we have to sit out here? It's freezing. And I'm in no mood for games, Andrew. I just got out of a hired car that I had to take all the way from JFK, after I got off a plane I spent way too many hours on."

He tapped the steering wheel. He toyed with the unicorn keychain that dangled from the ignition switch. The unicorn had been a gift from Cassie three Christmases ago: She'd bought it in the holiday store at the elementary school and had wrapped it herself in green foil paper and too much Scotch tape. "You should have told me you were coming," he said.

She laughed. "And you would have said it was okay?"

He rolled his neck from side to side, trying to stretch the muscles, trying to prevent a headache that would crash-land any moment. "What do you want, Patty?"

She sighed. "I want to see my daughter."

"You got her e-mail."

"Yes. And now I want to see her."

He didn't ask where her husband was or who was baby-sitting Gilbert Grape. "I thought if you'd agree, I would bring her for a visit in the summer."

"I want to see her now."

"You can't."

"Why not?"

"It's complicated." It was difficult enough trying to hold his breath around Irene Benson and the others. How could he handle this, as well? Andrew David Kennedy, once respectful, respected, now a victim of his own stupidity. "You have to leave," he said.

"I have visitation rights."

"You gave those up when you moved to Australia. You just can't swoop down and make claims on my daughter."

"Our daughter."

He leveled his eyes right on her. "*My* daughter," he said. He got out of the car and slammed the door. He walked down to the water, trying to clear his mind, knowing any second Patty would appear beside him and God knew what she'd try.

Sex, probably, because she knew that was one button that was tough for Andrew to ignore when it came to her, when it came to the way she could manipulate his dick. He drew in a long, slow breath of air.

The next thing Andrew heard was the sound of the ignition starting, then the treads of the old Volvo tires spit dirt and gravel as it sped from the lot.

Elaine was beginning to wonder why life had become weird.

"I understand Andrew Kennedy works here," the woman had said with an affected accent when she appeared at Second Chances. "I am his former wife. The mother of his daughter."

At least Elaine had been alone, able to cover for him, not that one more detail of his deception would be a big shock to the others, but Andrew, of course, didn't know that.

Elaine found it interesting, though, that with all the truth he'd told her, he'd failed to mention that Cassie's mother was Patty O'Shay. *The* Patty O'Shay. She supposed Elaine might have known if she'd paid more attention to celebrity gossip back when Andrew had been one of them.

By ten-thirty the commotion had subsided: Andrew and his ex were gone; Irene had scooted off with Jo and Sarah; Lily had decided it was a good time for a bubble bath. She'd promised Frank she'd go to a Christie's auction with him, for which, she announced, one should feel properly indulged.

Coffee seemed like the next best thing, so Elaine locked up the shop and dashed out for a jumbo latte. Inside the luncheonette she saw Jo's mother—they hadn't spoken since the wedding—who looked bright and wonderful. They chatted about the wedding and the honeymoon to Italy and then along came Gloria Wickham and her daughter, Maebeth, whom neither of them had seen since Marion's wedding, either, so the four of them talked right through the latte. Elaine ordered another to take back to the shop.

Stepping out one door, Elaine thought how wonderful it was that Marion was so happy. It was nice to think that by canceling her own wedding, Elaine had contributed a little to another person's joy. Two people, actually, if she counted Ted the Butcher, who had waited so long for Marion to accept his proposal.

Just as she reached in her pocket for the keys to the shop, footsteps approached. It was her father. And he was smiling.

"Your kitchen's clean and the dishes are put away," he said, buttoning the front of his red-and-black shirt. "I'm headed back to Saratoga, but I wanted to say good-bye."

They went into the shop.

He looked around, let out a low whistle. "Fancy," he said of the organza and velvet and pearl motif that Sarah had selected for the holidays.

"You know I can't thank you enough," she said as she sat down. He sat across from her.

"My pleasure," he said. "I'm only sorry I can't be here for the main event."

Elaine shrugged. "We'll work it out. I'm sure I'll find a caterer somewhere on the planet." She'd tried not to dwell on the fact that he wouldn't be with her, but with Mrs. Tuttle.

He fiddled with the buttons of his shirt the way she fiddled with the drawstring of the sweatpants that she wore at night. She wondered if the gesture was genetic.

"Thanksgiving is just around the corner," Bob said suddenly.

"Oh, good heavens, I nearly forgot. What with everything going on . . ."

He nodded. "I meant to tell you earlier: I've been invited to Syracuse."

She felt a small chill, not ice-cold, but a chill nonetheless.

"Larry's son, Dennis—you remember her twins?"

Elaine said that she did.

"Well, her son Dennis and his family are there. They invited us both. He has three kids, Larry's grandkids."

He had three grandkids, too, but there was no need to say it. "What about her other son, is it Danny?"

Bob frowned, then shook his head. "Didn't you know? Danny died a half-dozen years ago. Killed by a drunk driver."

No, Elaine hadn't known. "That's horrible, Dad."

Bob stood up. "Yeah. It's still hard on Larry, but she never complains. So I hope you understand, about Thanksgiving and all."

She thought about Mrs. Tuttle, who'd survived the death of a child. Loss, Elaine thought, comes in all kinds of ways. "Oh, Dad," she said, standing up, "it's fine." She gave him a hug. "I think it's wonderful that they want to include you." And then she realized that she really meant it.

"Christmas?" he asked.

"But your cruise..."

"We don't leave until the day after. And I'll want to see my grandkids... so I can indulge them."

She kissed his cheek, and that time, she felt no disappointment.

Bitch.

Andrew turned the word into a mantra as he repeated it with every cadence of his right, then left, foot.

Bitch.

Bitch.

Bitch.

He could have used some adjectives, but he wanted to keep it clean. Patty was Cassie's mother, after all: Cassie was half her as much as him.

Bitch.

He had no idea where she was going. To his house? The school?

Would she really have the balls to go to Cassie's school?

Or would she return to Second Chances and blow his cover? Not that it mattered anymore, because Andrew had a sick, sick feeling that he was about to enter into a custody fight for which he was not prepared.

But your honor, I have matured, she would plead with those huge turquoise eyes. *I have a home now. A stable home. Cassie has a brother who would love to know his big sister. Andrew has had her all these years. Isn't it time for me? I'm her mother, after all.*

Her mother.

Her mother.

What chance did he have?

And then he thought, *Oh,* God. *Would the bitch go to the police?*

40

He'd walked for twenty or maybe thirty minutes, which seemed like several hours.

He could have hitched a ride, but he was in the middle of goddamn nowhere. He could have used his cell phone, but it was in the car with the bitch that he'd been dumb enough to marry.

"Chemistry has no brains," John had warned when Andrew bought the diamond. He should have listened: John was, of course, older and an expert.

Stuffing his hands into his pockets, Andrew walked with hard, deliberate strides, head bent in concentration, eyes locked on the pavement.

He had no clue what he was going to do. He only knew that if Patty were given some kind of custody—any kind of custody—he probably would die. How could he live without Cassie? There'd be no reason to make blueberry pancakes in the morning, or brush up on his math tables, or plant a pumpkin patch, or any of the hundred thousand things he did because she was there, because she was his responsibility and she meant more to him than Andrew could express—not to Patty, not to himself, and certainly not to some damn judge.

Without Cassie he might as well go back to the city, go back to being Andrew David, immerse himself in a life where fame and fortune were great panaceas for all things that weren't there, things like love and trust.

He continued walking, trying not to think how his actions—and his lies—of the past few months would hold up in a courtroom, if it came to that. And if the media was going to have a field day with something as insignificant as the Benson wedding, what in God's name would they do with this story of the supermodel and the journalist-turned-recluse who was pretending to be gay?

And what would the judge have to say about that?

Just then an old pickup truck lumbered down the road, slowed down, then stopped. It backed up to where Andrew stood.

"Need a lift?" the driver, a man who was even older than the truck, asked. His white hair was unkempt, some of his teeth were missing, but he certainly seemed more harmless than Patty whatever-her-name-was-now.

Andrew climbed in.

"Car break down?" the old man asked.

"You could say that," Andrew said.

"Where you headed?"

"West Hope Elementary. I have to get my daughter."

She wasn't there.

"I was standing right here when Cassie left her classroom and walked down the hall to see her mother," Arlene Franklin, the school office manager said. "I told the woman she wasn't allowed to take her, that Cassie's father was the only one authorized to take her out of school. But then Cassie seemed so excited to see her mother. 'Mom! Mom!' she cried as she raced down the hall toward her. Then the woman said she was there to surprise her and Cassie said she'd written to her and asked to see her, and that you'd said it was okay, so what could I do? I tried calling you at work, but they said you weren't there."

Andrew stood there the whole time staring at the woman, wondering if he should choke her or turn her over to the police.

But violence had never been his method of day-to-day operation, and the police would ask too many questions, so he simply turned around and walked away without saying another word. Then, as he pushed open the front door, he saw a pay phone on the wall. It was a long shot, he knew. But any shot would be worth it.

He dug into the pocket of his jeans, pulled out two quarters, and dialed the number for his cell phone. Then he closed his eyes and held his breath.

"Dad? Is that you?"

He slumped against the green cinder-block wall in the school corridor. His eyes stung with tears. Thank God he'd left his phone on the front seat of the car. "Cassie. Are you all right?"

"Yes, Dad, I'm fine. Mom's here! I guess you know that!"

"Honey, tell me where you are."

"In the car."

"Where are you going?"

Cassie giggled, then didn't say anything else. He could hear faint music from the radio, and muffled voices of his daughter and her mother.

"Andrew?"

Shit. It was her.

"Put my daughter on, Patty. I want to talk to her."

"Sorry I had to leave you. I decided you needed a few minutes to cool off."

"Let me talk to Cassie."

"Cassie and I have a proposition for you, Andrew. You know she wants to visit me in Australia. You said yourself it was okay with you."

Oh, how he was beginning to regret that. "I told you I will bring her during summer vacation."

"Well, I'd like to take her now."

Now?

He blanked out for a moment, as if he had the kind of epilepsy where the seizures were like brain paralysis.

Now?

"She's not going anywhere," he said. "She has school."

"I'm sure we can arrange for her schoolwork to come with her. I can help her with it. I'm not stupid, you know."

He wouldn't comment on that remark. "Where are you, Patty? Right now. Where are you and where are you taking my daughter?"

"We're going to the mall to buy her a few clothes.

Things she'll need Down Under. It's almost summer there, you know."

He didn't ask how long she planned for Cassie to stay. "We need to talk about this," was all he said.

"Sure. We'll be home for dinner. Is six o'clock okay?"

41

Second Chances bustled the rest of the day. The phone rang several times.

The florist: "Samples of the white-and-silver floral soaps from the UK have arrived." Elaine knew Irene wanted something lovely and unique for the guest rooms at the castle.

The pyrotechnics manager: "The good news is we've been able to assemble a crew at such late notice. The bad news is you'll have to pay a premium. It's New Year's Eve, you know." Well, yes, they were aware of that.

One call had been more than positive: "Can you plan my second wedding for sometime in April?" They now had seven weddings booked after the Bensons'. It looked as if Second Chances might succeed after all. Elaine jotted down the name and number of the caller and explained that Jo Lyons would contact her. Jo was their official "front man," the one who knew how to get business rolling in their direction.

At four-thirty Jo and Sarah arrived back at the shop, having had a successful day in Boston with Irene, who'd caught the fast train to New York from there.

Andrew never had returned during the day. Elaine said she thought he'd had a migraine or food poisoning or something.

At five o'clock they locked up the shop and Elaine went home. When she walked in the door she was surprised to find Karen sitting at the kitchen table, staring into space, with no headphones on her ears and no TV noise in the background.

Elaine didn't want to ask Karen what was wrong. She had planned to have a quick dinner, then go to bed early. Tomorrow she'd have to start thinking about Kandie and Kory coming home for the holiday, in between trying to figure out what she would do about talking to caterers and picking the best one and worrying about how on earth she'd accomplish all that needed to be done.

But because she was a mom first, she set down her bag and said, "Honey? What's wrong?"

It took Karen a minute to reply, during which time Elaine took off her jacket, fired the gas under the teakettle, and sat down to listen.

"I've totally screwed up," Karen said.

Elaine didn't laugh. "Well, I doubt that."

"No, Mom, it's true."

Elaine waited.

"And now Thanksgiving's coming."

"Yes," Elaine said.

"Grandpa's not going to be here."

"I know. It's okay."

Karen lifted her eyes. "Mom? Would you mind if I went with Kory and Kandie over to Dad's?"

Lloyd's?

She wondered if something in the universe had decided it was time for children of divorce to switch parents.

"Well, honey," was all she said. Didn't her daughter realize that would mean she'd be alone?

Karen shook her head. "There's something you don't know," she replied. "And it's part of why I said I screwed up."

"What?" Elaine asked, mentally bracing herself.

"Dad wants me there at Thanksgiving so all us kids can be with him. He wants us to help celebrate that he and Beatrix got back together."

The whistle of the teakettle blew. Their eyes lingered on each other. *So much*, Elaine thought, *for Lily's belief that Lloyd still adored her.*

Karen got up, turned off the gas, and fixed tea.

"I don't understand," Elaine finally said.

"I wasn't surprised," Karen said.

"But he'd sent me all those damn roses." Had he been so annoyed when she'd told him to stop—had he been so annoyed that he'd gone back to his second wife?

Karen was silent. She returned with two mugs and sat them on the table. "Mom," she said, "it isn't his fault."

"What's not his fault?" Elaine felt as if she were in a dream. Yes, that was it. She was so tired, surely it was a dream.

"The roses," Karen quietly said. "I sent the roses on Sundays. Not Dad."

42

He hadn't been able to breathe right since Patty had arrived. It hadn't helped that she stayed at the cottage and Andrew had slept—or not slept—on the old lump of a couch again. The only good thing was that Irene had gone home, one less thread in his tangled web.

"You can't do this," he said to Patty, who sat in the kitchen drinking thick black coffee because, God knew, she rarely ate. Thankfully, Cassie had gone to school.

"Yes, I can," she replied. "Cassie is my daughter."

"How nice you remembered."

Patty drained her mug. "Don't do this, Andrew. Cassie has decided. She wants to come."

He was pleased to notice she looked old in the morning and not very attractive. "Give me until Thanksgiving.

If she still wants to go, fine." He wondered if that was a promise he'd be able to keep.

"What do I do until then?" she hissed. "Sit here and wait all day?"

"No," he replied. "You can't stay here, Patty. But there's a nice room up at The Stone Castle." It had been good enough for Irene, it would be good enough for Patty.

"I'll need a car," she said, "so I can do things."

"What kind of 'things'?"

She hesitated. "Boston. I could go into Boston. Or Albany, if there's anything up there."

"Shopping, you mean?" Of course it was what she meant. What else did Patty know?

"Well," she said, "yes."

"Or," he said as he leaned on the table and looked without fear into those turquoise eyes, "you could do some things with your daughter. She rides horses, you know, or maybe you don't. And she loves museums. But that might be too tame for you." He stood up and turned his back to her again because it was too hard to argue when he couldn't breathe.

"Never mind," she said. "I'll go to New York. I'll look up some old friends."

"Fine," he said. "You do that. But don't expect an answer until Thanksgiving."

So Lloyd didn't love her after all. Elaine supposed she should be upset, angry, or hurt. But the next morning, as she headed out to work, she realized she was none of those things. Instead, she felt oddly uplifted, unburdened, finally free to be Elaine.

It was a little bit scary, a little bit nerve-wracking, but Elaine suspected it was about damned time.

43

For days Jo wrestled with the decision about whether or not to tell her mother that she'd seen the "other woman," that she'd learned what she'd learned about her grandfather, and about Sam.

She waited until an afternoon when she knew the butcher shop would be open and Ted would be at work. Then she called and asked if Marion would like to accompany her to the secretaries' building to get a few more of her things.

The road from the new condo near Tanglewood toward Jo's apartment passed the rest stop that ran along the river. Though it was nearly dusk, Jo pulled in. She turned off the ignition and looked down at the water. It was churning steadily, a prelude to a chilling winter.

"The river never changes, does it?" Jo asked.

"Your grandfather loved fishing here. He loved it when you went with him."

Jo moved her eyes from the water to the riverbank, where frost had already hardened the fragile ground. "My father loved it, too, I guess," she said.

For a moment Marion said nothing, then, "Well, I guess I knew you didn't really bring me out to help you move boxes."

Jo shook her head. "I thought about what you said, Mom. About how you were to blame that Dad never came back to see me."

Marion didn't answer.

"It isn't true," Jo said. "It was because of Grandpa." Then she told her mother what she had done, what she'd been told, and how she now knew Marion had been right: There were two sides to every story.

When she told her about the threats her grandfather made to Sam, Marion quietly said, "I think I knew that. I think I knew that but I was too afraid to try and change his mind."

"Dad's mind or Grandpa's?"

"Either," Marion said. "Both, I guess."

They watched the river with its ceaseless motion. Then Jo said, "He bought a necklace for me for graduation. It has a silver charm of an oak tree. His way of wanting me to grow strong of body and of mind."

Marion nodded again. Jo sensed she did not want to speak because she feared that she might cry. She was going to offer to show the necklace to her mother—it still sat in the glove box, mere inches from her mother's knees—but suddenly Jo decided that wasn't necessary. If Marion wanted to see it, she would have asked.

"I have a new life," her mother said then. "I'm happy you've found some closure about your father."

Jo took her mother's hand, the left hand that now wore Ted Cappelinni's thick gold wedding band. "I think we both have," she said, and Marion nodded once again. "It will be okay, then," Jo asked, "if I move back into the house?" She hadn't decided until right then. It no longer seemed too big or in need of too much work. She didn't care that her furniture didn't match. The old house simply was home.

Marion smiled, and they sat and watched the water until the night grew dark.

44

The time passed quickly to Thanksgiving Day. Elaine had been caught up in menus and meetings with caterers, trying to find the right one for the Benson wedding and beyond. So far, she'd come up empty.

She had not told the others she'd be alone on the holiday; she knew they'd assume her kids would be with her. Jo was going to cook dinner for her mother and Ted and half of Ted's family, for Sarah and Burch (Jason was on the road again), and for Lily and Frank. Andrew had not been invited.

After the kids left for their father's (and apparently Beatrix's again), she made a cup of tea. She thought about her father and wondered if he'd make quail with chestnut stuffing and cranberry chutney at Mrs. Tuttle's son's house, the way he'd always made it at theirs. She wondered if Beatrix went to any trouble, or if she bought one of Ted's precooked "holiday family dinners and fixin's."

She looked out the kitchen window, thinking of holidays gone past. There would be new ones ahead, new memories as yet unmapped. But for now, Elaine knew in her heart that to look to the future, she must first come to terms with the past.

With that thought in mind, she set down her mug, went into the back hall, and began to unseal the cartons of her mother's things.

The only thing Andrew could do was go with them. Patty wouldn't like it, Cassie might or might not, but it was the only thing he could imagine. Which was why, the night before, he'd packed a couple of suitcases and shoved them under the sofa, next to his old copies of *Buzz*.

He sat through a late-afternoon Thanksgiving dinner with their neighbor, Mrs. Connor, at her house, with one eye on his cottage, waiting for Patty to show up. He and Cassie hadn't talked about it, but he knew her suitcases were packed, too.

During pie made from the pumpkins Cassie had helped Mrs. Connor can, the woman said, "So, Cassie, you're going to Australia!"

Cassie winced a little. Then she chewed her pie; she took a drink of milk. She turned to Andrew. "Maybe until Christmas, Dad. Will that be okay?"

He tried to be supportive, noble, strong. But all he could taste was defeat; all he could see was the disinterested look on Patty's face when she left them years ago. Still, she was Cassie's mother. And Cassie seemed to need her now. It was that women-thing, he suspected. That baffling shift in female hormones that he was ill-equipped to understand.

Andrew wiped his mouth, set his napkin beside his plate.

"I told you it would be your decision. What time is your mother coming?"

Cassie shrugged. "She said she'd have dinner in the city, then drive up early this evening."

So that was that, the deed was done. He hoped he'd still have time to do what needed doing now before breaking the news that he was going, too.

Andrew stood up. "Thanks so much for dinner, Mrs. Connor. Cassie, promise you won't leave before I get back? There's someone I need to see."

Cassie promised.

Then he was gone.

Jo had been spending more and more time at her mother's house since that jackass who lived in her building had duped her. Andrew assumed that's where she'd made Thanksgiving dinner, not that he'd been invited. When he reached the old colonial, he realized he'd been right. Cars were parked this way and that up and down the driveway; some were scattered like colorful pick-up sticks all across the lawn. Sarah's truck was there; Lily's pint-sized Mercedes, too. He felt the slight; he let it go. He was there for a much bigger reason.

He parked his car among the others, then went to the back porch.

"Andrew," Jo said. She was dressed in pale aqua jeans and a matching sweater. She looked beautiful but tired. Well, why wouldn't she be? She'd been working like crazy these past weeks.

"Smells like turkey," Andrew said through the screen door.

Jo opened it. "Please. Come in. Have you eaten?"

He nodded but stayed where he was rooted. "We ate with the neighbors." He supposed he should have said "neighbor" without the "s." Another lie that someday, he thought, he might have to confess too. He shifted on one foot. "Jo," he said, "I need to talk to you. Alone."

She stepped out onto the porch, closing the scents and sounds behind her. Folding her arms, she leaned against the railing.

"I've come here to confess," Andrew said. He tried to keep his eyes focused squarely on hers. The act was difficult. "I'm leaving for Australia later tonight, so I suppose I have nothing to lose. I had planned to tell you at the Benson wedding, though I doubt I could have lasted that long."

She didn't say a word. He wished she would.

"I want you to know the truth about me, Jo. I haven't been honest with any of you."

Someone inside the house—had it been Lily?—let out a boisterous laugh.

He blinked.

Jo blinked.

Then Andrew drew in another breath and, finally, he began.

He started from day one, as he had with Elaine. He started with the day he'd met John in New York City, when John asked Andrew to write "Real Women."

She sucked in her lower lip just a little and held it there with her teeth. But she made no comment.

So Andrew continued. He told her about his past: about his former career, about his train wreck of a marriage, about the fact that Cassie was really his daughter.

Still, Jo said nothing.

His throat was dry now. His lower back started to hurt from standing there, holding back his emotions while he spilled his guts. "And I never got the hang of doing brunch, so I guess I've even failed at being gay," Andrew added, hoping his words would pull her teeth from her lip and bring a small smile to her face.

It didn't.

"It was supposed to be simple," he said when he was finished, "and now it's so complicated. I'm so sorry. I only meant the best for everyone. Especially for you."

She didn't say thanks for coming or for telling the truth. If only she'd say something—anything—it would make him feel that this wasn't totally in vain. But Jo simply stood there and averted her eyes.

Andrew turned and said, "Well, I guess it's over, then." He meant to say more, to tell her how he felt about her, but he suddenly choked. It was apparent from her silence that she wouldn't have cared.

He drew in a last, humbling breath.

"Don't worry about the Benson wedding," he added.

"It will go on. Irene is quite taken by all of you, by Second Chances."

He nodded then, and left the back porch and Jo Lyons's life.

On the way home, Andrew stopped at Elaine's. He found her immersed in old pictures and musty memorabilia. He told her about his confession to Jo. He thanked her for keeping his secrets. Then he told her he was going to Australia.

"You couldn't find a better way of hiding out from the Benson wedding?"

He laughed. He shook his head. "Believe me, it isn't the excuse I would have picked."

Elaine offered a wry smile. "Will you come back?" she asked.

"I honestly don't know."

She held her arms out, then she hugged him. "I was counting on that dance. The first one at the Bensons' wedding."

"I'll be with you in spirit," he replied. "I really mean that, Lainey."

She wiped a tear from her cheek. "We'll miss you. Maybe me, most of all." More tears quickly followed. "Hey, maybe in your next column you can write about how sometimes men make women cry."

He laughed again, hugged her back, and couldn't help but wish he'd had that reaction from Jo.

After Andrew left, Elaine returned to the cartons, all opened now, their contents lined up on the kitchen table and counters. "I'm so sorry, Mom," she whispered. "I think I've finally forgiven myself for having made some mistakes, for not being perfect."

Then she grinned a wide grin as she surveyed the pieces of her mother's life, a life that had been gentle and trusting and grateful. She thought of her father: Her mother was gone, but he was still there. She would make an ongoing effort to bring him back into her life. It wasn't too late for that.

With that, Elaine set aside some of her mother's favorite jewelry, then put the photos and playbills and menus from McNulty's back in the boxes. Someday, perhaps, her kids would enjoy poking through them. But when she picked up a menu from McNulty's, Elaine had a sudden idea.

It was an idea as clear as the one she'd had that day on the lawn of Ted and Marion's wedding: She would stop interviewing caterers who'd never be like her dad. Instead, Elaine McNulty Thomas would start a catering business of her own, a business that would serve Second Chances and other customers, too.

She would either learn to cook or she would hire someone. But it would be done, and it would be hers, and its backbone would be rooted in the McNulty's of the past, with Veal Medallions and Toasted Basil Pasta and even White Chocolate Lace Bridal Veils, if she could master the damned things.

She resealed the cartons, looked up toward the sky,

and wondered if her mother had been up there all along, just waiting for Elaine to figure the whole thing out.

Marion had told Jo there were two sides to every story. Now Jo had heard Andrew's.

It would have been better, of course, if it hadn't sounded so innocent: a lonely man who'd given up a huge career and a well-connected lifestyle to give his daughter balance; a man who'd seen the chance to write the column as a chance to touch the world's periphery in a harmless way. A man who'd been dumped by his wife, who had nursed his wounds, who had never set out with malicious intent.

Andrew was not Brian. Maybe, like her father, maybe like her grandfather, he'd made a bad choice, but he was not Brian. All he had taken from her was a bit of her pride.

In return, Jo had ended up—they had all ended up—with what promised to be a wonderful business. And feelings for a man that she hadn't expected.

After her guests were gone, Jo got into her car and sat there a moment. The roads would be deserted on Thanksgiving night: most families would be home now, where it was warm, where love was safe.

Leaning across the seat, Jo reached into the glove box. She took out the picture of her father and the silver chain. She touched her father's gentle face, then moved her hand to the charm of the oak tree, with roots that ran so deep. She held it up to the moonlight, slipped it over her head, and let its coolness rest quietly, close to her heart.

She looked back to her father's picture, then she checked her watch. She wondered if there still was time, or if Andrew had already left.

45

Honey, are you sure?"

Cassie had been waiting when Andrew came back from Jo's, came back from Elaine's. Cassie had been waiting, but Patty hadn't arrived.

"She's not coming," Cassie said. "And I'm not going."

It was a good time to build a fire in the stone fireplace, to break apart a few twigs, to crumple some old newspaper sheets. Andrew wasn't sure how much more emotion he could pack into one afternoon. He opened the kindling box and got to work.

"What happened?" he asked, arranging the pieces on the wrought-iron grate as if he'd been a Boy Scout, not a city kid, as if he'd ever gone camping, which he had not.

"She didn't really want me, Dad. The way I figure it, she just didn't want you to have me."

He crouched in front of the fireplace. "Oh, honey," he

said, striking a match, then yanking open the flue because it seemed better to direct his anger there than at his self-centered ex-wife. "Why do you feel that way?"

His daughter shrugged. "A lot of the kids in my class have parents who are divorced. Custody fights are usually about the parents, not the kids."

He thought for a moment. He fanned the fire; he added a log. He stood up and surveyed his not-half-bad job. Then he went over to Cassie and sat down next to her. "I hate that you have to go through this," he said, because it was the truth, and Andrew was now committed to telling the truth. He put his arm around her. He ruffled her hair. Then he asked, "What changed your mind?"

"She called and said, 'I decided to check before I came all the way up there. Are you coming?' I said, 'I don't think so,' and she asked me why, and I said I didn't want to leave you."

He tried not to smile, but he couldn't help himself. "And then she said?"

"And then she said, 'Well, be that way, then.' And she said that you'd better let her know far in advance if you plan to bring me out there in the summer."

He nodded. "You're okay with this?"

"Yes, Dad. For sure."

The applewood crackled; little orange flames licked one another. "What if I said I had planned to go with you?"

Cassie laughed. "I know you did, Dad. When I came home from Mrs. Connor's, I came into the living room. I saw your suitcase sticking out from under the far end of the couch. That's when I decided. I know you love Jo. You went to her house and told her about all the lies, didn't you?"

He closed his eyes. Then he laughed, too. "You are too smart for a child of mine."

"Come on, Dad, you didn't want to go Australia, any more than I did. I decided it was more important to stay here. And see what happens."

He watched the fire again; he counted his blessings, or at least the most important one, who sat next to him. "So you're okay without a mother?"

"Sure, Dad. I'm okay for now."

They sat by the fire, just sitting, not talking. Then the doorbell rang, surprising them both.

"Andrew."

"Jo."

She stood on the back steps in the dusk, the tall, black fingers of leafless maples and oaks framing the backdrop against the gunmetal sky. "You're still here."

He pressed his teeth against his bottom lip, the way she had done earlier. "Yes. We're not going."

"Oh."

He couldn't imagine why she was there. He couldn't imagine why the two of them stood there, not speaking, as if someone had pushed the *mute* button on the remote. "Would you like to come in?" he finally asked. "I built a fire." He said it as if he'd built it for her. "Please," he added. "It's cold out."

But Jo shook her head. "No. I only wanted to say I'm sorry. I'm sorry for everything that's happened. I'm sorry I wasn't nicer to you."

At another time, he might have laughed at the off-the-wall idea that she—not he—had been the one who'd screwed up. But Andrew didn't laugh, he lowered his voice. "You were nicer to me than I deserved. Please. Won't you come in? Cassie would love to see you..." Cassie again. He must stop using her as a shield for his feelings, an excuse for his fear of getting too close.

But Jo didn't answer. Instead, she reached up and pressed her palm to his cheek. "Andrew," she said, almost in a whisper, "will you come back to work?"

He held his breath. Even in the gray light, he could see her green, green eyes. "But the wedding... the media..." He said it because he didn't know what else to say, because what he really wanted was to take her in his arms and hold her and kiss her and smell the scent in her hair and taste the sweetness on her tongue.

She paused; she held her eyes on him, her hand on his face. "We'll sequester you in the kitchen. If that's how you want it."

Her fingers were fire on his skin. Or was it his cheek that was fire on her hand? "You'd harbor a fugitive? From what, the paparazzi?"

"Please," she repeated. Her hand slid from his face; she folded her arms. She turned her head sideways, toward the backyard, toward his small pumpkin patch. Then she began to cry. "I was so afraid that you'd gone."

"Jo," he said, stepping forward.

Before he could embrace her, she held up her hand and whisked off her tears and said, "We'll talk again, after the wedding. Right now, we need you." She paused, then looked at him again. "I need you," she said.

Then she slipped away and she was back in her car and

had backed down the driveway before Andrew realized what had happened, that he'd been forgiven, that she had come to him.

On the drive back to her mother's house—back to *her* house—Jo brushed the tears from the edges of her smile. She wondered how it had happened that she'd was learning to trust, and she wondered if love would come next.

Epilogue

They stood on the terrace outside the ballroom of The Stone Castle, watching the magnificent silver-and-white fireworks that lit up the night sky. Lily, Sarah, Jo, and Elaine were tired but happy, validated by success.

John and Irene had been properly remarried without the slightest hitch; the media was heralding the women as the long-awaited experts on second weddings. The menu, the décor, the bagpipers, the dramatic White Chocolate Lace Bridal Veil—the press was gifted with abundant stories to bring Second Chances to the forefront, as Andrew had planned it.

"We wouldn't be in business if it weren't for Andrew," Sarah said. "We'd have closed up our storefront months ago."

"Instead we're expanding," Lily added. Frank had

offered them the space his antiques shop was in, because the town fathers (and the mothers) had finally approved construction for a new town hall, and he had bought the old one for his growing business.

Elaine smiled. She was glad Jo had told the others about Andrew's confession, that anger had turned to gratitude once they all knew the details.

Lily sighed. "But he was great as a gay man. Now he's just like one of the rest."

A moment of sadness passed over the group.

"At least he didn't leave us," Lily said. "And neither did you, Sarah." Sarah had made her decision not to go to New York—at least for now. Her relationship with Jason teeter-tottered, but Sarah said life happened that way sometimes. Burch would go with his dad for as long as it worked, Sarah said, with a catch in her throat.

So much for tranquility, Elaine thought, but instead she said, "I wish Andrew would come out and take a few deserved bows." She'd let him off the first-dance hook. He'd worked so quietly, diligently, these past few weeks. Yet he'd said it would be better if he blended into the woodwork, or, in this case, into the stonework.

Then Elaine saw Jo take a last look at the gala, close her silver shawl around her, and disappear into the night.

Elaine smiled, hoping her instincts were right about what would happen next.

She looked back to the sky, to the spiderwebs of silver etched on the darkness. The guests were mesmerized. Standing by the white-velvet-draped sleigh, Irene and John held hands. Cassie stood in front of them, cradled from the cold. Andrew, Elaine thought, was doing a wonderful job raising his daughter.

Elaine had done a good job, too, at this first event for McNulty's Catering. Most importantly, she'd done the cooking herself, helped out by her staff, with no outside chef, no outside caterer. When she'd told her father what she wanted to do, he had tried to talk her out of it. Then Mrs. Tuttle—Larry—called and told Elaine that if she wanted, they could cancel the cruise, that she knew Bob would much rather be cooking with her.

Elaine had thanked her, but she'd said no. Then Larry promised to make him visit whenever he was needed, to supervise if she wanted, as her special consultant.

Not that Elaine wasn't turning out every bit as accomplished as her father, or so everyone said.

Before the fireworks ended, before the New Year rang in, Elaine stepped back into the ballroom to check on the pastries and coffee.

"All set, Mom," Karen said. She'd been in charge of the presentations of teacakes and butter cookies, all white and silver, all lusciously tempting.

"Here, too," Kory replied. He'd been given the task of the silver carafes and fine-china cups.

"And in the kitchen," Kandie said. Elaine still couldn't believe Kandie had pitched in. Kids did the damnedest things when you left them alone.

"Does anyone mind, then, if I go home?" There had been chaos in the house for over a week; there were remnants in the refrigerator of Christmas dinner ("test runs" of the Bensons' menu) that needed cleaning out; there were piles of gifts from Bob and Larry and even from

Lloyd (and Beatrix) that still needed sorting... the only thing missing was Bob's book from *Patsy's* Restaurant—he'd been sure to pack that for the cruise.

Best of all, Elaine had told her father she was sorry. She was sorry for the past years; she was sorry for so many things.

He had simply held her and told her that he loved her and said she'd done what seemed right at the time.

Which, Elaine supposed, was what everyone did. And now it seemed right to do something else.

"Go home," Karen said. "Everything's under control."

So Elaine said good night, then took off her heels and dumped them into her bag. She had one stop to make on the way home, and there was no need to be gussied up.

"Martin," she said as he came to the door. "I hope I'm not disturbing you."

He wore an old threadbare bathrobe, the kind a bachelor might have bought twenty or more years ago, yet was still functional. "I was watching the ball drop in Times Square," he said. "Three minutes to go."

"Feel like some company?" she asked. He was, after all, such a nice, caring man. And Elaine no longer was afraid of what life would bring. She might not end up like them all—Lily, Sarah, and Jo—but she could be Elaine, and maybe that was okay. Maybe she'd even buy a few more new clothes—maybe a few things in bright colors, and a few with some splash.

Of all the things in the world women can have, I think they want love, respect, and peace.

Maybe, after all, they're the things that men want, too.

Maybe we should work on giving them to one other.

Andrew formed the thoughts of his next column as he stood at the far end of the ballroom, protected by the shadow of the balcony, peeking at the fireworks as if he were an intruder.

"There you are."

He turned and saw Jo, so lovely in silver and white, so lovely in the moonlight sprinkled by the fireworks and the stars.

"Jo."

She smiled. "In case I didn't say thank you: *thank you.* For this opportunity. For this gorgeous wedding."

He shrugged. "You girls are the ones who pulled it off."

She smiled again. She looked toward the window. "Remember the first time we came here?" she asked.

"And poor Martha Holland thought we were a couple." The words popped out before he'd thought about their implications, about the reminder that he'd lived so many months in so many lies.

Jo lowered her eyes. "It would have been nice if we were," she said.

Perhaps he'd heard wrong. Perhaps the cracks of the fireworks as they shattered the darkness had distorted his hearing.

"What?" Andrew asked, but then Jo turned to him and her lips were on his and his were on hers and there was no rowboat rocking and there were no orange life vests to come between them and, finally, this wasn't a dream.

About the Author

TWICE UPON A WEDDING is Jean Stone's twelfth novel from Bantam Books, and the second in the series about the women of Second Chances. A native of western Massachusetts, Ms. Stone sets her books in familiar places—this one in the picturesque Berkshire Hills. Her Yankee grandfather was an engineer on the Boston & Albany and New York Central Railroads, and she has drawn from many of his stories ("tall tales," some folks believed) to enrich her New England settings. For more information on the author and her books, visit her web site at www.jeanstone.net.

And look for the first tale of the Second Chances women in . . .

Once Upon a Bride

by

Jean Stone

On sale now

Read on for a preview . . .

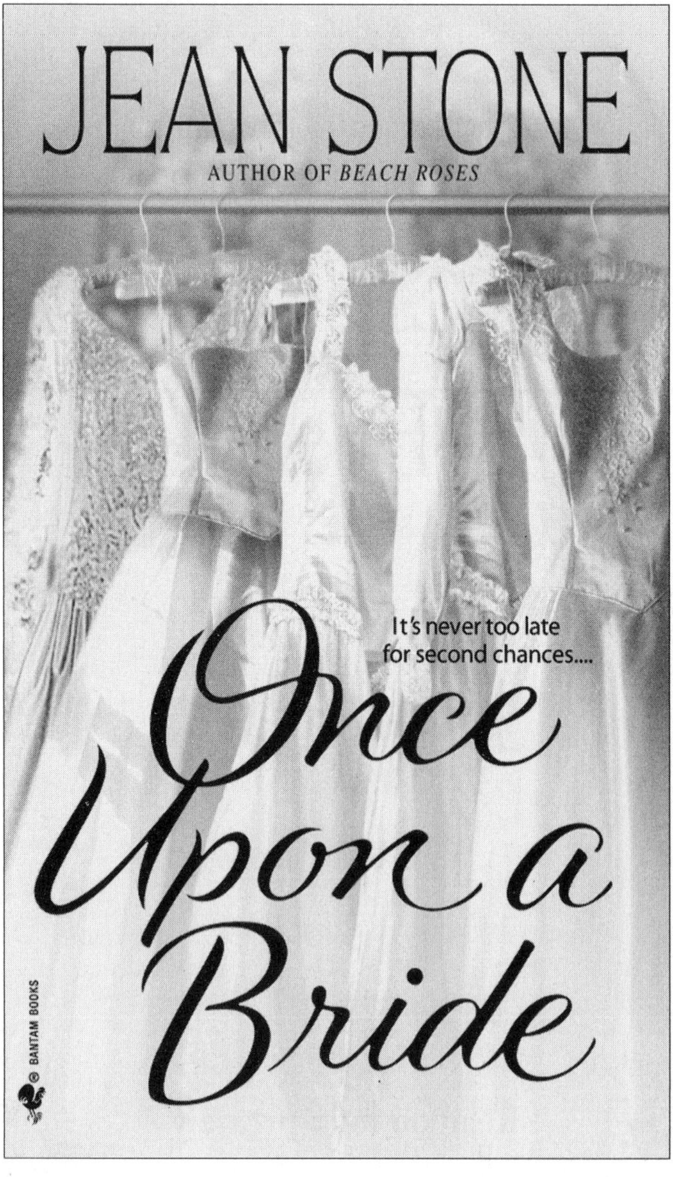
JEAN STONE
AUTHOR OF BEACH ROSES
It's never too late
for second chances....
Once Upon a Bride
BANTAM BOOKS

Once Upon a Bride

On sale now

"That's the ugliest wedding gown I've ever seen," Sarah said. She leaned back in her chair, her long black hair swaying with her movement, her dark eyes blinking with acerbity. "I can't wait to see what she's picked out for us."

Jo wanted to agree, but didn't dare. Elaine was only in the ladies' room and could return any moment. Sarah was right, however, the gown was horrible.

Lily shook her head, her short blond curls bouncing like little clouds of milkweed puffs against her pink cheeks. "We can't let her do it," she whispered in horror as she plucked the bridal magazine from the table at Le Fusion, the latest boutique restaurant in the small New England town that had once been quaint but was now tourist-choked. "She never had great taste in college. I guess that hasn't changed in all these years." She turned to Jo. "Josephine?" she asked as if awaiting confirmation.

Reaching for her wineglass, Jo glanced over at the picture of white satin bouffant with pink and blue organza roses set into excessive ruffles of tulle. The gown looked foolish, even on the angelic, eighteen-year-old model. On over-forty Elaine, it would look asinine.

Across the restaurant, Elaine emerged from the ladies' room. Her lavender polyester pants were too short, her eighties-style hair was dyed too brown and was too big. Yet Elaine marched along with happy steps, nodding and smiling as she passed the other luncheoning ladies who wore golf skorts and straw hats and had shopping bags from Ann Taylor and Lladró and Ralph Lauren. When Elaine reached her former college roommates, the women she'd selected as her bridesmaids for her "second-time around," she dropped onto her chair with relief.

"Mercy," she said, fanning herself lightly.

"I'm not used to drinking in the middle of the day." She smoothed the front of the pink-and-lavender-flowered big shirt, then adjusted her double-strand necklace of red and pink beads and the large dangle earrings that matched. Sort of.

Jo's eyes moved from flighty, elflike Lily to pensive, statuesque Sarah, extremes in looks and personalities, right and left wing, while Jo kept to the middle, with Elaine a few feet behind. Now Lily and Sarah expected Jo to break the news to Elaine. As the leader in the middle, it had always been Jo's role to be the obligatory mediator, the one with the most sense. Two decades apparently hadn't changed that, either. She sipped her wine. "Elaine, honey," she said gently, "have you thought about getting professional help?"

Sarah nearly spit her wine across the table.

Lily's pink lips peeled back in a grimace, revealing professionally whitened, perfectly straight teeth.

Jo smiled. "For the wedding," she continued. "Someone like a wedding planner."

She might have said that one of Elaine's three kids had been arrested on drug-trafficking charges, given the bewildered look

Elaine wore on her face. Then Elaine's eyes fell to the magazine that Lily still clutched. A wide grin appeared. "It's the white, isn't it? You think I shouldn't wear white!" She laughed a jovial laugh, then drank more of the wine she wasn't used to drinking in the middle of the day. "Well, this might surprise you, but I read that white no longer is a symbol of virginity. It now stands for 'joy.' I guess they had to change it because there are no virgins left in the world."

She drank again. No one laughed.

Jo leaned forward. "It's not the white, Elaine. It's the flowers. And the ruffles. And the, well, the *little girl* look. I know it's not fair. But even though there are tons of second and even third weddings, it still seems that all the books and magazines—and most of the fashions—are geared to twenty-year-olds." She hoped she'd made her point without hurting Elaine's feelings.

Elaine's wine-pinkened cheeks slowly darkened to red. Even her Miss Clairol-ed hair seemed to deepen a shade. She snatched the magazine from Lily's hands. "I'm not entitled to the wedding of my dreams just because I'm over forty?" She didn't have to mention that she'd been cheated out of a wedding when she'd married Lloyd because they'd still been in college and Elaine had been pregnant, so they'd married in haste at the town hall. The redness abated and fat tears slid down her cheeks.

Lily produced a clean lace hankie from her Asprey purse.

Elaine waved it away, then reached into her crocheted tote bag and located a travel pack of Kleenex. She blew her nose loudly.

The waitress appeared bearing three oriental chicken salads with dressing on the side, and a veggie platter for Sarah.

"Maybe we can help," Jo suggested once the waitress had left. "After all, as your bridesmaids, we have a vested interest." She grinned and patted Elaine's hand. "It's a little more than three months until the wedding, right?"

"I didn't want to wait," she said apologetically.

"Three months is acceptable," Lily interjected. "Only first-time brides need a year or more to plan."

Lily, of course, would know.

"Then we will do it in three months," Jo said. "Lainey, let us be your wedding planners."

Elaine blinked. "My 'wedding planners'? But you live in Boston."

Jo cleared her throat. "Actually, I've been thinking I might come back for a while. My mother's getting older . . . I want to be sure she can still live on her own." She tried to sound casual and hoped the others didn't notice the tremor that had sneaked into her voice.

"You might come back to West Hope?" Elaine asked. "But what about your business? What about your career?"

Despite a degree in elementary education, Elaine had only taught fourth grade between her second and third kids, then gave up on working altogether. For the past several years she volunteered part-time at the library and served on countless town boards, but as far as Jo knew, Elaine had no interest in business or careers, certainly not Jo's.

Folding her hands, Jo forced her best smile. "I've been thinking about branching out. The Berkshires could use a strong public relations firm. Attractions have grown. Tourism has escalated. We'll soon outpace any New England venue except the Cape and islands." All of which had little to do with Jo's recent debate with herself about moving back. The truth was, her life was no longer the same, and "home" was what now seemed safe. The others, however, did not need to know that. "But I haven't decided. In the meantime," she added quickly, "planning your wedding would be fun." She turned to Sarah. "You're so creative, Sarah. If I organize the wedding, maybe you can make it magical. Elaine's dream come true."

"I design jewelry," Sarah protested. "Not wedding dresses and reception halls."

Elaine lowered her eyes.

Sarah shifted on her chair. "Well," she added, "I suppose I could try."

Lily clapped her hands. "And I'll pay!" she exclaimed.

All eyes turned to Lily. Elaine broke the stunned silence. "But you live in New York."

"Don't be silly," Lily said, dismissing Elaine's comment. "It's a three-hour train ride from Manhattan. It isn't Timbuktu. Besides, it would be such a hoot to be together again! And how better to squander a chunk of Reginald's money if not with my friends?" Lily had recently become a widow when her much older, wickedly wealthy husband had sadly succumbed, leaving his beloved wife, Lily, (and his "beastly old sister, Antonia") a portfolio that probably bulged with more stocks and bonds than Lily could count. She laughed and said, "Think of it as a loan you won't have to repay. Think of it as your second chance." She raised her glass in toast to poor, dead Reginald.

Elaine gasped. "You mean it."

Sarah nodded. "She means it."

Jo held up her glass. "To second chances," she said, and they *clink*ed all around. Jo had little idea what had just happened. But for the first time in months, her spirits had lifted and she thought that maybe her life wasn't over after all.

She had been named "Most Likely to Succeed" by her high-school class. Josephine "Jo" Lyons had also been the captain of the debating team, the president of the student council, and the editor of the yearbook. She had been those things once. Now she was just a middle-aged woman sitting on the edge of the bed in her childhood home, wondering how it had happened that life had come full circle, with Elaine getting married while Jo was not, nor was Lily (perhaps to her chagrin), nor was Sarah, who no doubt preferred it that way.

They had always been different, the Winston College roommates. Lily said they were friends because of that, because they never were attracted to the same types of men, so there was no competition.

Jo had been the studious townie who had saved her money from waitressing during tourist season so she could live on campus and feel she'd left town, as if at last her life could begin. Jo had been attracted only to one man, Brian Forbes, who was tall and handsome, gregarious and a bit of a bad boy. He had been like her father, she supposed.

Elaine had been the domestic diva wanna-be (despite her dubious taste) long before such a label had been coined by a questionable marketing guru who might have had close ties to Martha Stewart or Pottery Barn. Though Elaine had come from Upstate New York, she and Lloyd had settled in West Hope because his family was there and she'd been embarrassed by the "premature" baby and all. Although Lloyd had gone to law school, Jo had thought of him as rough around the West Hope edges, a small-town boy without the polish, destined for a mediocre life.

Lily had been the orphan raised by a wildly eccentric, rich aunt. A fun-loving, cheerful city girl, Lily knew all the latest fads—like shawls and boots and the resurgence of miniskirts—long before West Hope got wind of them. Lily had been attracted to lots of men, mostly older, mostly wealthy, mostly those who doted on her with great sincerity.

Sarah had been the exotic roommate, having traveled from the West, a Native American with a mysterious ancestry that she'd turned her back on. She'd remained in the Berkshires, in a town even smaller than West Hope, deep in the woods. She never shared much about the men she dated in college, or about the now-famous musician with whom she'd shared her life for many years. He, too, kept their private life private.

Jo's mother used to say she could tell the difference between the roommates by the way they walked. Marion said that even with her eyes closed, she knew that Lily had the light steps of a ballerina; Sarah, the long strides of a slow yet deliberate woman; and Elaine, the short, clipped gait of a majorette. Marion knew Jo's steps, of course, because she was her daughter. She often described them to the others as steady and sincere, if not always heading in the right direction.

Throughout the years, it had been Elaine

who had kept the friends together. It had been her idea to meet in New York City each year in the fall for a weekend of girl stuff. New York, after all, was the best place to shop and to eat and to go to the theater. And to laugh. Despite all their differences, they always loved to laugh.

"Third weekend in September," Elaine announced every year, first by mail, then by phone calls, now by e-mail, though Jo suspected none of them needed a reminder.

Other than that, their meetings had been few. Lily's weddings. The birth of Sarah's son. The death of Elaine's mother. An occasional lunch or a quick "Hello" when Jo was in West Hope visiting her mother.

And now, another wedding, a second for Elaine, while Jo had not yet had a first. She'd been too busy being mature, responsible, dependable. Never a carefree kid.

Jo lay back on her bed now and stared up at the ceiling.

"Josephine!" she could almost hear her mother call. "Get a move on. Time's a-wastin'."

Time was always "a-wastin'" according to Marion Lyons, whether it was a school day or a Saturday or time for church.

"As pretty as your mother," Ted, the butcher,

said on Thursdays when Jo stopped by to pick up hamburg and flank steak and pounded veal chops for the week while her mother was at work as the clerk at the town hall.

"Such a smart girl," Mrs. Kingsley at the bookstore always commented with a knowing nod when Jo bought one of many books.

"A wonderful sermon," the congregation said, one after another, each month when Jo delivered the "children's" message from the purple-draped pulpit.

How Jo had hated West Hope.

She turned onto her side now and picked at the chenille dots that covered the twin bedspread, the same bedspread that had been there since the sixties and seventies, yet, unlike her, did not seem to have aged. How many nights had she picked at these same dots, dreaming of the day she'd escape the claustrophobic town and its smothering people for a real life of her own?

She had escaped, of course. The "Most Likely to Succeed" had succeeded for a time, in the big city, Boston, where she had a fancy condominium and a to-die-for wardrobe and men, so many men, who loved her, but Jo Lyons was too busy succeeding to bother to love them back.

She had succeeded, and then she lost everything, though she hadn't yet admitted that to her mother, to her friends, or, most of all, to West Hope.

And now Jo had a choice.

The closing on her fancy condo was next week; her movers awaited word as to where her worldly possessions should be shipped; the brass nameplate had been removed from the Back Bay office door: *JOSEPHINE LYONS AND ASSOCIATES, PUBLIC RELATIONS SPECIALISTS*. The "associates" were gone, the office was, too.

She could stay in the city, in a crowded apartment like the one where she'd started out, in a dark office building with no windows and no clients, and now with a reputation to repair and a bruised heart to mend.

Or she could go home. She could move back to West Hope, open a new office, and capitalize on the Berkshires' tourism as she had suggested. She could help plan Elaine's wedding; she could stay a year, maybe two, until her pain had subsided, until her strength had returned.

"Josephine!" her mother called up the narrow, steep stairs. This time the voice was not a memory. It belonged to the robust woman who was just past seventy and who hardly needed Jo's help to get through her busy days and her bingo-playing nights.